MW01199025

HOUSE
OF
BETH

KERRY CULLEN

SIMON & SCHUSTER

New York   Amsterdam/Antwerp   London
Toronto   Sydney/Melbourne   New Delhi

Simon & Schuster
1230 Avenue of the Americas
New York, NY 10020

This book is a work of fiction. Any references to historical events, real people, or real places are used fictitiously. Other names, characters, places, and events are products of the author's imagination, and any resemblance to actual events or places or persons, living or dead, is entirely coincidental.

Copyright © 2025 by Kerry Cullen

First Simon & Schuster hardcover edition July 2025

SIMON & SCHUSTER and colophon are registered trademarks of Simon & Schuster, LLC

Simon & Schuster strongly believes in freedom of expression and stands against censorship in all its forms. For more information, visit BooksBelong.com.

For information about special discounts for bulk purchases, please contact Simon & Schuster Special Sales at 1-866-506-1949 or business@simonandschuster.com.

The Simon & Schuster Speakers Bureau can bring authors to your live event. For more information or to book an event, contact the Simon & Schuster Speakers Bureau at 1-866-248-3049 or visit our website at www.simonspeakers.com.

Interior design by Carly Loman

Manufactured in the United States of America

1   3   5   7   9   10   8   6   4   2

Library of Congress Control Number: 2025936150

ISBN 978-1-6680-7459-6
ISBN 978-1-6680-7461-9 (ebook)

HOUSE OF
OF
BETH

PART ONE

CASSIE

OCTOBER

Every time I woke up, someone died. Usually my girlfriend, Lavender, or my dad, or my boss. Sometimes one of the other assistants. Or strangers I'd seen on the street, unlucky enough to have gotten their faces lodged in my brain, or people I remembered from long ago: the little girl I tutored in college, or Eli McKean. I saw them hacked to bits one by one, or force-fed poison, or tied up together and burnt like witches, their skins blistering over a blazing pyre.

The victims changed, but the murderer was always the same, always me. My hands smeared in gore, eyes alight with frenzied ecstasy. My smile, but wrong, more devious. In my real life, I sat up in bed to rub sleep out of my eyes, I stood in a shower I'd turned hot enough to hurt, I sniffed the armpits of my favorite dress. I kissed Lavender goodbye, or I smiled thinly at my roommates on my way out the door. All while the images poured through me, and I tried to convince myself that they meant nothing, that I didn't want them. I didn't want to kill anyone, I thought.

On Halloween evening, Lavender showed up at my office dressed like the night sky, holding a black umbrella, paper stars strung to it with fishing line. I was Donna Tartt in a blazer I'd thrifted on my lunch break—my old bedbug terror had surged like bile; I'd swallowed it down—and a low bun I'd fashioned to look like a bob.

We had initially planned to dress up as Tumblr lesbians, wrapping ourselves in cozy sweaters and twinkle lights. The plan was to spend the whole night entwined. We didn't mind. We'd been together for ten months, and we were near-telepathic. Often when we were separated, I would feel her heart flutter in my sternum; my palms would get sweaty, and I'd text her to ask what was wrong. Just like she knew when I ate stupidly and drank too much by the nausea curling in her stomach. "Would you stop abusing your body," she would say, laughing. "For my sake?"

Okay, the truth: I often faked it. Knowing me made her so happy. And she was so often anxious or sad that predicting her moods was nothing more than pattern recognition. Besides, I loved the way our supposed psychic connection lodged us closer together, made our story the stuff of fate, as if we weren't responsible for our own decisions. Sometimes I thought if I could keep swimming in the current of her love story, I'd never have to make another choice in my life; eventually, I would simply float, thoughtless and free.

For now, fights could take up days, told in three acts, replete with dramatic gestures: we starved ourselves, sobbed for whole mornings, all justified by our status as soulmates. I bragged to friends that it was a more intimate relationship than I'd imagined possible. I was exhausted.

When I added the fourth party to the schedule—a book party, right after work—I asked if we could decouple our costume. I didn't want to enter the infamous publicity director's personal home wearing my girlfriend like an ornament, nor to explain wlw meme culture to my bosses and colleagues. Being a twenty-eight-year-old agent's assistant was already humiliating enough.

I made 26k a year with shitty benefits, my days spent sending endless emails, my nights reading manuscripts on my phone: in coffee shops, waiting for Lavender to get off work, in the bathroom at the bar while she bemoaned nonprofit burnout with her coworkers, on the subway ride home, in bed after she fell asleep and before she woke up. My eyes burned all the time, like visual tinnitus. Lavender kept saying I should get them checked out, but I didn't have the cash for the copay. If I did, I would start with a gynecologist for the yeast infections I kept getting from wearing the same three pairs of black tights to work every day. After that, I'd see a dentist, once I had the mental wherewithal to handle the questions. *It's from the bulimia*, I'd have to practice saying in the mirror first, with a take-me-seriously face. *Yes, I know it was stupid. No, I don't drink soda. I never have.* After that, maybe a chiropractor, and then the eye doctor.

"I know," Lavender would say to my diatribe, settling in behind me on the old mattress my roommates used as a couch, working her thumbs down my spine. "But what if one day you couldn't read anymore?"

I had forcibly exposed myself to sickening thoughts before— *Stare at the word for ten minutes, but no longer*, I could hear my therapist saying—but this one was too horrifying to contemplate. Reading had been my truest love since I was a little girl. Growing up, I'd read at dinner, during recess and study hall, at parties, sometimes while hidden in the bathroom or the closet; I'd push my hand against the back wall every time, hoping for a door, for something fantastic and otherworldly to appear and change everything.

In publishing, I'd hoped to find more people like me. I hadn't been prepared for the social aspect of agenting: the lunches and coffees, or the secret rules of wardrobe and manner. I certainly hadn't been prepared for my boss, Arthur, with his thrush of gray hair and his stooped walk, like a wizard in a movie. His ancient suits, his eggplant breath. He was a legend in his late eighties. "Don't worry," a senior agent had murmured to me once. "He'll have to retire soon."

"Or die in his office," another agent said grimly.

And I had learned not to over-glamorize the reading itself at work—this was author behavior, waxing poetic on speakerphone while we all nodded, bored, in the conference room—and in fact, the older I got, the more starkly I saw that books were not magic and never had been. They were a coping mechanism that allowed me to ignore the outside world when I was small, and then I grew up and decided to turn that coping mechanism into a career. One that I was floundering in but terrified to leave. If I couldn't succeed at this job, which I'd essentially trained for my whole life, then what else could I do?

Maybe in a different life, I'd have made friends with the other assistants, but they straight-girl flirted with each other with heady desperation, as if finding a work wife was tied to their biological clocks. They clustered, laughing prettily, long-nailed hands stroking backs and shoulders, and I was never good at casually touching other women. I stayed at my desk, only extricating myself on the rare Fridays when Arthur invited everyone to his corner office, made us Manhattans, and regaled us with stories about the good old days in publishing.

When Lavender showed up, I was already a little buzzed, elated over having just learned the sleazy true story behind the '90s classic I'd loved in college. Lavender had broken away from work to meet me at my office before the book party I needed to make an appearance at. I was making myself sound more important than I was; I hadn't been properly invited, just DMed that morning by a cheery publicity assistant. I'd told Lavender that I could just meet her at her work party and save her the trip to Chelsea, but she knew I had a nasty habit of ditching parties. The trait had originated in high school, when I was afraid one sip of alcohol would coax me to project the inside of my brain like a snuff film on the nearest wall.

In college, I'd avoided gatherings entirely, which may have in part led to the breakdown, the transfer to community college, the dropping out, the fuck-it move to New York. I'd lucked into my assistant job because of timing; my second boss, Veronica, had read a Twitter thread about the racism/classism of requiring a college degree just before my résumé had landed on her desk. She whispered this excitedly in my interview, like we were in cahoots—fucking the man, together. She didn't seem to care that I was white and had grown up stolidly middle class.

After the book party, we had Lavender's office Halloween party in Gowanus, then my former barista coworker's in Washington Heights, and, finally, a low-key welcome hang for Lavender's best friend Alice, who was visiting the city for the week, staying with a cousin in the West Village. I hadn't met Alice yet—her friendship with Lavender had always been long distance; they'd met at ten years old, attending a summer camp for kids with gay parents, and been emotionally inseparable since. Alice was a textile artist who grew up in Connecticut and now lived in Salem, MA. She'd knitted me a scarf. I was excited. A cold front was coming that weekend, and I couldn't afford any more clothes.

The elevator released us directly into the open kitchen: an island that people were clustered around, flanked by gray marble counters holding bottles of red wine. I sallied forth into the open main room, Lavender behind me. I wanted her to be impressed, but also to know better. I wanted her to feel at home, even though I didn't. Maybe this was the purpose of a work wife: a companion who already understood every social event's subtext.

The author stood in a corner of the room, wearing a high-necked black dress. Her eyeliner was dark and liquid, the wings flaking near the edges. We were Twitter mutuals, but I was hesitant to introduce myself. She wouldn't remember me, and if she did, what would we have to say to each other? I hadn't read her book, and now that I saw her here, looking nervous and unreliable, I knew I never would. She was talking earnestly to Carl, a slightly older man I knew to be a pretentious ass. I'd danced with him at a party like this once, and he'd drunkenly told me that I should write books. "What should I write about?" I'd asked, cautiously flattered. I was trying to be a poet, but he didn't need to know that. "Sex!" he cried. "Everyone should write about sex," he'd continued. "But you should, especially."

I'd thought he was cute until that moment. Maybe even during that moment, and after. Maybe right up until he'd gone home with a different woman, with the tired eyes of someone who had spent hours waiting him out. Lavender proffered a small plate of cheese and crackers, but I shook my head—I'd read a nauseating proposal about dairy farms that morning. "That's the writer, right?" Lavender asked, jutting her chin. "Should you say hi?"

Carl's hand had slid down to the woman's elbow, and her gaze darted around the room. I drained my wine. "This party sucks."

Lavender tipped her glass back—I loved her throat—and shrugged. The less time we spent here, the sooner she'd see Alice. "Onward?" she asked, and took my hand. The elevator doors opened so fast that I startled, knocking over a giant vase filled with glass pebbles. I caught the vase, but the pebbles skittered all over the tile floor, the noise making people turn toward us. One girl stepped back and stumbled; another slipped and grabbed the counter. I heard a shriek.

"Go," I hissed at Lavender, and she stepped into the elevator. We descended.

Four transfers away—the trains were fucked—Lavender walked the empty sidewalk toward a converted warehouse full of nonprofits: a literary magazine that I knew of, a film company that I didn't, and

the mentorship program for queer and trans youth where Lavender
was an associate program director.

I'd met most of Lavender's colleagues at the annual gala they'd
hosted in September. I'd been rude at dinner, reading a manuscript
on my phone in my lap. Now, when we stepped into the warehouse,
a bespectacled person shrieked and launched themself at Lavender,
lifting her up and twirling her while I worked my arms out of my
coat. They set her down, both red-faced, laughing, and turned to
me. "Cassie! I'm a little drunk. Welcome!" They turned toward the
party with a flourish. "We're taking bets on who ends up sleeping
here tonight. My money's on JP."

I looked at Lavender and she mouthed, *Trish.*

Thank you, I mouthed back.

We wound through the small crowd for drinks. Everyone wanted
to say hi to Lavender, and I tried not to compare our work social
lives. I remembered now that I'd felt this way at the gala, too. My urgency over the manuscript had been out of an itching desire to prove
to myself that I was part of something superior. So what if my job
didn't love me back? There was nobility in fighting for appreciation,
I thought. Nonprofit types were easy to win over, I reminded myself.

Lavender handed me a drink and nestled her chin into my neck.
"Don't worry; we won't stay long."

"Why, do we have other plans?"

She laughed and squeezed my hand, hard. "You're my favorite
person here," she said in a confidential tone. Her palm was warm, a
little sweaty, and a chill tore through me, coaxing gooseflesh to the
surface of my arms.

On the way to the third party, Lavender's eyes were red-rimmed in
the blank subway light, a fake cobweb stuck in her hair. I was tired,
a premature hangover already pressing into my temples. My fears

were always worse after I drank, so I knew tomorrow would be hell; I would wake up feeling unclean, my head full of rot and blood. I shivered. Sometimes sex helped blot out the thoughts. At first, my brain would feed me a parade of horrors to get a reaction. I would try to let them fall like rain around me: okay, a breast being chopped off, okay, an orifice full of writhing vermin, disgusting, please let's not overanalyze it, the recoil is happening, but let's not worry about whether it's enough. Once I got turned on enough, they would fade away, which was always immensely comforting. And then once an orgasm had been achieved, my fears rose like puffy clouds over the teeming city of my brain. The relief could last for moments, even hours. It was the best feeling I knew. I probably would have become a sex addict in college if I hadn't been so leery of bedbugs.

I slid an arm around Lavender, my fingertips testing the waistband of her leggings. She wriggled away. "Later," she promised, and I pinned the corners of my mouth upward in a smile. I hated that I would use her for my own brief respite, and she would have no idea. I put her in danger every day I stayed with her. At any moment, the evil thing in my brain might finally take control and use my hands to cut her throat.

Nessa gave me a brief, bony hug as she ushered me into her apartment. "Hello, kitten," she said, her black lips shining as she spoke. "Who is this one?"

"Lavender," she replied.

"Beautiful to meet you. Did you warn her about me," Nessa asked, resting her elbow on my shoulder.

"Nessa is pure evil," I told Lavender.

"I don't know about pure," Nessa said. "Come, let me tell you Cassandra's secrets."

"Not my name."

"She's cute when she's contrary, no?" Nessa grabbed a round-eyed Lavender by the arm and slithered off.

I could have followed them. I looked around. I hadn't been here in months. Strange, as Nessa and I used to be the kind of friends who disappeared into each other's lives, emerging after days or weeks in a wardrobe of the other's castoffs. Grimy posters covered the walls, and the place smelled like smoke layered over cat piss. I hadn't been sure about bringing Lavender here. But Nessa's place still felt like home to me, as in: a disgusting place where I could be disgusting, too. The dim light and lack of order made me nostalgic. I stepped over a small pile of shoes and went to the kitchen for a drink.

Through the kitchen, a tiny room that sometimes belonged to a subletter was populated by a circle of folding chairs. No one was there. I took a moment, sitting on the floor in the center of the circle. Voices hummed in nearby rooms, but here I was alone, in the quiet. I was already too drunk and so tired. I wanted to go home.

Lavender stepped into the room, Nessa behind her, grinning. Lavender looked upset. "Cassie," she said. "Who the fuck is John Mark?"

Right. The night I met him—months before I met Lavender, came out, and changed my life—I'd just ended a situationship with an experimental cellist and I was feeling grandly morose, flinging my limbs around at a bar with my friends. I'd been cocooned with the cellist for months, so they were all annoyed at me, but still, they rallied. I was making a scene, dancing when no one else was, feeling everyone's amusement at my antics plateau and fade.

When John Mark wrapped his hands around my waist, I tipped my head back and looked into his eyes. He was attractive enough. Eventually, he guided me to a chair at a table full of empties. He went on about some Marvel movie. Eventually, he asked me to go home with him. I might have. But at one point, when he leaned toward me, I breathed in. His smell—not bad, just off, not like mold, not like sweat, something else; it was something less than what I wanted. So I lied, said I wasn't from around here, I was staying with a friend, I was sorry. He only asked the once. He left, and I forgot him for months. I guess I must have swiped left. I don't even remember it happening. My interactions with Tinder were rabid spells of loneliness and hope; I barely paid attention. I said it was a numbers game. All I know is that even though I said no that night, swiped left some other time, he screenshotted my profile. Screenshat, I told a friend later, enjoying my own crassness, not yet knowing to be afraid. With a first name, my college, and my face, I was easy to find. He must have requested scads of other people on my friends list first, so that by the time the ask popped up in my inbox, we had mutuals, and I just assumed I knew him somehow. I accepted. You never really know anyone, anyway.

He was in the gay dive I hung out in with my friends. He was in the café with the Eiffel Tower painted on the wall. He was across the street when I walked home, and when I waved, he started—cartoonish, overdone. My friends teased me about having an admirer, and I laughed along, laughed it off. "He's not an admirer," I finally protested one night, too loudly, when I was with Nessa and her newest shitty boyfriend. John Mark was sitting at the bar, nursing the same brand of cider I held. "He doesn't hit on me or even look at me. He's just there. Everywhere."

"Yo," CJ said. "That's actually kinda creepy."

Once he said it, we all knew it was. They looked at each other and not at me. Nessa said, "Catskin, maybe you talk with him."

"Yeah, tell that nerdass dick to leave you alone."

I sighed. I was starting to chafe at Nessa's performative irony around then—dating the literal worst dudes was part of it, I was sure, though she wouldn't admit it—but I hadn't yet met Lavender, who would so easily slide me out of my tenuous orbit around Nessa and take up all of my free time.

"You want me to fuck him up," CJ added.

"Nope!" I said. "I'll talk to him. You guys stay here, okay?"

I claimed the stool next to John Mark. Without asking, the bartender plunked down another cider. I traced the rim. I could feel everything I'd already swallowed sloshing in my gut.

"Cheers," I said to John Mark. "I'm Cassie."

"I know."

"Right," I said. "Um. Did I like, tell you that?"

"We're friends on Facebook." He spoke in a monotone with a weird flavor, something implicating in his emphases. Had he talked like that when I'd met him, that first night? I'd been so drunk; the only facts stuck in my head were the ones I'd kept to make fun of later. He reminded me of a group of boys I'd known in high school, video game obsessed, their every conversation a fortress of inside jokes. I'd had a crush on one of them, but I always felt stupid next to him, somehow deemed both stuck-up and inferior.

"So, I know you, right? From that night a few months ago. We danced?"

He nodded, sort of smiling.

"Okay," I said. "Did you want to talk or something?"

He stared flatly at me. I caught a hint of that scent. I gulped my cider, and the cold of it spread down my ribs. He slid his hand up my thigh, his hair shading his face; I couldn't see his eyes. I placed my hand lightly over his, wondering how to remove it without pissing him off. But at my touch, he looked at me, disgusted, slipped from his barstool, and left, letting the door slam behind him.

The next morning, he sat on a stoop across the street, talking to another skinny guy with unkempt hair, a couple of blocky tattoos, and a black T-shirt bearing some nerd-culture reference. I watched them for half an hour. They never looked at me. I went to my local coffee shop to read. Fifteen minutes later, he sauntered in and sat down across the room.

I walked over. "Okay, what the fuck?" I asked. "You need to get a life."

John Mark shrugged, a little cartoonishly. "Cassandra, this is my life."

"You don't even have coffee." I called to the barista, "This guy is not a paying customer!"

Her expression clearly asked me what she was supposed to do about that. I turned back. "What do you want from me?"

He waited. I felt myself starting to cry. Even when he looked right at me, I couldn't see who he was. "I'm getting what I want."

Now, I told Lavender, "It really wasn't a big deal."

"Doesn't he still live across the street?" Nessa asked.

Lavender turned to me. "Seriously?"

Nessa melted away, waving deviously at me over Lavender's shoulder. Asshole.

"Okay," Lavender told me. "That's fine. You can move in with me."

I allowed myself a moment to indulge this: living with Lavender, in her bed heaped with blankets, wearing her wool sweaters even though they irritated my skin. Smelling like incense, watching her wean off caffeine like she was always threatening to do, learning to love turmeric lattes with her. It looked like a beautiful life. More beautiful than I deserved.

I pulled Lavender around the corner into Nessa's room. "I can't move in with you."

I stroked the inside of her palm as she looked away from me, taking in the room. It was exactly as I remembered it—clothes everywhere, shoes buried like traps. Being here felt like stepping backward, into a former life. I led Lavender to the edge of the bed. She looked hesitantly at the heap of dresses there—castoffs, I assumed, from Nessa's pre-party try-on session. We used to get ready together, trading clothes and makeup. Now, I wore Lavender's hair tie and lip balm. I'd given her a sweatshirt in a pink too light for me, and she wore it sometimes in the soft hours before sleep.

Lavender's cheeks were flushed like the inside of a shell, smooth enough to house a living creature. Part of her always seemed raw to me, the things she felt writhing visibly close to her surface. I thought of headbutting her so hard that her skull crumpled in like a can.

She said, "I just can't believe you wouldn't tell me about some guy stalking you. What if he hurt you?"

"He wouldn't do that," I said.

"How do you know? Everything he did is fucking creepy."

"He never did anything to me."

"Not physically—but doesn't it freak you out? This sick person following you around, and you have no idea what they're thinking?"

"No one ever knows what someone else is thinking."

She tilted her head, squinting at me. "What's wrong, Cassie?"

I knew that if I told her the truth about my recurring thoughts, all the revulsion in her face when she talked about John Mark would turn toward me. Maybe she would try to cover it up, to be kind or polite, but she would watch me more closely. Eventually she would glimpse something real and haunted underneath. I couldn't bear to let her see me that clearly. I said, "I think we should break up."

She looked at me. "You're joking, right?"

"No. I've been thinking about this for a while."

She held a hand over her eyes, scrunched her face up, and let out a long breath. "Cassie, this is good. Really good."

I nodded miserably.

She looked at me again. She laughed. "And you aren't even going to try to fight for it."

"I'm doing this for you."

"Oh, come on. Cass, don't be a fucking child. If you'd just open up to me, I could help."

"You don't know that."

"So why bother trying?" She stood. "Almost a year and you still don't trust me."

It was me I couldn't trust. But I knew saying that would only make her ask more questions. I turned away, and eventually she left.

I stayed in Nessa's bed for a while, tucking myself inside her sheets, sweeping out the crumbs of the weird cereal she ate dry. Eventually, Nessa stood swaying in the doorway. "Poor Catskin," she said. "I liked her."

I sat up. "Fuck off."

"You can crash here if you want." Blood poured down her face, running into her mouth. I watched myself lift the hatchet out of her skull and bring it down again.

"I think I need to be alone," I said.

In college, I was diagnosed with OCD. My bedbug fear began during finals, freshman year. It was then that internet research and a series of therapists led me to a diagnosis. And with the diagnosis, much more about my life made sense: the hemophilia fear that had taken hold after my mom left, my preoccupation with leeches, even my anxious personification of inanimate objects. Many of my childhood oddities fell into place—which was especially satisfying for someone like me, I liked to joke, even though I didn't have that kind of OCD. My disorder had never had anything to do with order. Put me in a room of clutter and I suffered not at all. I didn't line up pens on my desk or color-code my notebooks. Sure, in college I carried a bottle of bleach in my purse, but that was to kill the bedbugs. More often, my compulsions involved research. I tried to build barricades of facts around my doubts, scrolling through Wikipedia, WebMD, Reddit threads. When I opened Google, the search bar autofilled with *how do i know.*

I suspected that my blood-drenched thoughts were a subtype of OCD that focused on harm. Every obsession or theme has a trigger: the moment that caused the person to ask the question that would then worm through their head and ruin everything. Mine was a manuscript I read a few months ago—a fictionalized memoir by a serial killer, written in fragmentary stream-of-consciousness ravings. It wasn't even good. I have no idea why it sank in my head and ruined my life. Maybe the guilty longing in the voice found a kindred spirit in me, a bisexual girl who had refused to know herself for years. Maybe subconscious rage boiled beneath my surface, and this self-torment was the only outlet I'd allow it. Or maybe my brain was just primed for a new horror that day, and if I'd read a book about bird flu instead, I'd be washing my hands raw instead of googling "common attributes of serial killer" twenty times an hour.

I'd thought of reaching out to Meredith, the therapist I'd seen back in college, before she'd switched practices, her fee no longer covered by my insurance. She'd offered me a lower rate, but I hadn't wanted to take up her time. Her other clients probably paid full price, and their problems were probably easier to stomach. Wives waffling over leaving their husbands, kids dealing with class bullies; real-world stuff. I knew OCD was not a rare diagnosis, anxiety far less so. But what if this time it wasn't OCD? What if Meredith took one professional look at my brain and called the police?

Back in my apartment, I felt wrung out and strange. I'd spent hours staring at a screen again, and it was getting dark. Who knew what might happen in the dark? I would stay inside, keep the world safe from me. I ate the rest of a pint of ice cream and binge-watched a comedy about roommates. I couldn't afford myself the space for new thoughts. I woke up with my lamp still on, a scrim of melted chocolate at the bottom of the carton, three episodes further than I remembered, and thank God, thank God, I felt a little better. I turned off the show, turned off the light, masturbated for the endorphins, and fell asleep as fast as I could.

On Monday, I woke up missing Lavender, like a normal person. I wondered if we would ever get to be friends. As I stepped into the shower, my horrible thoughts felt flimsy, almost nonexistent. Maybe they had left, I thought. And then the showerhead rained blood. I could see myself stuffing my roommates' fingers into my mouth and biting down, stabbing their soft bellies with a carving fork. We didn't own a carving fork, I reminded myself. My brain didn't care; it had new concerns. How would I pay my rent after I'd murdered my roommates in the kitchen? Let alone recover my security deposit.

Outside felt too bright. I couldn't see people normally. I used to like watching strangers chatting, but now, on the train, everyone's expressions looked off, plastered like bad makeup on their faces. Even interactions that seemed sweet—a mom holding her little girl's hand—carried menace; I imagined that the mother abused her daughter behind closed doors, pinching her hard on the soft spots covered by clothes, careful to leave no visible marks. The man smiling at the baby was a pedophile. A boy with John Mark's black glasses squeezed in through the closing doors and I turned away, facing my own faint reflection in the glass. Was it him? I couldn't look. I hated my transparent face. I lunged out the door at the next stop, twenty-two blocks from work.

I hoped no one would notice my lateness. Veronica, the boss I liked, was out of the office all week. Without her, my day would be emails, meetings, smiling sweetly at Arthur no matter what he said. I would forget to eat until after three, then lurch toward the office fridge for the cup of overnight oats that was currently congealing in my bag. The sun would go down while I was at my desk, and I would be spit out into the cold city, to be leered at on the subway, to go back home, where my roommates thought I was a freak. I would make mac and cheese and forget to thaw the frozen peas and toss them in anyway, little pebbles of icy sweetness melting into the hot noodles and watering down the cheese. I would eat it lying on my stomach in bed, watching an ostensibly comic TV show that only served to remind me I didn't have friends, not the way characters do. Maybe I'd read all three hundred queries in Veronica's inbox, find a novel that ignited me from the inside, and beg her to let me take it on. Maybe I'd submit more poems into the ether, trying to imagine that owning two contributor copies of a literary magazine with my name in the table of contents would change my life in any meaningful way. Maybe I would read my entire gchat thread with Lavender and cry. I would wake up tomorrow with a different kind of headache, and then I'd be here again. All this while battling an onslaught of gore that I couldn't control. Could I? I was so tired.

When I arrived, everyone was in the weekly meeting. Without Veronica there, I wouldn't be missed. Arthur didn't bother going anymore. Last week, he'd spent the time reading me a love letter from his ex-wife that he'd found in a crevice in his desk. He often beckoned me into his office to regale me with stories: of his youth, his seafaring background. Once, he told me I had a lovely figure. Another time, he asked when I was going to get married and abandon him. I was not out to him, a fact that caused some turbulence with Lavender. I stopped in at his office on the way to my cubicle and saw that he was slumped at his mahogany desk, his cane on the ground at his side.

I knocked on the open door. I'd caught him napping at work before, and I usually just let him sleep, but his posture was strange, one arm stretched out on his desk, his head hanging over the arm of his chair. "Sir?" I said, my voice low. I stepped in the room and smelled the hot tang of urine. I moved around his chair to see his face and yelped. There was a gash in his temple. Bright blood streaked down his cheek, staining his lapel and pooling on the floor below.

"Shit," I said, then clapped my hand over my mouth. My hand shuddered against my face, and I breathed hard through my nose. Lightheadedness blurred my vision. This was real; this had happened. I wasn't making this up. My vision blurred and cleared. I heard laughter down the hall, in the conference room. I shut my eyes and opened them. On the clean side of his face, his features looked slumped, like the skin wanted to slough away.

Should I burst into the meeting and tell them what had happened? But what had happened? My boss, who everyone knew I hated, was covered in blood. And I had found him, in his office, where my fingerprints were everywhere. If this was a crime scene, I would be a suspect. Could I have done it? What if I'd been here before this morning and my brain had neatly buried the memory? That's absurd, I told myself. But still, but still. The smell of blood reached down my throat. If I took another breath in this room, I would puke. I stepped backward out of the room.

My purse was still slung over my shoulder. Nobody knew I was here. In ten minutes, the meeting would be over, and someone else would walk by. I didn't have to be the person who had found him. I didn't have to be here at all.

I left my cubicle and went to the elevators. I walked the thirteen blocks to Port Authority, texting my dad—in Florida, with his snow-bird second wife—to make sure the spare key was still under the doormat. I bought a bus ticket to Elwood, New Jersey: adorable, an hour from the city, nestled along the Delaware, known for antique shops and fall foliage; my hometown.

CASSIE

NOVEMBER

On a sunny afternoon when I was ten years old, I walked home from my school bus stop and found the whole house sparkling clean. I remember feeling unnerved, and like I should be proper, to match it. I sat on the couch, my back straight, my knees together, my hands folded in my lap. Eventually, my mother came downstairs, weighted with luggage and wearing a dress. She stood in the doorway and when she saw me, her eyes filled with tears. She shook—her whole body, like a spasm—passed a hand over her face, and the tears were gone, though her eyes and the tip of her nose were still red. *Cassiopeia*, she said, *get in the car.* I wanted to ask if I should pack a bag, too, bring my toothbrush, put on a dress so I could look like her, but I didn't want to risk her changing her mind. I must have loved her. That day is a chasm in my history; I remember little of the years before it.

In that car, she took out a pack of cigarettes, something I had never seen either of my parents do. She stuck one between her teeth, lit it, and sucked in, making beautiful hollows in her cheeks. As we pulled onto the main road, she kept the tinted windows up, so that the smoke in the car made everything hazy and bitter to taste.

Then, she started telling me the truth. She told me about how my father belittled her, how he was callous. She alluded to them never sleeping together anymore, which I didn't understand at the time. She was unhappy. Maybe she had always been. *What is hap-*

piness, she asked with a sour laugh. *Anyway*. My father was a benevolent dictator, and she had entered the marriage pact knowing this, but over time his affection had atrophied. *The death of love is ambivalence*, she told me, an insider gleam in her eye. *Hate, I could work with.*

I love you, I said, with a child's idiocy. She said, *We're going to have a better life, you and me.*

At the restaurant, she ordered a martini and a steak. I ordered shrimp cocktail; I supposed we were being glamorous, to celebrate. She changed her mind about the steak. When the waiter brought my food, she touched his wrist. She asked him what he did when he wasn't waiting and he said, *I go to high school. I play football.* I was mesmerized by that hand of hers, rubbing.

She sucked her glass dry and stole half my shrimp as I struggled with the shells. We left the restaurant and pulled into a motel nearby. The tears were back in her eyes as she unpacked her silk pajamas, her bottle of water. She asked me where my clothes were, and I wanted to cry. Then she stood, the bottle still clutched in her hands, and locked herself in the bathroom. The water ran, and I could hear her voice. I wondered if she was singing.

I laid myself out on the bed like a snow angel. The ceiling had a stippled pattern of black dots, and I thought they looked like stars in reverse. I knew I was named after a constellation, though I could never remember how to find it.

When she came out, a cloud of steam came with her, billowing into the room and then disappearing. Her hair was sodden, and her breath smelled chemical. *Let's go to bed, Cass*, she said, all swoony and romancing. *We'll wake up to a new day.*

We woke up to a rapping on the door. She looked confused; I

think she looked confused. Her hair was only half dry. When she opened the door, my father lunged into the room. *You can't take her from me,* my mother cried, tossing her hair like a goddess. My father stared at her, dumbfounded. I remember him collecting himself. This I know for sure, because at the time I couldn't figure it out. He said, "Sylvie, stop playacting."

I think I put up a fight. I think I grabbed her hard around her waist. I think I held on to her skirts. I think he had to drag me away. But I remember that when I was finally loaded back into my father's car, a squished, humiliated part of me felt solid again.

When people find out that my mother left me, they assume that she must not have loved me enough. No proof I can give dissuades them: she made me pancakes, she took me shopping, she hugged me constantly, desperately, she told me I was smart, lovely, funny. Often, in the car, I would catch her watching me in the rearview mirror and she would put her hand back behind her for me to reach forward and hold.

"Sure," a boy said once in college as I drunkenly explained this. He was from the South, with two parents, acrimoniously married. "Sure," he repeated, "but you don't leave your child."

There were all sorts of things, I learned from him, that people didn't do. Mothers didn't leave their children. Fathers didn't ignore them so thoroughly that they felt only half existent. Girls didn't tease boys with kisses and with pushing their bodies together, relishing the pressure, and then refuse to give even a blow job to make up for it. Even a kiss on the cheek could be a tease, or a lingering look. I was indignant; I told the Southern boy about my best friend back in high school, Eli. How we'd spent each evening together, walking endlessly through the woods and winding roads of our small town. Sometimes when neither of us could bear to go home, we fell asleep together in his parked car, the seats cranked back and the stick shift between us. "He cared about me," I told the Southern boy, who laughed. "He cared about fucking you," he enlightened me. "Poor idiot."

The year after my mom left, my brain revolted for the first time. I remember those early months with a roiling, desperate resentment. That first bout with OCD still feels unfair, like I should be allowed to go back and fix it, to relive the rest of my life without its corrosion. My trigger was a book about hemophilia. On page sixty-four, I learned that hemophilia could lurk in a person's blood for years, and they might never know—but I knew now. Touching other people felt risky: their nails. I wore sweatpants and bulky hoodies, thick cotton socks; I was so afraid of being wounded. I made myself throw up to avoid gym class. I would not cut my food; I pulled it apart with my fingers or gnawed it into paste. Even a crusty toast could petrify me; small lacerations in the mouth and throat. I bit my nails down to harmless nubs. That whole year was drowned out by the drone of riot in my brain, and no one noticed.

All hemophilia carriers are female. If my mother were still around, I thought petulantly, I could have just asked her. Though of course, anyone can have acquired hemophilia. There's no family history requirement for that, and no warning before onset, either. One day you're healthy, the next you have nosebleeds, bruising, blood clots, especially during menstruation. I knew about menstruation; already I sat awake some nights, fingers anchored under my pelvis, ready to stopper the blood. Once I got my first period—on fucking rope-climbing day—every month was a crest in my spiraling thoughts: Were these normal blood clots? How would I know if not? The internet then was nothing like it is now, and I am grateful.

I was walking home from school, a book open in front of my face. I didn't care that we lived off a highway; after the day my mom left, I didn't like to take the bus. I was still convinced that if I stepped into the house quietly enough, I might catch her, back to pick up the rest of her things. On this day, about halfway there, I tripped over a cardboard box. The box mewled.

I'm not one of those bookish women who grew up imagining myself a spinster cat lady. I could never be like the girls who cooed over babies, bunnies, puppies. The theater of nurturing seemed performative, not unlike that of the girls who held hands and braided each other's hair, that sticky, saccharine closeness. It was missing something vital, and that was the very part I wanted, even as it terrified me: the real love, the bloody kind. As I reached inside the box, it scratched me.

"What's his name?" my father asked that night.

"Clot," I said sweetly, fingering her toe pad. The most beautiful word in the English language. Her little claws extended and retracted in my hand. Dad shook his head. "Sometimes you're too much like your goddamn mother."

How? I wanted to ask, but he was already out of the room. Clot stretched gleefully in my arms. I saw those claws sinking into my flesh, blood pooling in thick dark puddles around me. I didn't care. She needed me to feed her.

Over the next few months, I cheerfully suffered her scratches and snarls, love bites and other indignities, and my blood clotted just fine. I felt invincible. I told myself I would never become so consumed by fear again. Two years later, she died (escape, copperhead) and stupid me, I still thought I was safe.

"These thoughts are ego-dystonic, right?" therapist Meredith nudged me once, early on, after I went on a paranoid rant about infecting my classmates with a plague of bedbugs. "They don't align with what you actually want?"

I'd nodded mutely. "Right. Yes," I said, trying to sound sure. "I hate them."

"Of course you do," she said, believing me, and I cried like I always did. During exposure therapy, I lived my life in tears; I would wake up already crying, would cry at work, at parties, on the subway. The exposures themselves were only a few minutes out of my day. Meredith's commands were simple: watch a five-minute YouTube video of bedbugs every day for one week. The next, touch a chair left out on the street for twenty seconds; the next, a mattress. Not hard tasks for normal people. For me, they took hours of bolstering to accomplish. Right after, I'd usually fall asleep.

Now, I stepped off the bus at the Elwood gas station, feeling lightheaded and vaguely nauseous. I tended toward carsickness and hadn't eaten a real meal in days. I slung my duffel over my shoulder, crossed the highway that ran on one side of town, and ordered myself a whole pizza with sausage and peppers. I waited for it outside, head down, hoping not to see anyone I knew. I'd avoided my phone all bus ride, but now I checked it, expecting a barrage of worried texts. There were only three. *Arthur had a stroke in his office!!!* another assistant said. Then, *Sarah had to call an ambulance. They say he'll be okay.* And then, an hour later, *Can't believe you're ooo for this.*

In Elwood, every breath smelled like clean, wet bark. There were so many trees here, their fallen leaves bookending the streets. Down the main street, lined with coffee and consignment shops, ghosts and skeletons bounced happily in the light wind. When my pizza was ready, I trudged across the parking lot, down a short stretch of treacherous highway, and up the hill along the ravine studded with narrow trees, the ground below them red and gold.

Once I reached my dad's house, I put the pizza on the ground and let my bag fall off my shoulder. I didn't know where the spare key

was—my dad hadn't texted back yet—so I checked under the doormat, then in a flowerpot to the side of the door. The next bus back to
New York wouldn't leave until morning, and I rifled through friends
I could beg to get a Zipcar and bring me home as I turned over every
stone in the garden. I sat in the dirt and opened my contacts. Who
did I even still know in this town? I hadn't kept in touch with anyone from high school, surprising no one. Well, almost no one. What
would Eli McKean say, I wondered, if I called him out of nowhere,
ten years since I last saw his face, and asked him for help? I double-
checked the doormat and found the key duct-taped to the underside.

I had only been back to this house a few times since leaving for
college, and stepping back inside still surprised me each time. The
dark shades had been replaced by gauzy curtains; the whole house
felt lighter. I went upstairs to the room that had once been mine and
found a home gym with a rowing machine and an elliptical. It was
silly to be offended when I never came home, but I still felt strange
looking upon the evidence of my erasure. Twin water bottles stood on
a shelf, and I wondered if my dad and Fiona cared whose was whose.

Fiona had first appeared when I was in college. I came home to
stay one summer and she was there. When my dad picked me up
from the train station that June, he seemed new: cleaner, tanned.
"There's someone I want you to meet," he said. At the house, I noticed the clean floors, dingy carpeting disposed of, replaced by run-
ners and area rugs in creams and camels. As a child, I had not been
happy in that house, and my memory still colored it accordingly—all
gray, even the yellow bathroom taking on a shadowed tint. The furniture sagged. But that summer, the well-stuffed sofa pressed back
against my touch.

Fiona had come in without knocking, holding a bag of peaches.
She was taller than him, especially in heels. She was blonde and tan,
more so in the creases of her skin. "That fruit stand at the bottom of
the hill is so cute!" she thrummed. Her speaking voice was beauti-

ful; it trilled and burst like birdsong. "Gosh, it's dark in here," she said. She gave me the bag and moved through the rooms, sliding all of our heavy curtains aside. Buttery light flowed into the room. My father rose to join her, and I was left blinking in the sudden sun, feeling like one of the many dust bunnies that had been swept aside by all this new movement.

Fiona had clearly been led to believe that my dad was a more involved father than he was; I could tell by her questions. "I know you're a great singer," she told me once. "Your father raves about your cooking," she said, days later. Back then, I was taken with obsessive love stories about fatedness and twin flames. I didn't see that in Fiona and my dad. I saw two people who had made a joint decision to stand by each other's side. Their love was calm, as complete as a closed box. I went back to the city two weeks later, crashed on Nessa's couch until the dorms reopened.

Eli and I hadn't spoken in over a year by then. He had visited me once; he'd bought us both tickets to a show at Irving Plaza— a Christian rock band, which seemed weird to me at the time. I stood next to him while he mouthed the words, feeling out of place surrounded by shiny, too-clean people. I wished I'd invited Nessa, who was always game for a new experience; together we'd gone to a sex party (we were chickenshit and stayed at the bar, only glimpsing the playrooms in flashes of opening doors), a séance in an abandoned subway station, and two one-woman shows, both shitty, one literally. Nessa would enjoy the Jesus vibes ironically, maybe try to sleep with a believer for sport.

But Eli sang along to the corny lyrics like they had uncorked him. After the show was over, he wanted to walk to Times Square to see the lights. Instead, we got pierogies and ate them in Washington Square Park, other college kids bobbing up to us to offer us drugs or invite us to parties. I scowled at them while Eli demurred politely. He lay back on the stone bench, then leapt up when a rat skittered by.

"Remind me why you moved here?" he asked.

"I think it suits me. Like, some people are dog people, or cat people. I'm more like a rat person. I find a dirty little crevice to live in and hoard my treasures there."

"So what am I?"

"I'm not sure," I said. "But I think you belong somewhere open."

He nodded and kept nodding. Finally, he said, "Beth might be a bird person."

"Beth?"

"This girl I'm talking to."

I refused to jolt at the prick of envy. "Girlfriend?" I asked sweetly, goading.

He shrugged. "Want to see a picture?"

"Obviously," I said.

Lately, I've tried to remember precisely how I felt the first time I saw Beth's face on the screen of Eli's flip phone. The bridge of her nose was sunburned, and a damp tendril of hair curled along her ear. Her smile made her top lip disappear, and something about its shape made her seem boyish, adventurous.

"How did you meet?" I asked.

"She started at West this year. Her best friend moved away, too," he said, avoiding my gaze. He laughed. "We actually mostly talk about how much we miss you guys."

I jerked forward and kissed him clumsily on the mouth. He froze for a moment, then kissed me back, his fingers tentatively latching onto my shoulder, then moving into my hair. He cupped the back of my head so gently. Did I like being kissed by Eli? I wondered. Did Beth?

A few days later, Eli texted me with unusually formal grammar, saying he thought it was best if we took some time apart from each other. I knew he was disappointed: I'd spent years holding him at a careful distance, letting him idealize me in peace. When I kissed him that first time, I forced him to see me up close—my covetousness, my fickle whims. He'd thought I was better than that. I'd wanted him to think so. Ten years later, I still did.

A week into my grand escape from my entire adult life, I sat with a hardcover and an almond mocha in front of the big window at the coffee shop where I used to hang out after school. I took a picture of the book next to the coffee—a reflex; if I was in the office, I'd have posted it and tagged the author. I pretended the day was normal.

Heard Arthur's still in the hospital, another assistant texted me. *You working from home?*

At the best of times, Arthur didn't know how to log into Gmail or make an outgoing call from the office phone—I did those things for him. Even if he had reached out and complained to the other agents, they'd probably assumed that I was on vacation, that he'd known that and forgotten. Instead of responding, I'd deleted my work email from my phone.

When Eli McKean opened the door of the coffee shop, a little slice of light fell across my page. My body recognized him before my mind did; a shivery flush crept up my arms toward my chest as I stared at the back of his head. When he turned, I realized that the boy I'd known was different now. Some guys work out at the gym so much that their muscles look like they've been glued on; Eli's looked like they'd always been part of him, though I knew they hadn't. A shaggy mop of sun-blond hair escaped from his plain black cap and curled around his ears. I had known that cap, once, a lifetime ago, had held its worn brim in my hands. He didn't see me. A maroon bandana stuck out of his right pocket, grease-marked and tattered. His fingertips were stained gray. He ordered a dark-roast coffee with room for cream. I've always liked when men say cream instead of milk.

I'd hoped the small-town charm of Elwood might erase the creeping sense I'd had in the city that everyone was evil at the core, but so far, it was holding on—the barista, a peppy teen girl who was collecting donations for her chess club, might harbor dreams of peeling off her own fingernails and feeding them to her classmates. The older woman with six dogs I'd known since puppyhood locked them all in a too-small crate for hours, reveling in their whimpers. But right now, Eli was immune to my projections. Maybe because I'd once known him so well. Maybe because he looked hunched and sad standing in that line, arms wrapped around his ribs like he was holding them in place. When he paid for his coffee and turned back toward me, I let my hair hide my face.

The first boy who ever called me pretty was Gavin Lawlor, in the summer before seventh grade. We were at school: him for football preseason, me for cheerleading. We met walking toward the water fountain. He was older than me, in high school, his knees and chest grass-stained, his curly hair weighed down with sweat. "You can go first," he said. He stood back while I drank. I wanted to linger, to watch the bob in his throat. Later, I stole a boy's shirt out of Marjorie's locker—Marjorie was a field hockey player who wore her brother's hand-me-downs for practice. I brought the shirt to the boys' locker room, gingerly pushing the door ajar. Tyler Blake answered.

"I think someone left a shirt out in the hallway?"

A voice floated over. "Do Cassie."

Tyler grabbed on to the shirt, but I held on. We both listened.

"Cassie Jackson?" Gavin said.

"Splice!" a second voice said. "You're stalling."

"Alright, fine," Gavin said begrudgingly. "Splice: Cassie's face. Whose body?"

A third voice jumped in. "Helaine, obviously."

Helaine was the team flier.

"Whose brains?" the first voice asked.

Gavin laughed. "Jenny Richards," he said.

"Dude, she's such a ditz."

"I know," he said. I could hear the smile in his voice, the smile that had been stuck in my head all day. He said, "I like 'em dumb as shit."

Once, on a marketing call, I told this story offhandedly—we were representing a novel about the dark underbelly of Greek life, and I was making a point about teenagers. I laughed at the end, but no one else did.

A few nights after seeing Eli in the coffee shop, I walked myself to a bar on the river that I'd walked by plenty of times as a child. Sometimes Eli and I used to see our teachers drinking in the open windows. Now, I stepped inside, uncomfortable. I knew I couldn't spend every night alone in my dad's house, but I didn't want to see anyone I knew. I ordered a cider and sat at the bar. This was a mistake; the bartender—a red-faced guy who looked my age—asked my name.

"Cassie."

"I've always liked that name," he said cheerily. "Cassandra, the prophetess," he intoned.

"Cassiopeia," I countered. "My predictions are shit."

"My bad," he said. I half smiled, tired. My brain rifled through appropriate responses: I could slam my pint glass against his head, or I could shatter it against the bar first and slash his cheeks with a piece of jagged glass. I wished I'd ordered a whiskey so I could drink it in one gulp and leave. Instead, I sipped frequently, checking my phone.

"Cassie Jackson." Two hands clapped down on my shoulders. I

gritted my teeth and turned—then melted, sinking into his chest. "Eli," I said.

He stumbled back and almost took me with him.

"I never thought I'd run into you in a bar," I said.

"You're one to say," he slurred. He sat next to me, taking a moment to balance. "Another round," he told the bartender, including me in his gesture, even though I was only a third into my cider. The bartender delivered a pat on the hand along with Eli's drink—a whiskey—and gave me a softer smile, like Eli's presence put me in his good book. Well, Eli was a nice boy, through and through. He always had been. Now, he looked a little more like someone I'd be seen with—his hair longer, his jeans tighter, his Adidas switched out for scuffed combat boots. He was broader, too; in high school he'd been skinny and hunched, always a little furtive. Here, he sat tall, and seemed much taller, even while swaying on his stool.

"You drink now," I said.

"I've earned it."

Instead of asking what the fuck that was supposed to mean, I said, "Me too."

"Cheers to that," he said, and we did.

"So," I said, "what's happened since we last saw each other?"

He laughed quietly. "What's happened?" He shook his head. His exhale wiped his face clean of expression. That was fine; I'd always been the talker of the two of us.

"I'll start. I worked in book publishing until about two weeks ago. I dumped my girlfriend"—I watched him absorb this, a tiny wave breaking over his expression—"and now I'm here. Staying for who knows how long. Your turn."

He said, "I worked for a machine shop. Riley's, if you remember."

"Sure," I said. I didn't. "Do you like it?"

"I did. I'm a metal and glass—" He slurred another word, but I didn't catch it.

I said, "That sounds cool."

He nodded once, twice, then said, "Bag."

"Bag?" I reached for my bag and showed it to him.

"Bag," he said, his eyes roving over the bar.

"Bag," I said more insistently, shoving it toward his chest. His head sank down as if weighted, and he puked into it.

"My phone was in there," I said stupidly, as I checked my back pocket, relieved to feel my keys and wallet. My journal was also in the bag, half filled with lovedrunk couplets about Lavender, interspersed with work notes—drafts of pitch copy, potential blurbers, a list of authors to watch I'd been furtively keeping for years. Eli breathed heavily into the bag's mouth, his shoulders shuddering. A sticky mix of revulsion and compassion rose in me. I hadn't spoken with Eli in ten years, but I'd cared about him once, and I didn't like seeing him sick. The bartender was already rushing out with wet paper towels, patting his back, saying "It's okay, man, no big deal at all," which seemed like my job, it being my property that had been ruined. When Eli looked up, I saw he was crying. I hopped off the stool, took the bag from him, and looped my arm through his, the gesture so familiar still, like we were fifteen and sixteen again, best friends. I said, "Let's get you some air."

Outside, I dropped the whole bag into a sidewalk trash can. The stars were clear and endless, the night cool with an underbite of real cold. We walked a few blocks and leaned over the low railing above the canal. The moon was bright enough to see the reflections of black trees in the water, and I heard an errant frog on the bank. I had left my leather jacket inside. I hunched into Eli to keep warm. "Your Saturday night routine has changed," I said.

He laughed.

"Okay, that sounds like an improvement," I said. I didn't know whether to keep up the patter, and I didn't know what to ask him— I had no context for him anymore. I rubbed his back a little. Back when we knew each other, we touched all the time, but in the way of kids; we linked arms and skipped; we tripped and ended up on top of each other; we fell asleep on each other's shoulders and woke up embarrassed. We teased, poked, sometimes hit. I think I'd felt his forehead once and told him he didn't have a fever. This was different, more grown-up. More caring, less intimate. I said, "So is that bartender in love with you or what?"

He breathed in deeply, his ribs flaring under my palm. I pulled my hand away.

"He's just being nice. Everyone's so nice to me."

"You sound oddly bitter about this."

He waved a sloppy hand. "It's just because of everything."

"Okay," I said. "Let's pretend I'm a complete idiot who has barely come home for the last decade and hasn't kept in touch with anyone. What's everything?"

He looked at me suspiciously. Finally, he said, "My wife died."

I blinked many times. He was still talking. "Six months ago. Everyone knows. They—" He breathed in hard through his nose. "It sucks."

"Eli. I'm so sorry."

"Sure," he said. "Thanks."

I wanted to make him understand that I knew his grief must have depths I couldn't fathom, but also that I cared. But I hadn't known, and that fact showed a distance that couldn't be surmounted. "I'm sorry," I said again. "I really haven't been back in a decade. My dad is almost never here anymore, and after a few Thanksgivings, I just— But I should have kept in better touch with you. I wish I had been there, to help."

"Yeah," he said dryly. "Maybe you could have broken her fall."

"She fell?"

He didn't respond for a while. "I'm the one who should be sorry," he finally said. "I hurled in your bag."

"Yeah, that was pretty rude," I said. He didn't laugh. "Listen," I tried again. "I'm gonna be around for a while. In town, I mean. If you ever need to—talk. If you need a friend. I'm, you know. Here."

"Okay," he said.

"Can I do anything to help now?"

"I think I need to stand here for a while by myself," he said.

"Sounds good," I said, trying not to feel stung. I told him goodbye and went back inside. The bartender had stowed my jacket behind the bar. I thanked him and offered to pay both tabs, but he said that Eli drank for free these days.

"You think he's doing okay?" I asked.

"He'll be alright," the guy said. "I worry about his kids. But at least they have Joan."

I wanted to sit back down and ask invasive follow-up questions, but it wasn't my business. I settled up and left. Once I was out of the building, I ducked down a side street that looped around toward the canal. I leaned under the awning of a closed shop. Eli was still there, staring into the canal, his head bowed. I watched him for a while as clouds crossed over the moon, as lights went out one by one in the town above, until he straightened up, shook once all over like a dog, and shuffled off.

I first met Eli when I was sixteen. Bruce Rudd, a senior to my junior, had gone to a party out in the cornfields, where he'd set up the folding table that lived in his truck bed for beer pong. Bruce was a nice enough guy, a football player at a school that was known for losing at football, so he wore the jockish crown unsteadily. I had never spoken to him. That night, Bruce couldn't stop sinking ping-pong balls, so he wasn't drinking much. Maybe he didn't drink at all. No one could figure it out: how he wasn't drunk, but he still drove directly into a tree on his way home, all alone on the curving country road.

Half the school went to the funeral. Mostly students like me who didn't really know Bruce, who had never seen death up close and were not seeing it up close now, either. I liked the way my long black skirt swished around my calves, so I was ashamed as I added unnecessary half twirls to my steps. I wanted to be suffused with sadness. But my tights itched, my hair was full of static, and I was pretty sure I'd just failed a bio test.

Bruce's best friend Tyler gave a eulogy, breaking down into snotty tears fifteen seconds in. I shifted in my seat. I had never liked Tyler. And in my adult life, I've come to believe that there are two kinds of big grief: the kind caused by the unfairness of the cosmos—death, illness, natural disaster—and the kind caused by humans. Cosmic grief, I think, is more pure. Everyone bands together as a community. New connections blossom from these gatherings, and together, they carry the loved one's memory like a spark between held hands.

Back then, I was more familiar with human-caused grief. The bitter kind, the rotten kind. I didn't know what it was like for a parent to die, but I'd watched one leave, and the other turn away in myriad daily ways. My father didn't like to look at me because my face was too like hers. For school, I'd learned to forge his signature; I sometimes worried that one day he would wake up with the sudden, urgent desire to sign a permission slip and the school office would call it a fraud. I couldn't remember the last time we'd had a conversation that wasn't about pizza or Chinese. And I knew, I knew! I should have been grateful that my dad brought home takeout, that he didn't leave, that he wasn't dead. But I felt coated inside with resentment. I was jealous of mourners; at least they could remember their losses with fondness. Tyler blew his nose. I stood, skirt swishing, and burst out the big double doors.

A boy—Eli, a sophomore I'd seen around—sat on the steps, smoking a cigarette. I didn't smoke, but I wondered if breathing in fire might incinerate the corruption inside me. I collapsed next to him and asked, as if I did this all the time, "Can I have one?"

Once the expected coughing was over—him looking amused and faintly alarmed—I said, "Don't make a big deal of it, okay?" and he nodded. His hair was short back then.

"I'm Cassie," I said.

"I know."

We smoked in silence for a while. Finally, Eli said, "They'll be coming out soon. You want to go back in?"

"I can't."

He nodded. "Want a ride home?"

"You have your permit? What are you, twelve?"

"Fifteen. And not yet, but my mom doesn't care."

This intrigued me. "Sure," I said.

Eli said he needed to stop by his house before he could drop me off. At first, when we pulled into the driveway, I thought the sound was a movie, or music. "Shit," Eli said as he turned off the car. "Stay here."

I followed him as he trudged up the hill the house was perched on. He cast a look back at me, rueful or annoyed, but I didn't stop. I wanted to know what was hunching his shoulders like that. When he got to the door, he sighed loudly. I'm still not sure if this was for my benefit.

A lamp lay on its side in the hallway. The couch was bare, its pillows and cushions strewn around the room. I wondered if he'd been robbed, but he walked through the wreckage and up the stairs, where a long landing looked over the entryway.

"Mom?" he called, waiting outside a door.

A woman in a nightgown emerged, her long dark hair spilling down her back. She wore white athletic socks, one of them blotched red around the big toe. "Don't you dare tell me this is my fault, Elijah, you always take that little bitch's side. Always! Did she call you? She called you, didn't she?"

"I didn't!" A voice from down the hall, and then a long, loud scraping sound. Eli's sister—right, he had a sister, I remembered; she was in middle school—burst out another door. She looked like her mother in miniature but wore gym shorts and a T-shirt. "I did nothing, Eli, you have to believe me. She's a fucking psychopath." Her voice was hoarse, and her face—that was what made the two of them look alike. Their faces were red and raw-looking; they seemed looser at their joints, their expressions uncontrolled, like their mouths could open wider than they were supposed to, like they'd cried so much it had stretched out their expressions.

"Kim," Eli said, "go to your room and lock your door."

"I can't!" Kim screeched. "She unscrewed the fucking doorknob; I had to push my desk against it!" She kicked barefoot behind her, and her door rebounded open, a hole like a perfect round mouth in its side. "I'm packing," she said. "I'm going to Jenny's tonight."

Their mother laughed acidly. "And have her parents think I'm a terrible mother? Tell him the truth, Kimberly." She turned to Eli. "Your sister pushed the desk against the door while I was trying to come in, and the door shut on my foot." She raised her foot, displaying the bloodied sock. Eli stepped back. His mother sighed. "This is what I raised. My children, who I bore in my own body, who now pretend they have to protect themselves from me with locks and doors." Then she saw me. "Who is that?"

"No one," Eli said.

I waved.

His mother put the back of her hand to her head. "I'm so sorry. You've come on a bit of an off day for us," she said. "Can I get you anything to drink?"

Kim snorted.

Eli turned to me. "I'll be outside in a minute."

I went to wait in the car. A few moments later, he got in and pressed the heels of his hands against his eyes. Kim opened the door to the back seat, swinging a backpack in before her. Eli told me, "This'll just be a few minutes."

Kim put her feet up on the seat, folding herself up like a mantis, and cried quietly into her knees. Eli drove for eight minutes, then stopped in front of a blue ranch house with a swing set in the back.

"Thanks." Kim got out of the car and stopped at the open driver's-side window.

"Call me if you need anything," Eli said.

"Are you going back?" she asked.

Eli chewed his lip. "Yeah, but I'll probably drive around until she's asleep."

"Good luck," Kim said. She swung her backpack over one shoulder and trudged up the driveway.

Eli started the car. "Where to?" he asked me with forced brightness. I shrugged.

"Let's go to Wawa," he said as he pulled out onto the road.

"Is it always like that?" I ventured after a few moments.

"Not always," he said. "But sometimes it's worse. That was about mid-range."

"What does worse look like?"

He half smiled. "You'd be amazed at how many of our household objects have the capability of flight."

I looked at him.

"Not funny, I'm sorry. Kimberly and I make jokes. It helps."

"It's not not-funny. I'm just adjusting to the new information."

"She's insane," he said, then laughed desolately. I nodded. But I knew in that moment that I could never show Eli my most lost self, my pacing, frantic-checking, repeating-sentences self. If I did, he wouldn't trust me ever again.

"She can be really nice." He said it like a warning. "It can be hard to describe that"—he jerked his head back at the house—"to people who have only seen her good side."

"What do you think happened? Like, what did Kim do?" I wanted to ask if she might have deserved it.

"It doesn't matter. I'm her big brother," he said. "It's my job to protect her."

I remember thinking back then that he seemed good at protecting.

The morning after Eli puked in my bag, I was woken by the landline. I hadn't known we still had one.

"It's Eli," he said before I spoke. "I'm sorry about last night."

"I'm surprised you remember."

He laughed. "I didn't, actually. Or I thought maybe I dreamed it. I called Hank, who clarified things. Anyway, I thought I could give you a ride to get a new phone."

"You don't have to do that," I said. "It's nice, being freed from the tyranny of connection to the wider world." And it was. Last night, I hadn't spent my pre-sleep hours trawling the depths of the internet, hunting for a certainty that I would never find. I had simply fallen asleep.

"Says the woman staying alone in an old house who, I assume, still can't drive."

"You may not remember this, but I can yell really loud."

He took a deep, tired breath, the sound like the ocean on the staticky line. "I'm pretty embarrassed," he said. "Would you let me at least try to make it up to you?"

"Okay," I said. "Sure."

Eli's car was much cleaner than the one he'd had in high school, aside from some crumbs and a pink pig stuffed animal in the back seat. "Buckle up," he said when I got in.

"You remember when I used to stand up through the sunroof?" I teased.

"It's the law. By the way, this is on me."

"What, you don't need gas money?"

"The phone," he said.

"Oh, no, you don't have to do that," I said. "I can cover it." I thought I could. "Maybe I'll get a flip phone."

"I'm doing this."

"Fine," I said, with an edge that I hoped conveyed that I didn't need his help. But I did. I leaned my temple against the window and closed my eyes.

At the store, when I asked if I'd lose all my contacts, the bouncy employee said phones didn't work like that anymore. "Thank God, right?" She laughed. "Our whole lives are on there now."

"Can I wipe them on purpose?" I asked. Eli was an aisle away, perusing cases.

"Technically, I guess," she said. "Do you want me to?"

"Yes," I said, fast, before I could change my mind. "I want a new life."

She smiled the bright smile of a retail worker who has just realized they're talking to an insane person. "'kay, one sec!" she said, and disappeared into the back.

"Let me at least buy you coffee," I said to Eli as we left the store. He looked at the time before he said yes, and I wondered if this had been solely a duty-bound errand. His life seemed so different from mine—the nice car, the dead wife. Both conveyed a level of adulthood that I could only squint at, haplessly unable to understand.

At the coffee shop, I made him tell me about his life. He had married Beth, the girl he'd dated after I left town, and she'd died this past spring. He had worked his way up at the machine shop the next town over for years after high school. In the past five years, though, he'd moved on from machines—"I didn't particularly want to lose a limb," he told me, laughing—gone to night school, and gotten the certifications to become a metal and glass architect. He spent a lot of time in and out of New York and Philadelphia, crafting windows and fixtures for their office buildings. He loved the freedom, the aloneness, only wished he could be home more for the kids.

I'd been waiting for him to mention them, half terrified, half yearning to get it over with. "You have kids?"

"Oh, yeah," Eli said, as if embarrassed. "Two, a girl and a boy."

Before I could stop them, somehow before I even knew they were there, the images were a torrential rain dripping down inside my eyelids: little Elis with hatchet wounds in their skulls, dismembered, limbs lying in pools of blood, clutching their small pale throats as a malevolent version of me poured poison down their throats. Like always, it was all at once, and it didn't make enough sense to keep up. I clenched a thread of cheek between my teeth. In my head, a child I made up screamed, his face blubbered with tears and snot, as a shadow advanced. The shadow was me.

In the real world, I tried to impersonate a human being. "How old are they?"

He smiled broadly. "Nine and seven."

"Oh, wow. Cute," I said weakly as the beheaded toddler's limbs stretched. Beth must have gotten pregnant in my first year in New York. I felt dizzy, imagining a life so different from mine. I still didn't know if I ever wanted a child. How had she been sure when she hadn't even graduated high school?

Eli took out his phone. "Do you want to see a picture?"

"Do I," I said. Outside, a woman in a crimson scarf stood before the café window. I could just make out the ghost of my smile, blood red.

"Hey," Eli said, fluttering his fingers in front of my eyes. "Where'd you go?"

I focused on his face. The dimple in his left cheek, the scar on his temple from the time we were walking in the middle of the road late at night and a car came roaring; he jumped the guardrail and rolled down the ravine, me screaming with a depth I didn't know I had, him laughing the whole way down. The scar was faint now; only someone who knew it was there would see it.

"Show me," I said.

The girl, the younger one, took after Eli. His jaw worked, patterning his cheek as he clicked through a few photos. "I don't know how to be a dad anymore," he confessed.

"What did you do before?"

"I supported Beth," he said simply. "She homeschooled them, and I helped her—that was just doing what she told me. We went to church together, as a family. I haven't been since she passed," he said, finally looking at me. "I don't know if I'll ever go back."

Eli's conversion to Christianity had happened right after I moved, and I had never understood what it meant to him. I didn't have much vocabulary for the distinction between denominations. But Evangelicals had been in the news a lot lately, and now I wondered if he'd once been one of those rabid believers I'd been reading about.

Coolly, I said, "Why not?"

"Let's walk," he said. As I got off my stool, he took my jacket and held it for me to put my arms into. The gesture felt overly polite, but I didn't rebuff it.

While we passed the houses rife with gables and wraparound porches, autumn starting to feel threadbare in the town's corners— leaves in gutters, leached of color—I listened.

"I don't think I ever really believed," he told me.

"You seemed like you did, last time I saw you."

"I was definitely trying," he said. "I was really sad back then, maybe depressed. Not entirely because of you, don't worry," he said, laughing.

"I wasn't—"

"You were. But that's okay. I did have a pretty bad crush on you. And then meeting Beth, she was so different, and she seemed—no offense—easier to handle, back then. I thought she was so responsible. She liked caretaking. She'd had a complicated childhood. In some ways, she was like a tiny adult. She never really got the chance to be irresponsible."

"Like me?"

He thought. "It's not that you were irresponsible. But it kind of always felt like you were on this desperate search for something else. Something to save you, or change things. Beth had her something bigger, in her faith. And me—I wanted to have that, too, so I think I just pretended for years."

"You've thought a lot about this."

"I went to counseling for a while after she died. Pastor Jack wanted to help me. But nothing he said stuck enough to make it worth staying. I wanted to stay," he clarified. "For the kids, if nothing else. But I can't. I just—listening to the way they all talk about God, the promises he makes."

Gently, I said, "Does God promise that no one will die?"

He laughed. "I never expected you to defend organized religion."

"I'm not," I said. "But it seemed like it helped you. It calmed you down." I didn't say that I hadn't liked seeing him that way, that the lacquer religion gave him back then had felt false, too hard and bright.

"It kind of did," he said. "I wish it still did."

"I get that."

"You were never religious," he said tentatively.

"No. But I've had moments," I said, thinking of Lavender, and of my year of coming out, when every new conversation with another queer person felt like an awakening. "Of feeling like—I've found a way of living that will fix me."

"You don't need fixing."

I smiled softly. "You can't know that."

"I've known you for over a decade."

I didn't laugh, didn't tell him that this statement was ridiculous, true in only the most technical way, not in any of the real ones. I wanted to pretend together.

Later, the slick, puddle-studded street shone under our feet. We'd decided to have dinner, to keep catching up. A sympathetic neighbor was watching the kids. "Joan has a daughter, Felix, who's Preston's age," he explained. "They're best friends."

"We were best friends," I reminded him.

He smiled quietly. "We were."

I remembered talking about Eli to that Southern boy in college, how he'd refracted my version of our friendship and made it sadder. But I had always cared about Eli, and I still did. His presence was a reminder of my younger, braver self. I had lost that girl again, but he was safe; I knew this like prey knows where to sleep. I wanted to earn the right to stay near him.

"Hey," I said. I grabbed his arm and pulled him to me, then I reached around his neck and kissed him. His lips were cold, unmoving at first, but they warmed and changed under mine. He touched the small of my back, my shoulders, the nape of my neck. His hand moved into my hair, holding me caught between his skull and his palm. When I pulled back, he looked dazed. "What was that for?"

"I wanted to," I said with made-up confidence. "Didn't you?"

"I think so," he said. Then, more firmly, "Yes."

That night, in my father's house, I held Eli's chin for a while and scrutinized his face, trying to match what I saw with what I remembered. I thought his hairline crept back just a little at his temples, and I wondered if he'd grown it longer to hide this. I couldn't remember the freckle on his cheekbone or the slight bump in his nose. I wished we could slow down, sit across from each other and recount every detail of what the other had missed. Take our time relearning each other's souls before introducing our bodies. But we were adults. Besides, I felt that for a long time now; I'd owed Eli much more of my physical body than I'd ever given. I wormed my hand toward his belt buckle, but he pulled away. His smile was kind and disarming. "Maybe not so soon," he said.

"Of course," I said, flushed and apologetic. We kissed until we fell asleep nestled on the overstuffed couch, my heartbeat slowing to match his. When I woke up in the full glory of morning, he was still asleep. The sunlight felt honey-colored and viscous; I had to squint through it to see him, and he glowed around his edges. That light felt right around him.

I eased from his arms and heated a pan to make scrambled eggs with herbs. As the oil spat, he woke, yawning, eyes half closed. He sniffed the air and grinned. "You still love sage."

Warmth from the stove wafted softly over my face.

After breakfast, Eli dressed and went back to his kids. Without him, I was back to my scarred and rotted self. My decision to wipe my phone of contacts had felt brave and new in the moment, but I still had social media, and people still texted me; I just didn't know who they were. With the exception of Nessa, whose gleeful profanities identified her quickly. Some of the messages were annoyed—coworkers or roommates, maybe. One number was beseeching: Lavender? I didn't ask. I went back to the antique shops Eli and I had browsed, walked the gorgeous path by the river we'd traversed together, but without him, the small town lost its quaint simplicity, and the air carried a dim, foreboding color, a thickness like soup.

An internet fad called corpsing was raging through the town's teenagers; it wasn't uncommon to round a corner and be confronted with a body face down on a sidewalk, sometimes stained with corn syrup or raspberry jam; if you were a fool and showed fear or called for help, your gullibility would be recorded and posted and the nearby bushes would shake with laughter. A town meeting had been held, but they weren't breaking any laws. We learned to step over them, to cover our faces. I worried I was being followed. I thought I saw the glint of light off glasses in a near-empty bar and my chest clenched like a fist.

When we were kids and I was scared, I used to text Eli, even in the middle of the night, and he would come get me. He wouldn't ask what had happened; he just let me into his car and started driving. We drove through the graveyard to freak ourselves out. We parked by the canal and got out, carving paths through galaxies of fireflies. We walked to the wing dam that stretched out into the cold river like a numbed arm, where lone men stood with fishing poles before the sun rose. At the elementary school's playground, we claimed the swings while seniors did drugs in the covered slides. We snuck into parties even though we were never invited. The drunkest kids sometimes sought us out like we were oracles, as if by nature of not fitting in, we had a view of them that nobody else could see. I believed it, sometimes. Eli always knew better.

That was nice, someone texted me. For the first time all day, I recognized the number. It was the same one he'd had back in high school.

We texted all day, seeing what we remembered. Eli still loved pears and the smell of woodsmoke. He'd learned to appreciate blue cheese. His office was boring, but they got free bagels on Fridays. His sense of ambition had leapt before he'd left the shop, then plateaued right after. *Some of the guys want to design the glass on the fanciest buildings,* he said. *But I think windows are for looking through, not at.* He was charmed to hear that I had seen our classmate Tyler

Blake at the coffee shop, and that I still loved cherry pie. I didn't tell him that I'd hidden from Tyler, holding my book over my face. When I said that my favorite soup was tomato, Eli said, *That was Beth's, too.* Then he apologized. *You don't have to be sorry,* I said.

By sunset, he had asked if he could call me later that evening, and when he did, he asked if he could come back. The kids could keep on staying with the neighbor, Joan, he claimed. She was happy to help. She homeschooled her kid, too—unschooled, technically, he said, as if I should know what that meant—and didn't mind having two more around. I wondered if Eli had fans rooting for him to find love after Beth, if this Joan person was winkingly hustling him out the door to me. "Come back," I said.

His sneakers left scuff marks on Fiona's cream carpet. Scraps of metal and glass were always embedded in his soles; his shoes clicked on bare floors.

"Missed you," he whispered into my neck.

"Are you talking to my earlobe?"

"Yeah, actually. She and I have this whole other thing going. It doesn't concern you."

"I've got news for you: my earlobes are male."

He laughed. "Fine, I'm gay for your earlobe."

I said, "You remember that I'm bisexual, right?" He'd been so drunk when I came out to him at the bar, and I still didn't know if he was hanging on to vestigial Christian ideas.

He said, "Sure. You made out with Harriet Gould on that school trip to see *Sweeney Todd.*"

I laughed. Harriet and I had barely pecked, and I'd only done it to get the attention of Jimmy Dunn in the seat across the aisle. Now, I tried to remember Harriet's face. Her eyes had been brown; they'd crinkled at the corners. She'd tried to hold my hand later that day and I'd yanked it away. I wondered if she was out now, if she knew that I was, too. I wondered what she would think about me running

home to Eli. I felt a great distance open up between my current self
and every other self I'd ever been. And at the same time, here I was,
next to a person who knew my own past better than I did—and saw
it more simply.

"Right," I told Eli.

"I missed you," he said again. I kissed him. He was a good kisser,
and I kind of wished I'd known that back in high school, though I'm
not sure it would've changed anything. I've had people kiss me like
they want to possess my body, and people kiss me like they want to
possess my soul. I'd rather someone who focuses on the mechanics,
nothing more.

He leaned back on the bed and his shirt rode up, showing the
valley between his protruding hips, the dark shadow between his
waistband and his skin, the twine of hair that reached down from
his navel.

"Cassie," he said, like he was relishing the sound. I lay down, nestled in Eli's neck, and breathed in metal, oil, and sage. I read once
that smell is the sense most strongly associated with memory, and
I wanted to cancel out the last ten years with the scent of Eli's skin.

Eli asked if I wanted to meet his kids at Thanksgiving, but I wasn't
ready. My life felt tenuous and crumbling. My former employer had
finally sent me an email full of corporate jargon that amounted
to me being fired with no severance. I was still getting texts from
coworkers and old friends—I thought—and though I felt no need
to respond, the occasional dispatches from strings of anonymous
numbers, asking me where I was and what had happened to me,
were unnerving. One kept asking *are you alive* with no punctuation.
It was enough to make a girl wonder.

I had 862 dollars between my checking and savings accounts.
Sleeping on the couch in my dad's empty house was free, but I

still needed to eat. At least I had found a Craigslist subletter. I was charging him a hundred dollars monthly more than my rent, which was just enough to keep me in eggs, toast, and frozen spinach for the foreseeable future. Well, until my dad and Fiona sold the house, which they had recently told me they wanted to do as soon as possible.

Eli was painting his house. When he first spoke of this, he sounded beleaguered, defeated even. He should have done it earlier. September, ideally, and he should have powerwashed the siding back in August. He needed to do some small fixes, too, and those added up. He was taking a week off of work, and worried that it wouldn't be enough time. But of course, he couldn't have taken a week off in September; that was the busy season.

"When's the last time you went on a vacation?" I asked.

A wide and charming smile erased his brief frown. "Live a good enough life and you won't need vacation," he said.

It sounded like something one of the older agents might have told an assistant, breezily, sometime during the ten months of the year when they worked from the office and not from the Hamptons. But Eli's tone was hard and worn. He took his week off and painted the house; he didn't even have time to see me. On the one night when we did see each other, he was so tired he fell asleep at the movie theater, during the trailers.

But at the end of the week, he pulled into my dad's driveway fast, in a washed car. He'd shaven, his face bare and golden. "It's done," he announced.

"Can I see it? We'll just drive by," I added hurriedly. I didn't want to thrust more intimacy upon him than he was ready for. And I wasn't sure I was ready to see the house he shared with Beth, where his children lived.

"Why not," he said.

I expected to have a sense of foreboding or anticipation as we pulled down the road toward the address, but instead, I was distracted, looking at my phone when he stopped.

"Here," he said.

"Oh!" I squinted. It was a bright day, great for showing off new paint. The house was butter yellow, almost glowing against the green. It looked dissonant and strange, with a cheer that belied its distinguished nature.

"What color was it before?"

"Blue," Eli said. "Beth loved blue."

Of course she did. Blue was the easiest color in the world to love. But the house would look more right that way—a slate blue, maybe, muted against the oversaturated sky. A blue that didn't announce itself, one that had always been there, quiet, watching.

"We could go in," he said. "I could show you." He didn't move to open the door.

"I'm hungry," I lied. "Another time."

BETH

After I died, I woke up. At first, I didn't remember my life at all. I'm still waiting for some memories to come back; I feel incomplete without them. But I have lost so much: my house, my children, my body. What's a few gaps? Only I would like to know how I died.

Mostly, I reside in a particular tree. I don't know what kind; I was never good at those things. It's big, and the whole family could sit easily under its shadow. It has planks nailed into its trunk like a ladder leading to the first big branch, but then nothing. The idea of climbing toward nothing feels apt to me these days. I spent my life daydreaming of heaven, and now, here I am, stuck in the same woods I grew up running through.

Eli has painted my house. I didn't know I'd care so much until I saw it one morning—I'd been sleeping under a river stone—bright and shocking against the radiant sky. He wants to be ever more rid of me. Of remembering.

The new coat of paint leers in the sun, as if to say: All is well here; we are happy in this home. Yellow is an insistent color, and often a lie. But that's not new; this house lies all the time. It promises shelter, even though it will eventually crumble into dust. Everything turns to dust, except me.

More changes are coming. Today, Eli drove by the house. He passed me, and I felt with him a new presence. Not Joan. Joan I know like an old chair; she creaks and shudders under my weight.

This one feels ephemeral, like a breath of wind or the candle it blows out. I hope it stays long enough for me to get a look.

I could use a change. I've been living in these woods long enough for seasons to have moved through me; I'm tired of watching things bloom and perish. I can't relate anymore.

CASSIE

DECEMBER

Eventually, Nessa had started asking me when I would return to New York. I hadn't answered her texts. "She's kind of mean to you," Eli said once, after reading one by accident.

"She's essentially family."

He looked thoughtful. "Beth was close with her family," he said finally. Mention of Beth was a rare event. I put down my phone. He said, "Really close. Her dad gave her the house. Wanted to move into a log cabin in the woods."

"Woodsier than this?" I asked, gesturing past the porch railing, toward the dark thicket.

"Oh yeah," he said. "He went off grid. The closest grocery store is an hour's drive."

"How does he eat?"

"He hunts, forages, makes bread and jams. Beth's mom made most of his clothes, and he still wears them now."

"Could Beth do all those things?" I wondered if this was the kind of wife he wanted the second time around—someone with practical skills. Not exactly real world, more postapocalyptic.

"Some. She was a great cook, and she could mend a shirt."

I thought I could imagine it. The millennial with her version of her mother's antiquated talents. Maybe she gardened, wanted to raise chickens, flipped thrifted garments, making them fit perfectly. Or maybe that's just the version of homemaker I would be, if pressed. Something consumable, inspired by my Instagram feed. The holes between what Eli told me and what I could imagine always unsettled me. No matter how much information he gave me, I would never understand the contours of the space that she left, that I was living in. I worried that my presence colored outside her lines, or barely filled them.

"My dad and I are close," I said defensively. "We care about each other," I amended, "but we don't need to talk all the time. We're good at sharing space."

Eli said, "After you left, sometimes I'd see him with Fiona. She was memorable."

"Still is," I said.

"It's a shame she showed up so late," he said. I didn't have to ask what he meant. The teenage me could have used a stepmom like Fiona.

"I'm just glad she makes him happy," I said.

"Are they coming up for the holidays?"

"I don't think so. They're selling the house. They're done with this podunk town."

"It might be more podunk if you and all the other New Yorkers would stop moving here and driving up the prices," he retorted. This was a pet topic of his.

"I'm not a New Yorker."

"You're not a local."

"Ouch," I said. "I'm from another planet, actually."

He shoved me. "Still," he said. "Selling the house, that's huge. What are you gonna do?"

"Don't know," I said.

He leaned back, and I waited, very curious about what would happen next.

"Are you hungry? I'm so hungry," he said.

In New York, I had no job. I was admitting to myself that I had never learned how to be a professional person. I was terrible at boundaries. I had too many of them, and in the wrong places. I was polite, quiet, I think easygoing, though who knows. I assumed no one wanted honesty—wasn't that the point of a corporate job, of paying us so terribly they could pretend we weren't human? Occasionally I would realize that other people around me were forming real friendships, and then I would panic, sporadically try to connect, but it was too much.

Even when Eli was home with the kids, and I was living alone in my dad's house, knowing that I'd lose it soon, Elwood was still better than what I'd left behind.

I began to venture outside more by myself. I walked alone down into town and over the bridge, past the familiar Starbucks and the new sourdough pizza place. I dawdled in the ritzy clothing shops, saluted the long-closed anarchist ice cream stand, picked out the tourists from the city, who didn't know that I had been one of them. Dresses fluttered at me in open store windows, their ruffles like fingers reaching out. The town hadn't changed; still an erudite, kitschy, mostly white mix of charming and punk. Along it all, the river ran like a slow and powerful snake, its rapids like scales poised to shed.

Almost unconsciously, my feet took me to Franklin's Books. Like always, the place was crammed floor to ceiling with its wares. The aisles were narrow one-way roads, crooked and tricky to navigate. I breathed in at the threshold. Once, all the agents' assistants took a field trip to a bookbinder—a spry man in his seventies who was so devoted to his craft that I almost quit my job right there to beg for an apprenticeship. He told us that often, old books smell a bit like vanilla because of the lignin present in wood-pulp paper. Lignin is strong and resistant to decay as long as the plant it's in is still living. Once that plant dies, though, lignin loses control, breaking down rapidly into acid, yellowing and decaying the paper it's trapped in.

We don't use lignin anymore, not since the '70s, when acid-free paper was invented.

The cashier waved at me. I wasn't sure I knew him; I had spent many whole Saturdays here in high school, but I rarely spoke to any of the employees, and besides, he looked around my age. When I was fifteen and truly friendless—in my pre-Eli days—I used to walk here every day in summer, walking in and straight to the children's/YA section in the back of the store. I'd pick out a stack of books and read them right there, sitting on the dirty checkerboard floor. Sometimes the old tortoiseshell cat, Turtle, would try to crawl into my backpack.

The bookseller sidled up to me. "How's it going?"

I started, almost dropping a copy of *Jane Eyre*. "Fine," I said brightly, dismissively.

"Cool edition, right? It's from the forties."

"Wow," I said. "I love the book," I added. When I met other book people, I had a weirdly immediate urge to establish myself as one of them. The bookseller was cute, too—not like Eli, with his ropy arms and eyetooth grin. If Eli's beauty had grown wolfish over the years, the bookseller's was boyish, harmless, his cheeks round and sun-pinked.

"Of course you do. Eli told me you worked in publishing."

The past tense irked me. "You know Eli?"

"You don't remember me? I bartend down the road. I'm Hank," he said.

I nodded, not particularly wanting to dredge up that night. Lately, I'd been starting to wonder what my life would look like if Eli had never puked in my bag. Would I still be here? "Did you go to West?" I asked.

"Nah. I live in Elwood now, though. It's a fascinating place."

"You must be really into antiques."

He laughed. "Only of the rare-book variety. No, I meant the culture clash, all the new people moving in, changing things."

I frowned. "I guess I don't get out much."

"Well, it's pretty close to home for you, right? Because of Joan?"

"Joan?"

"Your neighbor?"

"I don't know what you're talking about."

He said, "You're staying with Eli, right?"

"No. I'm staying at my dad's place. I grew up here."

He looked down at the book in his hand. Something old; I couldn't make out the title. "I must have gotten things confused," he said.

"I didn't know I was notable enough for town gossip."

He smiled politely. "I should get back to returns."

"Right. Hey," I said. "There's a debut novel about a queer teen runaway and her cat out next month. I really loved it. I think it'll be big."

This smile was broader, more real. "I appreciate the intel. I'll order extra copies."

On my way out, he said, "You know, if you want a part-time gig while you're here, we could always use someone who knows publishing."

The *Jane Eyre* cover depicted two parallel lines of women in black and white, their faces haunted and severe. I opened it and flipped through the ochre pages. Even with the book closed, I could smell the must of smoke and bark, the lingering breath of wood pulp, once alive. "I'll think about it," I said.

I bobbed home, lighter than I'd felt in weeks. On my way, I gravitated toward the trails that wound up the hill, away from town, back into the woods. The woods encroached upon the town, as woods do. There was a line of tree and thicket between the towpath and the river, acres of trees between the canal and the highway. The sidewalk along the road that wound up the hill from town was flanked on the other side by a guardrail, past which was a rocky, near-vertical drop studded by boulders. The mouth of an abandoned water pipe loomed open a few feet under the guardrail, and sometimes when I was a teenager, when I couldn't stand to go home but I didn't want to be seen by anyone, I would climb inside it and read.

A few weeks after we first met, I showed Eli this spot. I had been reluctant, wanting to preserve a few places where nobody could ever find me, but he and his mom had fought badly the night before, and it had been a little bit my fault. I'd wanted to apologize. So, I directed him toward the rocks that were safe to step on. He had an easier time pulling himself up into the tunnel than I did. "This is really cool," he said, his legs dangling off the side.

"Do I ever lead you astray?"

He gave me a look. Deserved, since only a couple of days ago I'd coerced him into helping me climb onto the roof of a shed outside the gym, and then some asshole had taken the ladder and we'd gotten stuck up there. We still had two days of detention to fulfill next week. I knew my dad wouldn't care enough for me to bother telling him, but Eli's mom had, apparently. One side of his face was still swollen, and he kept touching it.

"I come here when I need to think," I said, lying back on the damp concrete. The inside of the tunnel smelled like dead leaves and animal fur. I watched my ribs rise and fall with my breath.

Eli tucked his knees up under his chin. "You ever spend a whole night out here?"

"Nah."

"I could bring a sleeping bag sometime," he said.

I imagined coming to the tunnel, thought-ravaged and tired, only to find Eli sitting happily on a plaid blanket, practicing his harmonica. "No thanks," I said.

"I wasn't offering it to you," he said.

"I just—it's my place," I said, too plaintively. "You can come here with me," I offered.

"Right, because this is your property." He laughed.

"You wouldn't know it was here if I didn't show you."

"Fine," he said. "I'm sure there are other abandoned pipes in this town."

"Better pipes, probably," I said, but he didn't laugh.

"I'm sorry," I said. "I just come here when I'm sad, when I need to be alone."

He turned his whole body to face me. "When I'm sad, I want to be around someone who cares about me."

"Well, I'm not like that."

His lips pursed. He smiled a little, then shook it off.

I shoved him. "What?"

"Nothing! Something that happened in history class."

"Tell me," I demanded, but soon regretted it when he launched into a story about two football players. By the time he was done, it was getting dark, the lights in the houses across the woods turning on one by one. "We should get going," I said, and he jumped out. "Bye, tunnel," he said cheerfully, patting it as we left.

I didn't go back for weeks; I was afraid I'd ruined it. But finally, I had a shit day of thoughts so bad I'd cut myself outside the corner store, certain that my blood would come out putrid and somehow wrong, sitting on a parking stop and feeling like an idiot martyr as a drop of crimson landed on my shoes. The wound was barely more than a nick. I wouldn't lick the blood clean, since I was still afraid to ingest it, so I grabbed some leaves off the trees and blotted it with them.

When I hoisted myself into the pipe, the smell was right, and I felt a cool mist cleanse my brain as I lay back. My shoulder landed on something small and sharp. A box, covered in duct tape to protect it from the elements. Inside, a stack of mini Twix, a deck of cards, a glittery bouncy ball, and a note. *For bad days*, it read, with a smiley face. The good feeling pooled uneasily inside me. I texted Eli. *you win. the pipe is yours.*

???
Dont be like that. It was a gift for you.

come back or don't, i don't care. i won't be here.

I dropped the rubber ball outside the pipe and watched it fall into the undergrowth.

Two weeks into December, Eli invited me home for Christmas. He assured me that this was an ideal time to meet his children, since they would be so distracted by the presents. I liked the idea of slipping into their lives, appearing like a fixture that they might hardly notice, that years later might catch their attention and make them wonder, *Has that always been there?*

But I told him that my dad might come visit after all, even though I already knew that he and Fiona had tickets to Croatia. Christmas felt too special, and I hadn't been in a room with any child in a long time. Occasionally, agents had brought their babies to the office; when everyone else gathered to coo and flatter, I slipped out on my lunch break. Even before, when I was only afraid that I might drop a baby, not that I might sink my teeth deep into a chubby arm.

One evening, Eli showed up at my house three hours late and impressively drunk. He banged around my kitchen, insisting that he was making dinner, but I had nothing in the house. "Pivoting to eggs!" he cried, brandishing a rubber spatula.

"I can make them." I closed three cabinet doors in his wake.

"You do enough," he said, an edge in his voice that I didn't understand. While the eggs cooked, he slumped in a dining room chair. "No one remembers," he said.

"Remembers what?"

"Today was her birthday." Eli put his head in a cave of his folded arms, resting on the table. The eggs were burning. I sat next to him and rubbed my palm in soft circles on his back. He didn't move, but I thought I felt some of the tension leave him.

"How would you have wanted it to go?"

He got up and turned off the stove, then went to the couch, where he lay face down.

I had forgotten her birthday myself. At some point, I'd known it. One night, weeks ago, I'd investigated her online presence thoroughly, seeking out all the digital leftovers of her personality. When he'd talked about her, it had been with cowed worship, her memory sweetly antibacterial, as if she'd had no faults. I didn't buy it. I'd wanted to see her for myself. So I'd watched her sing worship songs in grainy YouTube videos, her hands half raised, palms open to God. I'd read her sparse Facebook posts moving back in time through motherhood, then pregnancy, then her senior year of high school, all interspersed with Bible verses. I thought I could see her loneliness in her friendless selfies, her Instagram pictures of skies and sunsets. Even Eli didn't show up much, and when he did, he seemed more structure than person—his back, facing a sunset. His arms wrapped around his daughter's shoulders, his head hovering out of frame. There was one single picture of another woman with stick-brown hair, looking above the camera, her hand reached out, presumably to cover the phone. It wasn't a good photo, but it held something alive in it. The Facebook friends who wished her happy birthday over the years did so without flair or specificity.

Now, I went to the couch, where Eli had curled into the fetal position. I sat on the ground next to him and pushed my fingers through his damp hair, his scalp radiating heat. He breathed heavily and wouldn't look at me.

"About Christmas," I said. "I would love to meet your kids."

He stood, picked me up, and swung me around. I was so thoroughly surprised that I started to laugh and couldn't stop until long after he placed me gently back on my feet.

I did like kids. In college, I had participated in a program called Read-Along, which matched college students with underprivileged schoolkids. I'd been assigned a first grader named Caroline, who wore her hair in four pigtails. I'd sat cross-legged on her classroom floor with her each Wednesday and flipped through picture books, coaxing her through the words.

This was when my theme was bedbugs and I was grateful for the boundaries inherent in working with children—I wasn't to let her hug me or sit in my lap—meaning that Caroline was one of the few people in my life I wasn't afraid of. College is full of touching; near-strangers eat each other's food, sleep in each other's beds, share clothes and hairbrushes. I tried to want that intimacy, but every night I lay awake, certain I could feel them crawling on me.

Eventually, I skipped class for a week, scouring my room with a toothbrush dipped in bleach, washing my sheets every night until they tore open, the rip as long as my body. My roommate had been in a serious relationship for months; she slept in his dorm and only stopped by once that week, on Wednesday, to grab a dress from her closet. I was soaking my shoelaces in a bowl of boiling water, trying to convince myself to suck it up and go to Read-Along. I must have looked haunted, my eyes marker-black, my hair a sad halo.

"You should open a window," she said to her shoes. "This can't be healthy."

I choked back a laugh. What did she know about health? Bedbugs could cause allergic reactions as severe as anaphylaxis, could lead to anemia, strep, or staph, could infect the lymph nodes. I'd been to her boyfriend's dorm; he left food out to spoil, and his room-mate brought home a different girl every weekend. How often did he wash his sheets? If I had them—which I was pretty sure I did; I could feel them under my clothes—I'd probably gotten them from her.

"It shouldn't affect you," I said, trying to sound chill as I worried the cranny of a bedspring with a Q-tip. "You're never here."

"Right," she said. "Listen, it's not my business, but it might be good for you to know. I would stay here more if you didn't—" She gestured around the room, and I followed her gaze miserably, noting the pile of toothbrushes and paper towels stacked in my empty closet, every piece of clothing I owned neatly folded in the hamper, the desk cleared of belongings, my teakettle plugged in and heating water to be emptied into a basin so I could go over the floors once she left.

She backed out of the room, the dress slung over her shoulder like a body. I lay out on my mattress, knowing they were in there, sleeping between the seams, waiting to feed. But I was desolate, so tired of trying to keep them at bay. Let them have me, I thought. I never went back to Read-Along.

Now, I wondered if Eli's kids would like it if I read to them. I wondered if the corner of a picture book was sharp enough to puncture skin.

On Christmas morning, when Eli opened the front door, the children spilled down the stairs to meet me. I'd seen the picture of them on Eli's phone, and more from clicking through every individual photo on his Facebook page. I knew Preston was nine and easily embarrassed. Annabel, seven, basked in the spotlight. Now, she fell into a deep curtsy. She wore a sparkly silver dress, and the two giant bows perched on her head made her resemble a great horned owl. She brandished a fairy wand. "Can I knight you?"

"I thought you were an angel," Eli said mildly.

"Angels can knight."

"No, they can't," Preston droned.

I knelt.

She tapped me on each shoulder with the wand. I kept my head lowered until she said, "Please rise," and I looked her in the face.

Seeing a child up close was overwhelming. Her skin was smooth as bone, her eyes big and limpid, like those of a silent-movie starlet. I could feel the merciless tug of nature, my body wanting me to love her. But my brain felt the hum of dopamine and rushed in to ruin it. *So you don't want to hurt her?* the voice in my head asked. I tried to keep my face normal. Of course I don't want to hurt her, I told myself. My brain grinned deviously. It said, *Are you sure?*

Preston offered his hand to shake. "Welcome."

Both of them had the same eyes—a serene, alien blue. Not Eli's eyes. Annabel's French braid was off center. I itched to undo the scrunchie and rake the whole thing out. Preston shoved his hands deep into his pockets, like Eli used to do when we were kids.

Annabel plopped next to me on the couch. "I like your boots; they're so tall. Are you Dad's girlfriend?"

"We're close friends," Eli said. Somewhere, something beeped.

"Cinnamon rolls!" Annabel leapt up and clasped her hands together like a cartoon princess. Preston rolled his eyes into whites. I smirked at him and he looked away.

Eli said, "Who wants to frost them?"

"Me!" Annabel shrieked. In the flurry of her gown, I could see her thick, too-big wool socks as she ran. Preston trailed her, calling, "Use an oven mitt!" Eli bent and snuck a kiss from my lips, wiping his mouth before following them.

I sat primly on the couch and counted the presents to distract myself. I heard the oven door open in the kitchen. In my mind, I pressed Annabel's sweet face against the stove, heard the sizzle of her skin roasting.

In the corner by the tree, I heard squeaking. Then they were back with the cinnamon rolls, singing "We Wish You a Merry Christmas" to me, as if it was my birthday.

Presents began. Eli had apparently designated some of them as being from me, so I was as surprised as Annabel to find that I'd gotten her a stuffed bunny. My gift to Preston was a kit for making his own barometer. Eli and I had exchanged real gifts the night before: a wallet and a bracelet, both sleek and anonymous. We had never given each other gifts as kids, and we didn't know how to start now. The kids got me a too-sweet vanilla candle. Eli lit it with a flourish before he lifted the last box out from the corner behind the tree. The squeaking came back, louder. Behind Eli's back, Annabel looked at Preston, her eyes wide. He mouthed *Puppy?* and she writhed with excitement. Eli opened the box and lifted out a cage. "Hamsters!" he declared.

Annabel sagged just barely, and Preston touched her shoulder. The movement was so brief that Eli didn't see it as he fiddled with the cage door. I wondered how often the two of them comforted each other when their father wasn't looking.

"The girl is for you, Banana, and the boy is—oh shit," Eli said. "Kids, come look!"

At first, I saw a pile of berries, pale pink. A berry moved—they were baby hamsters. "Six," Preston announced. "That's eight altogether!"

"We'll have to find new homes for the babies when they get older," Eli said, watching the writhing mass apprehensively. "But we can name them all today."

"I want to hold a baby," Annabel said.

Eli reached into the cage and scooped out the mother, then the father. The father circled in his palm. Annabel patted the squirming mass. "Oh." She jolted back. "Their little hands."

"I think you're supposed to separate the father," I said. "I think he can be dangerous to the babies."

"Dangerous how?" Preston asked.

"Tickle attacks," Eli said somberly. Annabel ran upstairs for a shoebox.

As we watched the male hamster explore his box, I found out that Eli had a penchant for naming animals after other animals, and that his children hated this. Annabel preferred names with multiple nickname options. Preston suggested Thunder first and stuck to it. Finally, Annabel said she could live with Thunder as long as the full name was Thunderbolt, and she could call him Bolty if she wanted to, and she got to name the girl by herself. Everyone agreed. Annabel went to the other cage and screamed.

I saw the mother pop the last of her babies into her cheek. Preston eked out a panicked giggle. Eli looked like he might cry. Annabel was already crying, her mouth clownishly downturned as she stumbled back into the coffee table. The candle tipped and rolled off, landing in a snowdrift of wrapping paper. Flames shot up.

Preston and Eli lunged toward the kitchen. Annabel crawled under a chair in the dining room. I was alone, still sitting on the couch, dumbly watching the fire. The flames were low but growing fast. In the kitchen, Eli yelled about a bucket.

I could just leave. I had come back to Elwood to escape chaos, and this house was all chaos—grieving children, dead animals, holidays on fire. If I left now, the children would forget me quickly. Eli, eventually. Maybe I'd get another disgruntled text. Maybe I'd go back to New York. A flame flirted with a low branch studded with paper snowflakes.

"Um," I called, too quietly. In the kitchen, the faucet ran. I cursed, gathered my dress high around my waist, and leapt with both feet into the center of the flames.

Embers scattered under my boots, and I crushed them. I felt crazed, cursed, like a dancer from a fairy tale, stomping out tongue after tongue of flame. I was starting to make progress when Preston skidded back in and hurled a bucketful of water at me. Steam hissed and I felt like an idiot, soaking wet and coughing in the wreckage. The carpet was ruined. My boots squelched when I moved.

"Sorry?" Preston asked, and I laughed awkwardly. Annabel barreled into me, threw her arms fiercely around my waist. "You saved our lives."

Later, I was back home and replaying it all, working to quash the part of my brain that wanted to tell me I had purposely set up the whole situation to convince them of my false heroism. Annabel's hug was imprinted on my body; I could remember the exact weight of her head pressing against my belly, her ridiculous hair bows digging in under my ribs. My dad's house was quiet, devoid of cannibal hamsters and house fires. I kept remembering the turmoil with blushing warmth, like it was a celebration or a kiss, a little embarrassing in its intimacy. I wondered if they were all still replaying it too, telling the story over and over together like I was telling it to myself, alone.

BETH

Underneath me, the insects seek shelter. They have tasted the rain, felt the air's shifting pressure against their fragile wings. My roots itch with crawling things, burrowing into nooks to keep safe. It's a retreating feeling, like goosebumps drawing inward instead of rising rash-like on a surface. I used to retreat, often, from everything. Now, I simply am. I stay mostly in the tree where I last lived, but I can flow into others. I can spread myself out under their bark. I have been in blossoms unfolding with slow grace, in a raindrop as it slides down a rock and seeps into the earth. I know what it feels to be a blade of grass, to be the dew that encases it. I like being a twig. I like being cracked underfoot.

I feel freer now. I'm not free; I can't leave these woods, can't even go very far within them. But my waking life is no longer eaten by worry. I can sleep as late as I want. I can bury myself in dead leaves and let whole days go by. I can let the wind sway through me, sweeping all thought with it. Now, I experience all sorts of things that my embodied self could never have imagined. I take storms down my throat and leave them empty, spent and aching. A storm is coming. The bugs know, the ground knows, the trees know; we hum with awareness as the clouds thicken, as the hair on humans' necks goes sharp with static.

I would like not to care about what happens in my house, or in the rest of the human living world, but I can't help looking through the windows. I saw her there, raging against the flames. She looked ridiculous, jumping up and down like that. I almost laughed, until I remembered that no one can hear me. I think I miss being heard. I think all my life, I was never listened to enough, and now that I've died, I want to spend eternity screaming until someone, anyone, turns their face toward me.

CASSIE

My dad was officially selling the house. A Realtor named Dawn kept walking happy couples through. They were usually in their late thirties, with one kid or two; they seemed settled. These people were wholly unrelatable to me, talking about property taxes, imagining renovations—kitchen islands and lofted ceilings, machined floors, tearing down, ripping out. I didn't love that house, but I had never viewed it with the disdain that Dawn and her potential buyers seemed to—sure, it was dark, all nooks and close spaces, the floors scratched, the appliances unreliable. But I'd never lived in a place where everything worked. These people seemed to yearn for an ease that ran contrary to nature.

I spent more dinners at Eli's. I braided Annabel's hair and looked over Preston's schoolwork. I tried to view the house with a canny eye: Had he chosen these kitchen tiles? The Shaker-style cabinets, the warm wooden floor? Or had it been Beth? Usually, I loved being alone in a romantic partner's space, putting together clues of who they were—Lavender's room had housed an absurd number of blankets—but here, the picture was muddled and unclear, shaded with her absence. Soon enough, I was reading Annabel's bedtime stories, proofreading Preston's five-paragraph essays. I cooked dinner occasionally, though not very well. I adorned the table with flowers and candles, and I strung up fairy lights in the dining room window. I liked imagining the way we looked to outsiders, two adults and two children framed in glow. The pretty picture distracted me from the idea of sticking Annabel's pinky into the mouth of the big nail clippers and squeezing. Sometimes, while I cajoled them into listing their daily gratitudes, making them laugh and show off, I noticed Eli watching me.

"It's been nice having you here so much," he said one night, after I emerged from Annabel's room. We were downstairs, curled up on the couch with glasses of wine.

"It's a nice place to be," I said.

He looked around. "I guess it is. Sometimes I still feel like I don't know how I ended up here."

"Did you have something very different in mind?"

"I always wanted to stay in Elwood," he said. "But maybe I'd have moved closer to town. I like the houses on the river. But the flood risk—I wouldn't want a house that was also a job. For how old this one is, it's remarkably low maintenance."

"I was thinking I might get a job," I said. "At the bookstore; your friend Hank offered. And I'm going to have to find an apartment or something soon."

"Right," he said. He scratched the stubble under his ear. I tried to keep my face pleasant, devoid of annoyance. I didn't know if I wanted to live with him, but it seemed rude of him not to ask. A bookstore job wouldn't pay enough for rent here; the town was too cute to sustain life. And his house was so big. Once, on my way to the bathroom, I'd accidentally opened the door to a walk-in closet that was almost totally empty.

"Would you work at the bookstore full time?" he asked.

"I think they only need part time," I said. "Weekends, maybe."

"I'd miss you on the weekends," he said. "So would the kids. You're good with them."

"I love them." I meant it, or I wanted to mean it. I wanted to be the kind of person who gave up her former life to take care of two children she barely knew. It felt like an act big enough to erase every bad thing I'd ever done. Tired, I rested my head on his shoulder. His heartbeat was slower than mine; it soothed me.

His chest thrummed as he spoke. "I love you."

I sat up, my hair tangling in my mouth. "What?"

"This can't be a surprise," he said.

"No," I said. "I mean—of course I love you." I'd said these words to him a thousand times—affectionately, jokingly, never with import, and not at all recently. Of course I loved Eli; we'd stolen endless bags of chips from CVS together. I'd watched him break his wrist learning how to skateboard, had felt his anguished howl in my throat. And now, he was older, more knowing and wounded. Both confident and fumbling as he hugged his kids, puzzled out recipes, tried not to cry. He was crying now, I realized, a tear streak shining in the quiet light.

I kissed him once, then again. We still hadn't had sex—I'd wanted to, but Eli always stopped me, gathering my hands together and giving them back to me, a gesture I loved, frustrating as it was. I assumed it had to do with Beth, or maybe with some remnant of Christian guilt. This time, though, he let me move my hand into his jeans. I scratched his hip gently, enjoying his shiver.

"Dad," Annabel called from upstairs.

I yanked away. Eli climbed over me, pulling up and buttoning his jeans; he was gone before I knew he was leaving. I pulled my dress down, arranged myself artfully, and waited. Eventually, I checked my phone, sitting up, finger-combing my hair. On Twitter, a mental health tag was going viral and I thought about joining in, but I didn't know what I would say. Eli came back downstairs. "You're still here."

"Should I have left?"

"No," he said, drawing out the word. He sat next to me. "But I think the kids will have questions if you're here when they wake up."

"Right."

"Can I drive you home?" he asked.

"No. I'll get a Lyft."

The closest one was over half an hour away, and I considered walking, but I knew Eli wouldn't let me, so we waited awkwardly together, him yawning every three seconds. I told him to go to bed, but he refused, and I wondered if he wanted to make sure I would leave. When Louis R. was two minutes away, Eli said, "I know my situation isn't ideal."

"It's not your fault."

"I know that. I just—I don't want to destabilize them any more than they already are."

I wanted to ask why he had pushed my meeting them, why he was letting me become a part of their lives, if he'd meant it when he'd said he loved me. But I remembered Eli's mom's many terrible boyfriends. I could understand why he would want to move more slowly. That was okay. I could fit into any box he made for me once I figured out its shape.

The next time I saw Eli, he was goofy, bouncing on the balls of his feet. I remembered him teenaged, that year when it seemed like every time I saw him, he was taller. He swept me into his house and told me that he was taking me out, that Joan would watch the kids. I still had yet to meet Joan, and I had many questions about her, but Eli didn't understand my curiosity, so I'd stopped asking, not wanting to seem obsessed. We dropped Preston and Annabel off at her house next door, and as I waited in the car—"You don't need to get out," Eli had said when I'd taken off my seat belt—I caught a glimpse. She was taller than I'd expected.

He drove me out to the river. We walked down the canal path, which smelled like river water and goose shit, and we turned together at the right spot, hopping over boulders until we reached the wing dam. It was freezing outside; he'd brought a picnic basket, but we gave up quickly and trudged back to the car. There, the windows fogged up while we ate slices of ham wrapped around cubes of cheddar cheese and drank a bottle of wine he said he'd had for a long time.

"I really wanted this to be nice," he said, dejected.

I ruffled his hair. "It is nice."

He gave me a look, then sighed heavily. "I want to ask you something, but I don't want to do it in a way that will scare you."

I swallowed my dissolving cheese cube.

He said, "I was going to ask you to be my girlfriend. But—I was thinking about it, and that doesn't make sense for us. I already know you. You read stories to my kids. What would be the point of dating?" His voice was fervent, with the cadence of a sermon. I felt myself flush. His breath was hot, the car too small.

"I know you, Cass. I know what you need. I know how to make you feel safe. I want you. And I want—you know, my life got ripped off its track last year. I want to be moving forward again. I don't want to *date*"—he spat the word—"someone. I want to have a life with a person I know and love already."

My throat still felt stuck; I kept swallowing, trying to fix it. "What are you saying?"

He gathered my hands together, but instead of folding them back to me, he pressed my palms against his chest. His heart was beating as fast as mine. He said, "Cassie, I want you to marry me."

My body lies to me all the time. My gut makes up dangers to torture me with; my intuition fucks with me just for fun. I am always relearning that I can't trust my impulse to run, because if I did, I would never stop. Right then, I was seized by the conviction that Eli, in his passion, would step on the gas and launch us into the river. Never mind that the car was turned off; I couldn't stop seeing us plunging together. And if I was about to die, as I was so often sure I was, would I prefer to have him with me, over being alone? Yes, I thought.

"Yes," I said.

After we threw out the ham and cheese cubes, after we walked to the silversmith across the river and picked out rings and went out to dinner at the nicest place in town, where a waiter I was pretty sure I'd once babysat poured us champagne, Eli told me, his eyes bright with tears, that nothing in the world mattered to him anymore except me. This was an obvious lie, but I had to admire the drama. It made me wonder if he wasn't more fucked up than I gave him credit for. As we drove home, I felt for the buzzing sense of onrushing doom that had been present in the back of my mind since Dad had suggested selling his house. It was gone, and the hush in its place felt soft and pliant against the inside of my skull. Casually, almost psychically, Eli said, "Now you won't have to get a job."

When we arrived home, a familiar-looking car was in the driveway. Joan's, I realized as the front door opened and light spilled out around her form. Eli muttered something I couldn't hear and strode across the lawn while I half jogged to keep up.

"Preston had a nightmare. He wanted to be in his own bed," Joan said to Eli. She was a few years older than me, narrow-bodied with short brown hair and a rasping voice. I didn't know how to react to her: whether to thank her for all the babysitting or wait to be congratulated—did she know what he'd done?—or tell her that I liked her sweater. I didn't like her sweater, but I tend to flatter when I'm not sure what else to do. Joan stepped aside to let us in. "Felix," she called. A girl Preston's age stepped into the hallway, hugging a puffy pink coat. Lanky like her mother, she looked otherwise very different—where Joan's eyes were hazel, Felix's were a clear lime green; her hair blonde, crew cut with two long strands framing her eyes, but the real difference lived in the ways they carried themselves; Joan quick and jerky, Felix more serene. "I'll be outside," Felix said, her voice high and chiming.

Joan said, "I want to talk to Eli for a moment."

"I can watch YouTube," Felix said. She slipped by us and out the door.

"It's nice to meet you," I told Joan.

She nodded. "I hear congratulations are in order."

"Thank you," Eli said.

"Thanks," I echoed. I wished I'd had more time to practice arranging my face.

She looked at me for the first time, distracted, like she was working through complex calculations in her head. She said, "Beth used to follow a Christian curriculum with the kids, but lately we've been working with more of an unschooling model. You know Preston and Felix are like conjoined twins these days; I've been schooling them both, but maybe we can work out some kind of shared schedule."

"I—"

"We still have a lot to talk about," Eli said smoothly. He squeezed my shoulder.

Joan wasn't the warm elder neighbor I'd imagined her to be, and I realized now that I'd been hoping she might be a kindred spirit, a possible friend.

"Well," she said. "Congratulations again."

She shoved between us and outside, where I could see Felix's phone light flashing like an alarm.

"She seems nice," I said to Eli.

"She's usually not like that." He shrugged.

"I don't mind homeschooling the kids," I said, hoping he would tell me I didn't have to.

"Cool," he said, distracted. He looked at me like he'd just remembered I existed, then kissed me, hard. I wondered if I'd finally made the greatest mistake of my young life. I hoped so. I was tired of things only getting worse.

The next morning, I woke up alone in Eli's bed. We'd finally had sex the night before. I'd been pleasantly drunk, the room rocking like waves, and I couldn't hold on to much. He had gone down on me for a while, and my face flushed now as I remembered him breathing my name between my legs. I'd come by touching myself on top of him, and he had watched me like I was showing him a magic trick. He kept telling me to open my eyes and look at him. The intimacy peeled me open, but I'd done it.

Now, I buried my face in his pillow, relieved and embarrassed. The low din of voices downstairs reminded me of childhood. I sat up in bed and felt the chilled morning air around me. The big window on one side of the room looked out into the densely tangled woods. When I padded naked to the glass, I saw that its edges were delicately printed with frost.

I heard a too-loud creak and dove for my duffel bag, pulled on black leggings and an oversized hoodie. In the cool morning, my new ring spun loosely around my finger. I pressed my thumb against it, and the cool ridge of it reminded me of who I had become. I looked around the room, acknowledging five things I could see, four things I could touch. Though I had been to his house plenty of times by then, I'd never been in his bedroom. The room was done in shades of blue, from navy to turquoise. I thought absently that I wouldn't have expected Eli to decorate with such intense color saturation before realizing this must have been Beth's doing.

One might expect a blue room to be peaceful or melancholy, but this wasn't that. The carpet was crisscrossed with moody stripes, the oceanscape above the headboard a wave about to break, light-shot at its crest, the urge radiating through it. A clay vase of dried navy flowers stood by the mirror; when I looked closer, I saw that the vase was carved with hundreds of tiny cerulean eyes. All of it made me uneasy. I had understood that Beth was a simple, godly girl, and I expected lightness and absence of personality from her spaces. I thought of all her blandly captioned Instagram pictures. I remembered that one strange shot of the blurry woman mid-protest. I realized now that it was Joan.

Downstairs, Preston complained, "When is she going to wake up?"

My cue. I opened the door, leaning back against the force of all that golden light.

CASSIE

The wedding was tiny, just me and Eli, Preston, and Annabel. I told Eli to invite Joan, or his work friends, or Hank, but he said she was busy, they were all busy, and I wondered if he was ashamed of me. It took place at the town hall, just a certificate. I told Nessa about it, knowing that she wouldn't leave the city. She sent black calla lilies to my dad's house, along with a condolence card. Annabel was thrilled—we'd brought her shopping, and she'd picked a gold dress with a bell-shaped skirt—but clearly confused, too, repeating how excited she was for me to be her big sister. Preston barely spoke in the weeks leading up to the ceremony.

I had called my dad and told him the news. "You can come, if you want," I offered.

"If I want! My only child is getting married; of course I'll come. When is it? Fiona and I are supposed to be in the Galápagos all June, but—"

"This Saturday," I admitted, shame flushing my whole body.

He paused. "As in, two days from now?"

In the background, I could hear Fiona saying, "Phil, what's happening?"

"I'm sorry," I said. "I mean, it's okay. It's basically an elopement. No one else is coming." I meant the words to be a comfort, but coming out of my mouth, they sounded pathetic.

"I'm sorry, Cass, I just don't know—"

He and Fiona must have had a conversation of expressions; she had taken the phone. Her voice sounded bright and sweet, like always. "You send us your registry, honey," she said. "We'll get you the biggest thing on the list. And who knows, maybe we can find tickets and someone to feed Priscilla—"

"You really don't have to do that."

"Well, we might not be able to. But we'll try."

Later that night, she texted me with their regrets; I was so embarrassed I couldn't even bring myself to open the message. In my whole life, only one other phone call with my father had humiliated me so deeply. I'd been in college, between classes, when his number flashed on my screen. He and Fiona were on their honeymoon somewhere in Europe, hours ahead of me, and he was drunk. He asked a few vague questions, which I answered, bemused. Then he took a deep breath, like wind through a thicket.

"I was a good dad, Cass—right?"

"Sorry—what?"

"I worry," he said. He gasped, sounding pained. "I know I didn't always do the best I could."

"No, Dad, you were amazing. You were great," I said, horrified. "Dad, is Fiona there? Nearby, I—"

"You won't tell me," he said. "But I know. I neglected you."

"You did your best," I said.

"No," he said, sounding sure. "I could have done better. I failed, with your mother. I was afraid to fail—to try and still fail again."

I waited.

"I'm learning how to be a good husband," he said. "I'm going to do right by her."

"That's good."

"I fucked up with you," he said. "Sometimes I wonder if that's why—" There was a jostling sound, then a crack, like a phone hitting stone. A flurry of voices, then nothing.

I spent the day before my wedding writing an open letter in my head: Okay, true soulmate, this is your last shot. Show up now, clear and irrevocable, and change everything. I wondered if the doorbell might ring, if Lavender might be on the other side. Or someone else, someone I couldn't see clearly, diffused at the edges. This anxious hope lasted all night, all morning, even while I walked toward him, his hair pulled neatly back, me wearing the cream silk dress from the vintage store that clashed with my skin, making me look paler. Even then, I still wondered if someone else might call out my name with urgency, with certainty.

No one came. I got married.

The Monday after we married, Eli showed me the massive schoolroom, with the circular desk in its center. A hulking computer sat encased in a chestnut rolltop off to the side. I saw myself slamming the top of the desk down on their fingers, the bones cracking like chopsticks. Instead, I focused on the bookshelves. One whole wall was lined with them, stuffed with haphazard stacks, flanked with piles of more books. The walls that weren't bookcases were painted in chalkboard paint. One section of the wall held a half-filled map of Europe; another boasted drawings of sea creatures both real and not; a giant squid tentacle reached lazily to scratch the toe of Italy's boot.

"It looks like Beth did a lot of work," I said carefully.

"She swore they mostly learned on their own. Preston, especially. She had more trouble with Annabel," Eli said. "But I'm not too worried about her. She has a mechanical mind."

"Is there anything I should be focusing on in particular?"

Eli sighed. "Preston's going to be ten this summer, and the district has agreed to let him jump a grade and start middle school. I didn't want to start him in a place where everyone already knew each other, but a couple of different elementary schools flow into the middle school, so it's a good time to start out. And I don't think Annabel will want to stay home once he leaves. So, it'll really just be the rest of this year, until the fall."

"So, essentially babysitting?"

He thumbed his jawline. "Well, it'd be nice if you could keep them busy. I think they need distraction. But right, I don't think you need to worry too much about administering tests or anything like that. Not like what Beth did."

For just a second, his expression slipped, and emptiness crawled over his face like a rash. "You'll do great," he said.

At first, spending whole days with the kids was physically taxing, like taking cold shower after cold shower—the grisly thoughts still came, but I was too occupied to allow them much room to flourish. I was making sure they were safe in actuality; I didn't have the brain space to indulge in hypotheticals. I could scroll through them quickly—okay, me stabbing Preston in the chest with his pencil, okay, me dragging Annabel down the hall by her pigtail braid—and move on. I wanted to prove myself to Eli.

Teaching children didn't feel that different from working with authors: being cognizant of their egos, keeping their natural predilections for rash decisions from ruining their lives. I knew how to soothe, how to present a necessary course of action as if it was a thrilling possibility. The first night Eli got home, we showed off the play we'd spent the afternoon writing together, replete with many costume changes. The second night, they read the poems they'd written at lunch—Preston's about the life and death of a dog violet, Annabel's about her sandwich.

Homeschooling put me and the kids in our own small, separate world. Looking back on those early days, I remember myself either teaching the kids or hovering nervously in the corners of the house, still awestruck by my own presence there. Before, I had been on a career track, making my way up a ladder, trying to be a person who could one day have an effect. I was a child, too; in the hierarchical nature of the office, I was on the lowest rung, but I knew what I wanted to become, and who I should emulate in order to move forward. Here, I was simply an adult, the only adult, for days at a time. In fairy tales, the stepmother came from no past, inexplicable, and her presence changed everything.

One morning, I woke up to Annabel bouncing on the bed between me and Eli. I was wearing an oversized T-shirt, thank God. Sometimes Eli woke in the night wanting to fuck, and neither of us could be quite sure the next morning whether it had been a dream until we confirmed with each other. Those midnights were strange; he was more aggressive than he was when fully awake, and I liked the hunger, the way he wasn't careful. Sometimes he wouldn't even open his eyes, and I loved the idea that I could have been anyone.

"Annabel, what are you doing?" I asked.

She fell into a crouch. "Oh no," she whispered, aghast.

Eli stirred. "Banana?" he asked.

"I was trying not to wake you up." She looked like a small, sad clown.

"Then why were you jumping on the bed?" I asked.

Eli shook his head. "We've been over this."

"It's the only bed I can jump on," she explained. "Mine has the slanted ceiling."

Eli sat up, snatched her by the waist, and pulled her, laughing, into his chest. "You know, Banana, you're not allowed to jump on any bed when no one's watching. That's how your grandpa Randy broke his leg."

"I know." She pouted. "That's why I came in here."

"We're not watching when we're asleep."

She rested on her father's shoulder. "Maybe you could read me a story." She gave me a sly smile.

"Cassie will do it. I have to get up for work."

"But it's only seven."

"I'll read you two stories before bed tonight. How does that sound?" He shunted her over to me, stood, and stretched. I patted her head timidly. "What story would you like?"

She retrieved an Angelina Ballerina book from underneath the dust ruffle. As we settled in, Annabel mouthed the words along with me, her brow furrowed. She looked satisfied enough when the book closed, when Eli, now dressed, kissed her and then me on the tops of our heads before loping out of the room and down the stairs, and out the door, letting it slam heavily behind him. Annabel seemed to lose some of her buoyancy. I could relate.

"Hey," I said, startling us both. "Do you want to wake Preston up? Tell him we're going on an adventure."

She raced out of the room. I threw myself back on the bed and covered my face with a pillow, breathing through a thicket of down. Moments later, Preston staggered in. He wore a baggy T-shirt and PJ pants with dinosaurs on them. As always, he looked faintly disappointed to see me. Down the hall, the sound of springs and then a thump. I sat up. "Did Annabel fall off the bed?"

"She would scream," Preston said flippantly. "We're not going on an adventure, are we?"

"We are, we are. Give me five minutes."

"Fine," he said, pulling the door shut behind him. "Banana!" I heard him screech, muffled through the door. "Are you okay?"

The day was overcast, both gray and painfully bright. The grass, still wet, stroked our ankles as we walked. After we saw the cows, Annabel tromped through the long grass next to the road until Preston pulled a dog tick off her knee. "How did you see that?" I asked. "They're everywhere," he said. "You have to check yourself every night, especially for deer ticks, or you could get Lyme."

At the creek, I watched them play, resisting visions of slamming their heads against the rocks, their blood mingling with the water and rushing downstream. Annabel bit the tail off a salamander, leaving a swipe of mud along her mouth. Google revealed that salamanders were poisonous if ingested, leading to dizziness, cardiac arrest, paralysis.

Sweat bloomed like frost in my palms. "Preston. Do you know the name of your doctor?"

"We don't go to the doctor."

"Never? What about vaccinations?"

"Joan used to be a nurse. She does them for us at home."

Fifteen minutes later, I knocked on Joan's door for the first time, Preston bouncing on the balls of his feet, Annabel insisting that she was fine.

The door swung open. I craned my neck to meet her eyes, feeling like a child. When she offered her hand to shake, it was surprisingly warm, a little damp.

"I'm sorry to come over without warning. Preston said you were a nurse."

"Years ago," she said. I was still having trouble fitting this abrupt person with the legend who cared for Preston and Annabel so altruistically.

"Can I play with Felix?" Preston asked.

"Sure." Joan inched the door open wider, and he scurried in. To me, she said, "What seems to be the problem?"

"Annabel ate a salamander. I guess they're poisonous? Well, part of one. I wanted to take her to the doctor, but Preston said—"

"No need," Joan said. To Annabel, she said, "Come on in, hon."

Annabel stepped inside. I stayed out on the steps, feeling foolish and uninvited. Joan said, "You can go home. I'll drop them by before dinner."

"Oh. Okay," I said. "What should I tell Eli?"

"I usually recommend the truth," she said dryly. She shut the door.

After we put them to bed, Eli found me in our bedroom, reading about other poisonous creatures of the American Northeast. I wanted to be ready. He held an open tub of ice cream and offered me a spoonful. Eli said that I'd done the right thing. Joan had induced Annabel to vomit and she was fine.

"How do you stand it?" I asked. "They're so vulnerable. And sometimes it really seems like they're trying to die."

"Oh yeah. Parents say that a lot." He ate the bite of ice cream. I wanted to wring the nonchalance out of his voice.

"I know she's fine, but the kids say they don't go to doctors?"

"They've been to the doctor. Beth just didn't like to take them unless it was necessary. She was raised differently, her family—they didn't trust institutions."

He sat on the edge of the bed, the tips of his hair sliding over his shoulders as he nodded. "When Preston was a baby, Beth was terrified like, all the time. We had this helpless creature, totally reliant on us—not just to feed him and change his diapers, but to do things that he had no idea he needed, like sterilizing his bottles. And the internet will tell you that everything you're doing is the wrong thing. For me it was actually harder with Annabel—Beth was focused on Preston, so more of that fell to me. But now it's like, they can feed and bathe themselves, and they can communicate in words when something's happened? Amazing. Every day they're more capable, you know?"

I wanted to tell him that accidents could happen at any age, that life felt more dangerous, not less, the older I got. And he had to know this already; his own wife had died by horrible accident, right? But I knew that was too invasive, too accusatory, for even me. All I knew was that I could not abide fear of something unpredictable going fatally wrong. But I was going to have to find a way. I took the ice cream and ate a spoonful. Butter pecan, Beth's favorite, which Eli still bought out of habit.

After we'd brushed our teeth, making foamy faces at the mirror, and padded into the bedroom and undressed together, I went to the kitchen to get a glass of water. I was wearing Eli's shirt and boxers, the room silver with moonlight. I looked out into the yard by the woods and saw, along the tree line, three pairs of glowing green eyes. I squinted, but I couldn't discern the outlines of the deer's bodies. Maybe they were only eyes, floating in the dark. I turned the faucet on slowly, as if they might hear the water running and leave me. My water glass filled. I was transfixed, my feet flat against the cold tile floor, my bare hip pressed against the counter's edge. I would have stayed there forever. They watched me, six suspended orbs, then all at once they spooked and dove into the woods.

I switched on the stove. I pressed my hand against the electric burner, feeling it warm under my palm, missing the dramatic whoosh and flame of my old gas stove in my old, shitty apartment. I filled a saucepan with cold milk and Hershey's syrup.

Preston appeared on the stairs, rubbing his eyes at me. "What are you doing?"

"Hot chocolate. Want some?"

He sat. I felt a private thrill and added more milk and syrup to the pot.

"Mom made it with real chocolate."

"And I make it this way."

He brought a chair to the cabinet and clambered up to get us mugs. We sat at the table, watching the steam rise. He said, "I had a bad dream."

I waited. He blew on the surface of his mug, making ripples. Outside, crickets keened, the occasional frog peeped. In the top corner of the window, the moon glowed, full and knowing.

"It was about Mom," he said.

"Tell me more."

"Dad told me and Banana not to talk about her in front of you."

I sat back. He sipped, eyes on me. Kid eyes were so round. I saw my thumbs forcing into his sockets, popping them out. I jerked my gaze to the window as he said, "He thinks it'll hurt your feelings."

"That makes sense that your dad told you that," I said. Outside, the eyes still shone amid the trees. "But listen, you probably need to talk about her sometimes. And if you do, like if you're having nightmares, I am here."

I looked back at him and realized uneasily that he was crying, his face crumpled like a washcloth. I didn't know what to do. I pressed the mug between my hands as the lamp above us gleamed coldly down. His sobs calmed.

"I'm so sorry, Preston," I said, my voice low.

His chin was slimy with yellow snot. I gave him a napkin and he wiped.

"You know," I said, "my mom actually left my family when I was about your age."

He folded the sodden napkin into squares and smaller squares, already composed. He picked up his hot chocolate mug. "Can I take this to my room?"

"Sure."

BETH

Cassie sits slumped in the kitchen while Preston leaves the room. Moments later, he reemerges in his bedroom, stepping carefully with his full mug. He sets it down on his nightstand and waits. Before too long, I see the shadow creeping behind the house, hunched under the windows. Felix climbs the tall pine, scampering too far out on the branch that hangs over the porch roof. She drops cat-like on the roof and taps on the window until it scrapes up and lets her in.

Before I met Eli, I had a best friend named Zeke. You imagine a boy with spiked hair, zooming by on a skateboard, leaving sarcastic one-liners in his wake. He was that, too, but not at first. When I first met him, Zeke was bird-boned, with colorless hair and an unsteady gait, a slice of gold in one of his sea-blue eyes. Church ladies made strong declarations about that eye—a blessing, a mark of the Divine, a heartbreaker, when he was older. Once, I overheard his father telling mine that it creeped him out.

Before my mom died, Zeke used to come to my house for home-school lessons. My mother enjoyed teaching him at first, said he was a riot. Years later, after seeing it in Annabel, I figured out that Zeke probably had ADHD. He was always bouncing around, changing subjects. I knew a doctor had recommended medication for him, but none of our mothers trusted doctors or pills; they preferred herbs, oils, prayers. Still, my mom once sighed and said that it might be worth the risk. Some days, when he asked too many questions, she would give up and wander out of the room. She was often unwell then; she would take to her bed for days at a time. Her eyes could fix you with a look that didn't feel like seeing at all. After she left, I would take over with Zeke's lessons.

I liked teaching Zeke. The best way to counter his questions was to ask them right back, and to listen to him talk until he landed on the right answer. The way he smiled when he understood something made me feel like we were discovering the world together.

Because of this, and because a church lady once called me "a remarkably calm little girl," Zeke became my responsibility. I was always placing a still hand on his jiggling knee. I was making sure two hamburgers at the church potluck were set safely away from all condiments for him. He was always simmering into a boil, his outbursts frequent, red-faced, sticky with mucus and tears. I knew how to see when one was coming; I would shuttle him into the coat closet and talk him down. Parents—not just ours—told me how I had a way with him, and how one day, I would be an amazing mother.

No one else saw that when we were alone, we were equals. We were running through the woods together, tripping over roots, and he was helping me up, brushing the leaves out of my hair. I was daring him to climb the tallest trees, to bring me back the prettiest leaves so I could fold them into my pockets and dress my dolls in them. I wasn't like Zeke—my energy rarely built like steam or rattled me open—but I wasn't like anyone else, either. I had reread *Anne of Green Gables* too many times in my youth; often when I spoke, I sounded like a nineteenth-century orphan. Later, in high school, I would start watching TV, rehearsing current slang until I could get it right. I practiced my smiles in the mirror before debuting them in public. If Zeke was too careless, I was too careful, and together, we could be typical enough.

Besides, I was in awe of him. He had an eidetic memory and a guitar. He couldn't write anything new, but he could play songs after having heard them just once. He used to flip through radio stations, mimicking every voice he heard. "Showers this evening in Philadelphia, moving up the coast—side effects may include nausea, sores, depression, blindness—call now and receive a free garlic press—now, if you're in the mood for love, here's a little ditty—and Lord, we pray that those listening will be saved." His ability to copy was uncanny, and sometimes I worried that nothing he ever told me was real. Sometimes I wondered if, without him, I might have settled into the group of church girls who couldn't wait to be mothers. They were always nice to me, to everyone. But they bored him, and I didn't want to be boring.

In eighth grade, Zeke shot up to over six feet tall. The other girls started noticing him. They'd spent years rolling their eyes at his distracted way of talking, his disheveled clothes; now they made up excuses to brush his hair out of his eyes. They were syrupy to me, too; faux-reprimanding him for putting me through so much. Once, after Ally P. spent an afternoon flirting with him by listing his faults in laughing tones, we walked home together, him quiet, kicking a nub of a broken stick ahead of him down the sidewalk.

"You could make other friends," he said abruptly.

"I don't want other friends."

"Maybe you should."

I didn't respond, but I still followed him all the way home. I often felt like a martyr with Zeke: patient, misunderstood. I liked that feeling. I imagined my face in stained glass, looking up at him, hoping to please him.

Eventually, the church ladies began to retell our bond as a romance. They said we would marry one day. I wasn't opposed—I knew I would eventually have to get married, so why not to the person I knew best? Still, the thought rankled him; I could tell. As we moved into our teens, he would roll his eyes more dramatically at their pronouncements. I never asked: If not me, who would you want?

*　　*　　*

We went together to homeschool prom and danced to every slow song, holding each other at arms' length. I wondered if I wanted to kiss him as he swayed in a rented tux and I tried to keep my balance in new high heels. I had over two hundred bobby pins in my hair, and every time I turned my head, a new part of my scalp pricked.

After the dance, most of the others were going down the shore to a beach house—chaperoned, of course—where they would stay for the weekend. A few couples were rumored to have clandestine hotel room plans. There was a lock-in at the church, but only the utterly friendless were attending. Zeke and I had no plan; we almost never planned anything; we just followed his momentum. We ended up at the local diner, still dressed in our finery.

"I have to tell you something," he announced when the food arrived. He dunked an onion ring in his peanut butter shake and crunched, greasy crumbs on his lip. I reached for his mouth with a napkin, half tenderness, half revulsion. He swatted my hand away, and I returned to my rice pudding. "I'm leaving," he said.

"But we're not done eating," I said idiotically.

"No." He grinned, my favorite smile of his, his slightly buck teeth biting his bottom lip, the corners of his mouth straining toward his ears. "I'm going to Philly."

"Oh." I laughed, sat back. "For college? Temple sent me a brochure."

He said, through another onion ring, "I'm not going to college."

I frowned. I had assumed we would do college together like we did everything together. "What are you going to do?"

"I don't know. Wait tables. Odd jobs. I'll find something. It doesn't matter, B, I'm dying here. This place is ruining me."

I tried not to take offense, as I always did when he ragged on our town. He said it was where culture went to die. I didn't disagree;

I knew there was appeal to a city, and I wanted to explore other places, too. But I planned to leave the normal way, with a place to go, where I would have orientation and assigned reading.

"You could apply and just see what happens," I pointed out.

"I have no desire to be a pawn in another institution," he said. His breath smelled like peanut butter. I knew he was just speaking in the voice of the last book he'd read, but I didn't want to tell him that. "Okay," I said slowly. "Well, we have time to figure it all out."

He looked at his phone. "We have, like, an hour."

"What?"

He reached across the table and grabbed my hands. His were cool and wet with condensation.

"Tonight, Beth. I'm going tonight."

"Why?"

"Why not? Sometimes you just need a change. I made a Couch-Surfing account online. I'm gonna crash with this guy in Fishtown until I get on my feet. He's cool; he's in a band. And," he said. "I want you to come with me."

My fingertips went numb. I pulled my hands out of his grasp. I could feel him watching my face. "I think my dad would be lonely."

He lifted an eyebrow. "He's an adult. He can make friends."

Zeke had always loved me without asking what I thought about anything. I was passive by nature and mostly happy to travel in his wake. But sometimes when he got me wholly wrong, I felt years of resentment gathering, like I was a magnifying glass under sun, smoking before the spark.

Now, I said "I can't," and he looked at me as if I was one of his own limbs turning against him.

"Fine," he said. He tossed a twenty on the table and got up. I stood, too, stepping on my long dress. I wanted the rest of our night back, the night I'd imagined, where we'd leave the diner hand in hand, then drive to our favorite spot overlooking the graveyard, lie down in the grass and stare at the stars, dream of leaving this town together one day, in the diaphanous future. "Are you still going to give me a ride home?" I asked.

He did look sorry. "Can you call your dad?"

I did. The next morning, I called Zeke seven times, even though his phone was dead. Hours later, he sent me a picture of the Liberty Bell. I never saw him again.

Halfway through summer, I asked my dad if he would enroll me in public school for my senior year, and this was done without any great fanfare.

CASSIE

MARCH

That Saturday, Eli walked the kids to Joan's—the weather was uncannily warm, so Preston was knock-kneed in shorts, and Annabel had insisted on bringing her swimsuit, even though Joan didn't have a pool. Eli and I walked down into town and into the café where I'd first seen him again. I felt eyes on us and remembered Hank's assumption that we'd been living together back in December. Months ago, now. Time unspooled differently around children, each day an overwhelming task that, once survived, was pushed out of mind to make room for the next.

We meandered toward the river, turning before the bridge to stay on the Jersey side. Around the corner, a limp body lay out across the sandy towpath, and when I gasped, the boy jumped up, yelling, "That better be good, I got goose poop in my mouth!" Three other teens emerged from the bushes, doubled over with laughter.

Eli shook his head, but I laughed, too. I was a little giddy, free of the kids for the first time all week. "I didn't expect to be so tired," I said brightly. It was a good tired.

"You've been doing a lot."

"I like it," I told him. We walked the sandy towpath between the canal and the Delaware. The canal smelled faintly septic, but the sun gleamed on the river water, glinted through the trees. I remembered the worship concert Eli took me to, freshman year of college when he was newly Christian. The front man had raved about heaven, how the rivers would be made of diamonds. They already are, I wanted to go back and tell him. I sipped my coffee, burning my tongue as we stalked through a gaggle of geese on the path.

"When they were little, Beth spent all day every day teaching them. But in more recent years, she basically just gave them their lessons and let them teach themselves."

"Really?" I preened. "Maybe she was tired. It's hard work."

"Well, you might be working yourself too hard," Eli said.

"What do you mean?"

"I just don't think they require that much," he said. "They're pretty independent. And remember, we just have to get them through the year."

"I don't mind," I protested. "I mean, I have to do something so I don't die of boredom."

"Sure. Well, there's always other stuff to do. Cleaning, especially the kitchen, and cooking," Eli said. "I bet you could come up with some fun ideas."

Beth had a shelf of vintage cookbooks over the stove, mostly French, their broken spines falling open to complicated dishes that I was afraid to ask Eli if she had ever made. Soufflé, bourguignon, and worse. Too often, I made pancakes with raw centers.

I hadn't needed to cook in my adult life. I was happy subsisting on kid food: macaroni, rotisserie chicken, undressed vegetables. Nessa used to throw dinner parties back in New York, where she always made pierogies and didn't trust me to bring anything but alcohol, rarely a necessity here. I missed being drunk, being out, stumbling across avenues with friends and strangers. When I remembered the city, I always pictured it in the middle of the night, just after rain, windows freckled, streets pearlescent.

I felt caught. Clearly Eli had seen some deviousness and malice in my interactions with the kids. I had been so careful. And mostly, I hadn't needed to be—I thought I'd been doing a good job.

Maybe I wasn't made to excel. Maybe I was made only to find a place that would do the mercy of taking me in, to make myself as unobtrusive and grateful as possible. Maybe the best I could offer this world was a version of myself small enough to stay unnoticed, useless enough to do no accidental harm.

"I could learn to cook," I told him. "For a family, I mean."

Cleaning was its own beast—my OCD wasn't triggered by uncleanliness, but I did sometimes find that when I set upon a deep-cleaning task, I couldn't stop, eschewing meals and social interaction. I wouldn't tell Eli that. He didn't know about my OCD at all. He had only just legally bound himself to me; I didn't want to display my flaws just yet. He would find out eventually. And maybe after a few years, once the kids were grown and had their own independent lives, I would explain exactly how fragile I'd been during this time. Maybe we'd be dressed up at a nice dinner, maybe a little too drunk. By then, I would be able to tell it all laughing. Ideally, he would marvel over how well I'd kept the secret of myself.

That night, at dinner, I couldn't look at Annabel without a torrent of blood pouring out of her mouth. There was no shoving it into the background; I was too tired, and what was the point? So my brain reveled in the details: a film of red left on her teeth, the dark cracks between them, the stain on the tablecloth, the smell of iron. Eli had brought home hamburger meat, and Preston had made Kraft macaroni because he knew it was my favorite, and it all stuck like bones in my throat.

The next day, I told Eli that I needed a few hours out of the house. I walked down into town, but as I neared that café, I started to feel nauseous. I didn't want to step inside and wonder what people thought about my life with Eli. I wondered if they knew I had already proven myself shit at schooling kids and had been basically relegated to the role of housekeeper. If any of them were clicking their tongues, wondering what the fuck I was doing here. Or if I was wrong, if no one cared, if no one knew me, if I was really alone here, in the place where I'd grown up—where, even during all those years in New York, I'd still always considered home.

I kept walking. I stopped in a consignment shop where long dresses fluttered outside the window. It was cold outside again, but the store was clearly anxious for spring, all their display dresses florals and pastels. I wondered if Beth had ever shopped here. I couldn't imagine her in a mall, flipping through identical skirts. I ran my hands over the long rack of sweaters. My skin was susceptible to scratchiness, but I liked the way wool reddened my skin around the neck and cuffs, reminding me that no matter what my brain said, I was also a body.

I didn't have the money to go shopping. Eli and I hadn't talked about setting up joint accounts. As I understood it, if I needed money for anything kid- or house-related, I could ask him for it. I dreaded this kind of interaction and hoped to avoid it completely. I left the store, crossed the bridge, the chill wind off the river cutting through my coat, and walked to Franklin's Books.

Hank was behind the counter when I walked in, clicking through something on the ancient desktop computer. I wandered, feeling uneasy in the maelstrom of new books—there were so many I didn't recognize. Which ones were being bet on in my old offices? I saw the teen runaway book I'd mentioned, sitting face out on a shelf. "That one's selling pretty well," he said. "You were right."

I plucked it off the shelf and scanned the blurbs, even though I knew them all by heart. "The author's big on Twitter. The editorial assistant got so many galley requests that she ran out and they had to order more."

"The book is great," he said. "It's nice when that happens."

"I'm glad you liked it."

He waved a sheet of paper at me. "Now for the sad part. Returns."

I pursed my lips in a frown and followed him as he plucked copies from the shelves to send back to the publisher. I said, "What other industry works this way?"

"It does help us, you know, keep the shop open."

"If you must." I grinned. "Here, I can hold some."

He handed me a few hardcovers. "I know you're glad we exist. Even though you haven't been here in months."

"I've been busy."

He climbed up on a stepstool to retrieve a dog-centric sob story.

"Too busy for that job I offered, I take it?"

"Stepparenting is full time, turns out."

He glanced at my hand. "So you're a McKean now."

"It has a nice sound, right? I like the consonance."

He straightened a skewed stack of memoirs. "I'm a bookseller, not a poet."

"And yet you knew the term."

"I considered grad school for a while."

I rearranged the books in my arms by size, to better hold them. "What stopped you?"

"The money. The fear. Oh, and I didn't get in."

"People say your odds get better the more times you apply."

"When you've earned your weight in application fees?"

"I'm just saying. There's still time."

"Sure," he said. "I could go to the city, spend all my savings, and end up right back here."

"Please do. I'm hoping to earn some ad revenue for my existence."

He laughed. He seemed like he might keep on—I hoped so; Eli wasn't one much for banter, and I missed it—but scooped my books away and walked toward the front, calling back, "Thanks for your help."

I thumbed through a new novel about a family hot-air balloon business before leaving. I wasn't sure I wanted to read novels about families now that I was in one—I was afraid my version wouldn't measure up. As I passed the checkout counter on my way out, Hank called out, "Be careful!"

"What?"

"Loose floor tile," he explained, but I had already tripped.

Later that week, Joan came over. She stood outside the door, even after I invited her in. She shifted her weight, and I wondered if she might turn and run. "I'm sorry," she said in a low voice. "I wasn't very kind the other week."

"Oh. That's okay," I said. "You did save Annabel's life."

She nodded reluctantly, like she didn't want to admit that she had.

"I've been meaning to tell you," I said. "I know you've been an incredible help to Eli over the last year. I wanted to thank you in person."

She sighed. "Eli said you want to learn to cook," she said. "Why don't you come over while I make dinner?" She called "You and your sister, too" toward the top of the stairs, where, when I whisked around, Preston's mop of hair was disappearing.

I thanked Joan and watched her leave, her bony ass swaying. She wasn't my type at all—I liked girls who bubbled and spilled over, who told me everything—but I was curious about her. Maybe I was just desperate for a friend.

For dinner, Joan roasted a chicken and tomatoes. "And you remember how to make it," she prodded as Preston went for seconds.

"It seemed pretty straightforward," I said. I'd been amazed by her sure hands as she'd mashed herbs in butter, then worked it over and under the skin, as she'd poked grape tomatoes with a fork so they wouldn't burst while roasting.

"Where did you learn to cook?" I had asked once the chicken was in the oven. I was washing the cutting board while she smoked a cigarette with the back door swung open. Outside, the sun was setting, the light violently bright through the treetops. Once the board was dry, I reached for the knife—the last thing left. I let the images wash over me—me stabbing Joan in the heart where she stood, blood pouring down her front, pooling on the beige tile floor. Joan's house was set up similarly to ours, with the kitchen leading out to the back porch, but the kitchen itself was smaller, more cramped. Homey, I thought.

"I worked in restaurants starting at fourteen," Joan said. "Bussing tables, then waiting them, then bartending. I tended to hang around the kitchens, and the cooks taught me."

"This was in Boston?"

She looked at me sharply.

"Eli told me you were from there."

She nodded. "Right, yeah. I grew up outside the city. Always thought I'd end up there."

"Why didn't you?"

"Met Felix's dad," she said. "He was from Pennsylvania, so we went there. The school in that county is bad enough that I figured I could do better for Felix myself. Then when the piece of shit left me, I figured there was no reason to stay. But I didn't want to go back home, either. I wanted to settle in a place that was completely mine."

"I thought you homeschooled Felix for religious reasons."

"Ha!" She threw back her head and everything. "No, no. I don't believe in anything. No offense."

"None taken; I don't, either."

She nodded. "Beth was very devout."

I put the knife to rest on the counter. I wasn't sure whether this pronouncement was a judgment, and if so, of whom. I had so many questions about Beth, but I was afraid to ask them, lest I seem unhealthily obsessed. Even the details I gleaned from Eli felt overwhelming, each fact about her a new warped lens through which to view myself. She was a better cook, a tidier homemaker, a more dutiful wife. I had never before cared about occupying these roles, but now, when measured against her, I found myself wanting, and I wanted to prove myself. I wanted, too, to ask Joan about Beth's worst traits. Was she a gossip, a weakling, a prude? I wanted her insecurities, her faults. I wanted to already know these things, to be able to talk about her, not just listen. Instead, I said, "It smells good."

"That was so good, Mom," Felix said now, as I scooped ice cream for dessert, the sound of crickets chorusing around us on the porch. Joan passed around a bowl of cut figs, but Felix refused to eat them, since she'd recently learned about their symbiotic relationship with wasps. "They die inside them," she kept saying.

"Mm, bug guts," Annabel said, happily chomping. Preston put his half-eaten fig back down on his plate. The sun had fallen by then, and Joan had turned on a string of globe lights that cast the table in a yellow glow. Joan touched her daughter's head. She could touch the kids; their innocence didn't burn her. A hand on Preston's head, casually tucking the tag in on Annabel's collar. They climbed all over her like she was furniture. She was more natural with them than she was with me. She barely looked at Eli, except to frown at his jokes. Maybe she was skeptical of men after having been left by her ex. Annabel licked her bowl clean, and I imagined sinking my teeth into her arm, gnawing the tendons from the bone.

Eventually, under Joan's tutelage, I would learn to let a chicken thigh brown in the pan without checking, and to salt everything more than I thought necessary. I would continue to be awed by her confidence in the kitchen: matter-of-fact, almost brutal in its swift decisiveness. She always knew exactly what she wanted a dish to taste like, and she knew how to take the correct steps to make it so. I waffled, making decisions out of panic, adding extra ingredients without considering them fully, half astonished when anything I did had any effect at all.

BETH

In both houses, new scenes play out behind the windows. At Joan's house, Cassie and Joan grow more familiar with each other; Cassie laughs at Joan's joke, Joan plucks the lemon Cassie struggles with from her hand and squeezes it into the pot, her other hand poised underneath to catch the seeds.

At my house, Preston and Felix sit on Preston's bed together, poring over a graphic novel. Preston tells Felix he's ready to turn the page if she is. Annabel stands on her head in her room; falls and tries again. Below, Eli walks from window to window with urgency. He goes out to the porch and stands, gazing into the woods for a while. Then he turns. He can't see into Joan's windows, can't know that right now, Joan offers Cassie a spoonful of broth. Cassie takes the spoon from her hands, sips, and nods. All Eli can see from his vantage point is the forsythia bush in full bloom, as bright as a scream.

Once, shortly after Eli married Cassie, she brought the kids outside. They ran right into the woods, and I felt it, a shock like they were breaching the bounds of my body. I think I'd half convinced myself that they had become as faded and translucent as I was. It wasn't true. Preston's boots thudded in the snow. Annabel grabbed a handful, crushed it into a ball, and took a bite. I felt her teeth cut exquisitely through me; the shadow of me filled with a sweet, fine mist. She spit out the snow, and I ran like a tear down her chin.

When Cassie knelt to tie her boot, Annabel stuffed a handful of snow in Cassie's hood. Cassie shrieked, ripped off her coat, and spun in circles, the coat flying like a body in her outstretched arms as the kids laughed. Eventually, she put the coat back on. It was still wet, and she tried not to tremble in front of them. I understood why Eli had swept her back in when she'd washed up on his shore, why the kids giggled so contagiously behind their lit windows when she read them stories. There was something raw writhing helplessly just under her surface, like a baby animal new and furless; anyone would want to touch it.

I reached out. Wistful, unthinking, I swept through her hair, found the crevice of her ear, and dug in. At first, all I understood was blood.

It was my own babies in her head. Their bodies twisted and mangled. And a third body, rocking in a corner, its bones roiling under its skin, pressing its head forcefully into its knees. I was afraid. My babies were murdered again, and the figure shook. Again, and she raised her head to vomit in her lap. Cassie.

I yanked myself out of Cassie's head. It was a little jarring to see that she had been laughing and joking with Preston the whole time, an approximation of herself. Her joy took effort. I could see the strain in her tense shoulders, her hesitations. The children didn't know. I wondered how she lived with them without them feeling her revulsion. But I was a mother once; a thousand times I'm sure the kids thought they had my undivided attention when I was rifling through mental to-do lists, seething at Eli, wondering about Joan. I watched longer, trying to understand. She loved them, I thought. Preston snuck up behind her and shoved a handful of snow into her scarf. I held still, afraid as Cassie shook off a flinch and knotted her hands behind her back. Preston cracked up at something she said, and she cupped his shoulder quickly, then jolted back, surprised by her own bravery.

I remembered my own surprising bravery—every time Preston did anything helpless and gross, humanly debased. Baby shit on my fingers, spit-up dripping down my chest. I'd been afraid that the viscera of babies would disgust me. During most of my pregnancy, I'd tried to find things to think about that wouldn't trigger my urge to vomit. The only objects I could hold in my head without gagging were trees. I don't know why they were allowed. I watched them sprout all over the landscape of my imagination.

I was afraid the nausea was simply a new part of me, that I would spend the next eighteen years trying not to breathe through my nose. But it faded, as it does, and once Preston was born, his need eradicated my disgust. It was so clearly more important. It erased me.

When they came back, it was only Preston and Cassie. Snowdrops had nosed through the decay and hung their heads in small choruses. The light had begun to linger, painting the damp bark of the trees. Just before spring, I liked to hover in the topsoil, feeling tulips grow into me. I lifted when I heard Preston's voice.

He was growing, too. His jeans stopped just short of his ankles, and he walked with a new gait, his head bobbing uncertainly on his shoulders. He wasn't used to his new height. He was eye level with Cassie's shoulders. She wasn't tall. She would probably be the first adult in his life he would surmount. That would have been me, once.

She gave him her headphones and played him a song. I thrust forward and swam into the wires; it sounded new, peppy and electronic. The world would keep moving on without me, I grumped. Or Cassie's music taste was just different from my preferred stomp and holler ballads. I smoothed into the air around their heads, Preston's bangs tickling my throat. His eyes were closed as he listened, so I oriented myself to see her face.

The way she looked at him caught in my chest. She longed to brush the bangs off his forehead; she would not let herself. Her love carried loneliness in it, tender and bereft. I bolstered my strength by taking in the sweetness of all the blooms about to burst above-ground, and I reached both hands into her mouth.

The same room, dank and cold. I hadn't noticed the stench before, like metal and rotting. This time, I sat down with her and watched the movie playing on the walls. Annabel was there only in flickers; this time, the main event was the death of Preston. The mangling, the gore. I probably shouldn't have been able to bear it. I'd been angry with my kids; I was no saint—but still, seeing them so ruined in someone else's imaginings should have destroyed me.

She didn't know I was there. I didn't know if I should touch her, tap her shoulder or try to hold her. I wasn't afraid of her for seeing what she saw, but I was afraid of the furious storm of her pain. I knew she couldn't hurt me, but I worried that if she knew she was being witnessed, she might do something horrible to herself.

I sat a while longer, letting the images paint themselves around me, then peel off like rotting wallpaper to reveal more, even worse. I knew they weren't real, which made them easy to abstract from meaning: just colors, reds and flesh tones. I toyed with the thought that death had made me sociopathic, but even that didn't bother me much. I felt enough. Eventually, I receded.

CASSIE

APRIL

The next morning, the clouds hung dark and heavy. I sat on the front steps with my coffee as the kids gathered sticks to make into fairy houses. Now that I didn't have to teach them, I just watched them, zoning out on my phone, ears pricked for signs of distress.

As the afternoon dimmed, a pinkish light filtered uncannily through the sparse front-yard trees: the fraying white birch, the three maples, the stout apple tree. I was beckoned toward the window by the strange glow.

Outside—when did they get out of the house?—Preston and Felix sat opposite each other, staring into each other's eyes. As I watched, both tipped their heads slowly back to stare up at the sky. Unnerved, I went to the door. "Come on in, guys, it's going to storm."

They pretended not to hear, so I called again. When they trudged inside, grumbling, I felt more like a mother than I had in days. Soon, thunder crashed around us. Even the inside of the house glowed with a strange orange tint.

"It's creepy out there," Felix said.

"Where's Annabel? Annabel!" I called, and she emerged at the top of the stairs, peering down at us like a tiny god. "I'm on You-Tube," she said, rubbing her eyes. "Learning about frogs."

"Come down with us," I said. She descended, holding her iPad to her chest. When she reached the floor, all the lights went out. Felix screamed.

"It's okay." I had to keep them calm; if they got scared enough, it would seep into me. I clapped my hands together once and said, "Let's pretend we're from another time."

Moments later, Preston had gathered and lit all the candles in the house, and Annabel had collected every snack that didn't need to be heated up. I brought down all the blankets and pillows, and Felix dragged the container of art supplies down from the schoolroom.

"There was a time when whole families slept in one-room cabins," I told them.

"Like Laura Ingalls," Preston said.

"Yes, exactly. We're going to do that. For entertainment, we will tell each other stories. No tablets or phones. No TV, no lights except for candles."

They looked excited, and for the first time in a long time I felt like I was bringing something new and interesting to the family. Annabel was already rooting around in the art supply box, telling us she was going to paint pictures of all of us.

"Dad told us that you and him had the best fort of all time," Preston said.

"The old pipe?" I was surprised he would tell them about that.

"The cafeteria."

"I forgot about that one. I guess we did," I said. "Do you want to hear about it again?"

"No."

Preston and Felix pored over a fantasy novel together. I looked through the novels myself. It was a hodgepodge collection—a few romance novels and thrillers, some selections from well-known series, and a random array of tearjerker bestsellers from years ago. Books accrued by people who didn't know books.

"I'll be back," I said, jumping up from the blanket nest, my feet slapping against the wooden floor at the threshold of the room. The children didn't look up.

In the bathroom, I felt my way around, avoiding the mirror. I stared through the rain-flecked window. Lightning brightened the sky and the trees stood stark on the lawn, and then twilight fell again. The eerie red glow had receded; just a normal storm now, but it still felt off, its wrath somehow tilted, unusual and snakelike in its fervor. I heard a scream from downstairs.

Preston and Annabel had gotten in a scuffle and she had fallen back, landing badly on her elbow, which seemed unbroken but bore a growing lump. I sent Felix home and made them take down the fort. Preston solemnly gathered the books and art supplies with Annabel's down comforter draped over his shoulders. After they were done cleaning up, I sent them to bed, still shaking, the potential for catastrophe tense and coiled within me. I sat at the table in the kitchen and tried to think of other things.

Eli and I hadn't created a fort so much as found one. We'd figured out while ditching gym class, looking for a place to hide, that there was a space underneath the stage in the cafetorium where a small group of people could fit comfortably, if they hunched. We skipped a whole day of school there, periodically making sudden noises and enjoying the flurry of curiosity outside. Nobody found us. We talked about how we could smuggle in clothes and snacks, books and blankets, and live under there until graduation. Eli always wanted to make new homes out of every place he saw. Over the years, I had learned to indulge him in this; it made him so happy. And I came to like playing house with him.

Now, while I waited for him, I skated through the internet, clicking and refreshing. Back in New York, Nessa had gotten a new tattoo. She had gone to the weekly queer party in the West Village, and now her sweaty, glittery face was all over the Facebook promo material for next week's show. Lavender was there, too, dressed like Amanda Seyfried dressed like a mouse, duh, and was up onstage grinding with a man in glitzy assless chaps. I liked the photo, then unliked it. Did I miss her? It was tough to tell. *Because you're a psychopath with no heart*, my brain muttered, but I shooed it out. I felt like I'd disappeared out here.

When I heard the front door open late in the night, I jumped, clattering the chair backward on the kitchen tiles. Eli shrieked. "Who's there!"

"It's me, just me," I said hastily. I dragged the chair upright and there we were, staring at each other, both afraid.

He laughed, and then I could laugh, too.

"God, those dishes," he said, staring at the mountain in the sink. "I can smell them."

"I'm sorry; I should have done them while you were gone. The kids were a lot, with the storm, and then I was just exhausted." I was babbling. I had been sitting in the kitchen for hours by then, working myself up to do the dishes, unable to convince myself that lightning wouldn't strike the house and electrocute me while the water was running.

"It's fine," he said. "Let's do them together."

While I rinsed and scrubbed off the harder spots, he loaded the dishwasher. He hated how I arranged the dishes, said it wasn't practical.

"Preston said you told him about our fort under the stage."

"Oh, yeah. Man, that was so long ago."

I wrung out the sponge. Dishwashing was the cleanest and grossest chore. "Why weren't we ever together in high school? We obviously both wanted to be."

He snorted. "You're really asking me that? You would never have gone for it."

That might have been true, but I wasn't going to admit it. "You never tried," I shot back.

"Of course I didn't. Do you remember what you were like in high school, Cass? You made Troy Garfield cry when he asked you to prom."

"I thought it was a prank."

"Why would it be a prank? Everyone knew he liked you. Anyway, I was lucky we were friends. I spent half our friendship worried you might turn on me at any second."

"What do you mean, turn on you? I never turned on anyone."

He hummed, thinking as he fit the last cup into the top shelf of the washer and shut the door. We migrated to the table and sat opposite each other. "You're right. That's a little unfair. What I mean is—I knew all the snarky, brutally honest things you thought about everyone else. I was scared that if I ever ruined things between us, you'd find another me, and you'd talk about me like that to him."

"I don't think I would have done that."

"You would have," he said with supreme confidence.

"Fine, then why be with me now?"

"Well, you've changed. You've matured a bit," he said, then chuckled at my face. "Is that so hard to hear?"

"How dare you imply that I was ever anything less than the pinnacle of maturity?"

"Right. But really, I think it was more that I grew up." Carefully, he said, "Once I was in a relationship with Beth, I started to understand . . ."

"What?"

"Oh, I don't know. This is hard to explain. Beth was super gentle. She didn't like to talk badly about anyone—even when she was furious, she would get all flustered and start stammering. It was easy to ask her out, to kiss her, because I could tell that even if she said no, she would do it so gently; she would be embarrassed for me. At times, years later, I wondered if she said yes just because she couldn't bear to reject me." He half smiled. "You, high school you, was the complete opposite of that. Back then, I thought about trying to kiss you, and I wondered if you might turn away not because you didn't want to, but because you did."

Would I have? I had no idea. Sometimes even now, waking up in this house still felt like a supernatural mistake, like a toddler god had picked up the box holding the world and shaken it out of order. But I was here, and the sight of Eli across the table, careworn and stronger, touched a tender spot in my chest that I didn't think anyone else quite could.

"I wanted to," I said.

"I know." The dishwasher clicked to a new setting, filling the kitchen with the sound of rain. He sighed. "I'll always miss Beth. But after she passed, I realized that I didn't want to be with someone who loved me out of a sense of duty."

I wanted to ask more, but I was afraid to say the wrong thing. I could feel myself folding inward under his gaze. Beth. The only way to avoid her was to stick to the present. I yawned luxuriantly. "We should probably get to bed."

Was he disappointed that I didn't know how to have these conversations with him? Beth wasn't like an ex; an ex I could have disparaged in a gentle, exploratory way until I figured out the boundaries, which parts of this person remained sacred. Beth's whole self was holy ground, and boundless. And besides, I didn't want Eli to know how much I craved a clearer picture of her—it felt voyeuristic. I had no right to her; wasn't it enough that I was living her life?

In bed, he took my hand reverently to his lips and bit it. Not hard enough to break skin, but his teeth pressed against bone. I kissed him, running my other hand up his neck to his nape and yanking the scruff of hair there back, pressing my hips against his. The size of him still sent a thrill down my spine, a kick in my stomach. He slid his hands in my nightgown, bookending my hips in his wide palms.

I pressed myself hard against him. The storm was still raging, rain pooling bright and silver in the grass.

After, I couldn't sleep. I wrapped the quilt around my shoulders over my tank top and Eli's boxers, shoved my bare feet into combat boots, and went outside. An uncanny mist sluiced through the air, cooling the inside of my throat, pressing like fingertips against my eyelids. The wind howled weakly, sweetly, calling for me. I walked toward the woods.

Once I stepped inside the woods, the path like a dirty mouth, the rain stopped—or maybe it was just halted by the cover of leaves. The air changed around me. Under the branches, the path was dry. I saw that my first few steps had left wet footprints, a weather report from another world. Something moved in the brush, but I wasn't afraid. What had beckoned me here would keep me safe.

I walked down the winding path. My hair snagged on thorns, but I kept going. I had been caught in a tide, and I was bobbing along. I wondered if it had gathered me intentionally. Maybe I was just errant, unnoticed flotsam.

"You think no one cares about you," Lavender had told me once in a fight. "You think there are no consequences for what you do."

Odd pockets of wood far away looked almost sunlit. I saw a tree I couldn't name in full bloom, pale blossoms dropping from its branches one by one as I watched. Though I remained bone dry, I thought in a moment that I could hear the sound of torrential rain, and then it was gone. A smattering of leaves crunched under my feet.

Finally, the yearning looped around me, circling like a dog about to nap, and I was halted gently in my tracks. I stopped in front of a great tree that had been split in two, the wood raw and scorched, its rough bark veined with pale gold. As I stood before it, it bloomed.

I could have stood there for decades. Eventually, a flower dropped into my cupped hands. It was golden, beautiful, the petals unfurling against my fingers, warming my palms. I smelled it, then brought it to my mouth and tongued its petals. Suddenly ravenous, I stuffed the whole thing down my throat. It tasted viscous and strange going down, like a mushroom or a living organ. I shuddered and clamped my hand over my mouth to keep it inside me. Finally, it settled.

In my old life, I thought dreamily, this was what I was so afraid of: someone swallowing me whole, then regretting it, realizing that I was too complicated, too anchored to my past, too resistant, to everything. I had refused to be devoured.

In the morning, I checked the Instagram stories of everyone I still followed from high school. Earlier in the night, all of it was good-natured "stay safe!" messages, pictures of the restaurant lit by candlelight, the antique shop's signature elephant statue holding a paper umbrella. Later, though, the messages got more fraught—reposts of the news story that kept going around about the family on the other side of the river who died after abandoning their car, a missing-persons alert for a startled-looking boy with a buzz cut.

Interspersed with these were stories from my New York friends. My roommate was out on a rain-slicked street, smiling widely with my replacement. Nessa was drinking a bloodred cocktail in a dim bar with Lavender. I took a picture of our puddled lawn, captioned it *the afterlife*, and posted. Later, I saw that Nessa had commented *wht the fuck is this uspposed to mean lol* and Lavender had liked it.

When I went downstairs, I saw that water lapped at our front steps.

"Does the creek overflow?" I asked Eli.

"It has before," he said. He came over to look. "But not like this." He was mesmerized by the ripples. I thought they might look peaceful if not for the rain, still falling into them like nails, like all the stars in the sky sliding down the side of the world and collecting before us.

Eli went into the kitchen to make a call. I was back in the kitchen making eggs in baskets. I turned and he was there, standing like he'd been waiting for me to notice.

"Randy's basement flooded," he said.

"Randy?"

"Beth's father."

"Shit. Is he okay?"

"Fine, but—" Eli pulled a piece of egg toast from the plate and blew on it. "He needs some help."

"You're heading over, then?"

He took a bite, and yolk dripped down his chin. "Supposedly the roads are clear enough. I figure I might as well bring the kids. We might stay over, maybe for a couple days. Randy tends to underplay, so there might be more wrong than he's telling."

"And you want to bring the kids?"

"It's good for them to learn. This area will only flood more over time."

"What all should we bring?"

He picked at his crust. "Well, someone should stay here and watch the house."

"Oh."

"It's just Randy—"

"You don't have to explain," I said. I could easily guess plenty of reasons why Eli might not want to let me meet his Christian father-in-law. "It'll be nice to have a weekend to myself."

"Right," he said, relieved. "That's what I thought."

I turned back to the stove. I figured I wouldn't look for Eli's wedding ring after he'd gone.

*   *   *

Once they left, I walked by the TV and it turned on—a baking show. I went up to the bedroom and dove into the internet. Hours later, I woke up craving salt. I wanted to fetch the family-size bag of Ruffles that had been sitting uneaten in the pantry since before I moved in. But I knew myself; I would eat it all, unable to stop, then feel bloated for days. Better not to eat. There was cleaning to do, always, and with this much time, I could finally tackle the unnameable smell under the sink, wash the humid weight of sweat from the duvet, really scrub the hardwood floors, rid the corners of their dust clots. I read online that dust is 80 percent human skin, and I read later that this had been debunked, but I still believed it.

I cleaned into the night. Once the bathroom was clean, I couldn't convince myself to leave it; by comparison, the bedroom felt layered with dust and stagnant smells. I covered myself in a towel and fell asleep in the bathtub, the faucet dripping into my hair.

When I woke, it had stopped. My phone was dead, and the late-morning sun streamed through the window. I couldn't bring myself to disturb the perfect dishes by using them to eat. When I charged my phone, I saw that Lavender had texted me a picture of the Delaware, saying, *isn't this where you're from?*

When I hadn't responded, she went on: she was visiting a friend at an artist's residency on the Pennsylvania side of town. She asked, *are you free to meet up?*

wild coincidence that you're here of all places, I said.

She said, *???*

I held my overheated phone between my palms. Lavender reaching out when Eli and the kids happened to be gone felt fateful. Maybe seeing her would pitch me back in love. Maybe I'd blow my life up again, but backward. Or maybe I'd see her and feel nothing, return home clarified in my resolve. This certainty would be a gift to Eli, to the kids, to myself.

I got to the café early, my favorite dress on and my wedding ring in my pocket. She was there already, of course, outside the door, petting a dog whose leash was tied to a bench. "New friend?" I asked. She turned and smiled hugely, enveloping me in a tight hug. Her hair still smelled like sage, and my body still knew hers. The last time we'd hugged, we were still together, and my whole life had been different. A faint sob caught in my throat.

She pulled back, her hands on my shoulders. Her red hair glowed in the sun. Our eyes met without me craning my neck. My whole body missed hers, but I pulled out of her reach. If this wounded her, she didn't show it.

"I'll get us coffee," I said. "What do you want?"

"Chai. I'm cutting back on caffeine," she said warily, ready for an argument. "But I can get mine."

"I've got it," I said. "I don't pay rent anymore."

That made her face change, though she recovered quickly. Moments later, we were walking past the restaurants and consignment shops on Main Street, and then down a side street. Lavender was always an easy conversationalist. She got new dinner ideas from strangers at the grocery store, made lifelong friends at concerts. Now, she told me funny stories about her coworkers and commented on the cute houses, the sound of birdsong, the rare smell of fresh air. And of course I missed her, while we walked together. I wished I could reach out and grab her hand and listen for the contented sigh that had always followed.

I knew that as the initiator of the breakup, I was supposed to be the gracious one. But I also knew she would be wary of my new life, and so I couldn't help proving myself, prattling on about Elwood—how I felt so at home here; I'd always missed it, had never fully realized how much of my sadness was intrinsic to city living. A lie, but she didn't need to know that. I stopped short of raving about

Eli or the kids. Still, I reveled unfairly, watching her grow smaller as I spoke.

We passed a forest-green Victorian with a wraparound porch. She said, "If I had a porch like that, I'd eat every meal outside."

I imagined her hanging from a noose tied to the brackets and breathed in deeply. "It's pretty, yeah, but the river floods every couple of years, so there's a lot of turnover down here. My husband"—I refused to choke on the word—"and I live up on the hill. With his kids."

She pulled her arms in against her ribs. "So you *are* married."

I retrieved my ring from my pocket and twisted it on. "I hadn't decided whether to talk about it."

She nodded, her lips pursed.

"What? You can tell me what you're thinking."

She took her time before saying, "I guess I just have to know: Did I do something? To you? I still don't understand why any of this happened."

Over the past six months, I had read our old handwritten notes, gchat messages, texts, and emails, listened and relistened to the playlists we'd made for each other. Sometimes when I woke up next to a snoring Eli under the covers, when he turned over, I expected to see her face. Sometimes I felt like my body was living in this life and my mind was still in the past. Those were nice days. I could remember the good parts and nothing else.

Now, confronted by her presence, I remembered more. The way she snaked her arms around me when I was trying to sleep. Coaxed me away from pages I needed to read. I caved to her desires too easily. She made my body, my longings, feel right, for a while. She had introduced me to her queer friends, her queer world, and showed me how to exist in it. Queer spaces were healing, everyone around me told me. But they couldn't heal me. I had kissed Lavender so many times, hard, my tongue stroking hers, my greedy hand in her shirt, while my detached brain asked me if I was feeling enough, and if I wasn't, then what was I, and was I being unfair? And when my brain forced me to retreat from the world, she took it personally.

"You wanted me to be happy," I said slowly, "but only when you were making me happy. You didn't want anything else to make me happy."

"Come on, Cassie." She laughed with a crueler edge than I'd ever heard from her. "You weren't ever happy. You hated your job. You and Nessa weren't even speaking when we met. I pulled you out of this huge sadness, I introduced you—"

"You saved me," I said. "You're absolutely right. But saving someone is not a permanent state, Lav. You wanted to be my savior forever. That's not a relationship."

"I think you kept me in that role more than you'd like to admit."

"Sure, maybe," I said. "It's nice being taken care of."

"You seem to think so now, too."

Shame, like an arrow shot straight at my heart. I shivered. "I guess so."

She touched her face, and I saw that her eyes were teary. "We could have moved out here if that would have made you happy."

"I find that hard to believe."

"I had no idea what you wanted, ever. I was always just guessing. Trying."

She bit her lip, and I imagined myself reaching out to clamp her jaws together, forcing her teeth through flesh, coating her chin in blood. I controlled my flinch as she said, "Nessa and I went by your office, you know, to get your stuff. Everyone was so confused. They kept asking what happened to you. I had no idea what to say."

I considered asking why she and Nessa were spending so much time together. But I couldn't make myself want the answer. I said, "Thanks for doing that."

"Don't be too grateful. I threw it all out."

"That's fine."

She exhaled through her nose. "Are you seriously going to stand here and tell me you don't care?"

"I don't know," I said. I remembered the books I'd kept on my desk, each one tangled and complicated. The bestseller I'd rejected. The bestseller I'd loved but couldn't get anyone else to read. All the books we'd sold excitedly to publishers that had gone on to barely sell in bookstores.

"I'm really worried about you."

"I'm sorry," I muttered.

She straightened her back. "Yeah, me too."

We didn't have much to say to each other after that. I left her back at the coffee shop. We hugged again before parting and it felt wooden, final. As I walked home, I kept feeling the urge to turn around, to find her, to beg her to forgive me, but I knew it wouldn't work. I couldn't lie back down in the hole I'd left; I didn't fit there anymore.

PART TWO

BETH

When Cassie first stepped into that house, following Eli like a shadow, my first thought was: finally.

I knew her, too, back when she was in high school, but she doesn't know that. She doesn't remember me; I can't imagine why she would. I didn't go to school, but I'd seen her around, at the diner, the coffee shop. She walked around our town like she owned it. I didn't own anything. I was boring. I wore my hair in two blonde braids every day. I was faithful, rereading my Bible. I spent my life waiting for my life to begin, and then it ended.

When Cassie came to the woods, she wore his boxers under the quilt I made. The gall! And I was annoyed to be woken by the sound of heavy steps through the brush. I had been sleeping inside my tree, between the bone and the bark, dreaming of the children. In the dream, I was inside that house, cooking dinner, and—strangely— I was happy. I wasn't anxious or itching, wondering if there was any more to life than what I'd been given. I was delighted by the simplicity—the smell of meat roasting, the sound of the children bickering, the somersaults in my chest when Eli grabbed me around the waist and swooped in to kiss me. I had no ambivalence.

But as I stirred awake, Cassie stopped walking. For the first time in my entire life, I looked closely at her. I remembered all the times I'd thought of her, getting out of Elwood, living the kind of life I was too scared of, while I made my world of her leftovers.

She was less perfect looking than I remembered. Her arms were sickly pale, the elbows knobby. All of her bones looked loosely connected under the skin in that way that looks anorexic chic in pictures but jarring in real life. And there were dark circles under her big black eyes. More than anything, she looked afraid. And the nurturing thing in me, the mother thing, rose up, and I wanted to give her something. So, before I thought it through: the flower. As it fell, I don't know what I expected: that she'd keep it in her pocket, maybe press it into a book. It's not my fault that weird fucking girl decided to eat it.

Now, she feels me pulsing like a firefly in her chest, and I can feel her curiosity. She tells herself it's nothing; I'm nothing. But I'm not; in fact, I'm getting stronger. I can see out of her eyes. Only sometimes, when she isn't paying attention. Just after waking, and during daydreams. One time, I woke her up to walk her down to Preston's room. I missed watching him sleep. I could feel her body wondering what had brought her there. She decided it was a growing motherly instinct. Poor dear.

I feel no pain watching Cassie with Eli. She doesn't need to worry so much about making my memory jealous. If anything, to see him again as desirable is a charming feeling, honeyed in nostalgia; I almost miss that want.

Now, I only want to taste more of the world.

I deprived myself, alive. In life, I got the man, the house, the children. I had my faith back then, too. I had everything I claimed to want. But there was always Cassie out in front of me, like a will-o'-the-wisp; someone to look toward; someone to think of, to think: I could have left this town. I'd think, I still could. I could travel the world, I could live in a city, or by the sea. I could go anywhere. And stupid, silly, small-minded me, I chose to stay right here. Now Cassie is here too, and now I am with her.

CASSIE

MAY

I craved more time in the woods. The trees called to me, and the chapel-like sense of quiet calmed me when I entered it. The kids and I stepped over twisting roots and bursts of unfurling ferns. I stroked neon-green patches of new moss, trailing Annabel, who cleared our way with mighty swings of a felled branch. Sprouts winnowed up through the cloud cover of decayed leaves. The sun found veins of mica and turned them on like lights. Oak leaves curled in on themselves, silhouettes of human bodies, maple leaves shaped like stars. Acorns dropped from trees and nestled in the hollows between exposed roots. Dog violets were everywhere, and crab apples, sour and tangy, sap puckering our fingers.

Preston told me about the histories of the trees around us: the mulberry at the edge of the woods, stooped and crooked, that dropped fragrant plummy berries on our heads, coating the earth around its roots with smashed dark spots. Later, in June, we would eat the berries and they would stain our hands, the juice drying in black crescent moons under our fingernails. In later June, the wineberries, a relative of raspberries, growing in clusters from branches sheathed in a red fuzz of thorns. After that, in August, the rare blackberries, their spines more evil-looking, like rose stems. Are they related, I mused, and Preston informed me that no, it was apples that were related to roses. I considered the relationship between romantic love and original sin, but I didn't raise the subject with him.

Black currants grew in the woods, too. They would be ripe in late June. "They're technically illegal," Preston said. "We don't know how they got here."

He told me that when they were first planted in America, they carried a fungus that caused blister rust, threatening the existence of the white pine, a linchpin of our lumber industry. They could have been the downfall of an industry. They were considered so dangerous that they were banned from the entire country. But in Europe, especially England, the black currant still thrived: they appeared in drinks, in jams, in bags of vegan Starbursts.

Online, later, I found out that black currants had been making a slow, quiet comeback. New, disease-resistant varieties had been developed, and eventually, after much beseeching from farmers, the government left it up to the states to choose when to lift the ban. New York State had been producing small-batch crops for almost a decade by then. Still, I felt tender for the American black currants that had been purged, before. They couldn't help what they carried.

Now that my father's house had sold, he and Fiona were flying up to take the things worth keeping, and they wanted to see me. Well, they wanted to see "the whole family," Fiona wrote in an email from their shared AOL account. "Your father says Eli is a charming young man."

Had my father and Eli encountered each other very much after I'd left? Or was he remembering Eli as a reedy sixteen-year-old, nodding emphatically at every adult until the interaction ended? What had we seemed like back then, from an adult perspective? Had we been like Preston and Felix, almost mythically close? Or had we been normal, awkward teenagers, friends only due to lonely circumstance? Probably my dad was just being polite and didn't remember Eli at all.

*   *   *

A week later, he and Fiona arrived at our house in a U-Haul. Fiona leapt out and hugged me tightly while my dad shambled after. I always expected Fiona to be a little bit mean; she had the look of someone who probably was, but never to me. She knelt to meet the kids. "Aren't you precious," she said to Annabel, who preened. My dad watched from a few steps back as Fiona folded Annabel into a hug. Had she wanted a daughter? I wondered. A real one.

Felix and Preston ran down the stairs two steps at a time, breathless. "Have you seen Rasputin?" Felix asked.

"Sorry?" I asked.

"My snake," she explained. "He's missing. Can you help look for him?"

"You guys can stay here," I told my dad and Fiona, but they were already peering under their chairs and in cabinets. "When did you last see him, sweetie?" Fiona asked.

"Is it poisonous?" Eli asked.

"Venomous," Preston corrected. "And no. He's a ball python."

"He likes warmth," Felix said. "And the dark."

"I thought there were only two kids," my dad said to me as he helped me take off couch cushions.

"Felix lives next door," I explained. "Her mom helps with home-schooling."

As if summoned, Joan walked in. "Felix texted," she said. "I told her not to take that thing out of our house."

We searched every room on the first floor with no sign of Rasputin. Felix started to hyperventilate. I took her aside, letting the search continue without us. Fiona lingered on the stairs, and I waved her away. "I want you to try something with me," I told Felix. "Let's breathe in for one, two, three, four seconds, and then hold it for one, two, three, four. Then let it out." I let out a long gust of air. "For four seconds, and then start again. Ready to do it with me?"

She breathed in while I counted. After a few moments of this, the splotches of red in her cheeks had faded. "Rasputin is fine," I told her. "Snakes are very resourceful. He's probably found a comfy hiding spot, and he's excited to surprise you when you least expect it. Okay?"

She rolled her eyes, but she still smiled. "Okay," she said.

"Fiona says you have a way with the kids," my dad said at dinner, just the three of us. We sat outside at a restaurant by the river.

I said, "They're good kids."

Fiona put down her fork. "Okay, but what's going on with that Jane person?"

"Joan? She's kind of amazing. She's teaching me how to cook. We switch off with homeschooling the kids. She was friends with Eli's first wife, I guess. She's been helping out since she died."

"Okay, but why?" Fiona asked.

"I don't know. Kindness, I guess."

"I don't buy it." Fiona picked up her fork and stabbed her salad emphatically. "No single woman hangs around another man's family unless she sees something in it for her."

"I think she's just glad Felix has a friend. I like her," I added. "A lot of the time, she comes over because I invite her over." This wasn't exactly true, but I didn't like when Fiona talked like the world was greedy and transactional. And the heteronormativity in her assumptions bothered me.

"Well, I'm very happy for you," my dad said. "It's a good life you've found."

"And a beautiful house," Fiona added.

After we'd hugged goodbye and they'd told me they would make sure to come back and visit soon, after my dad, embarrassed, shoved a too-big check into my hand, and I, embarrassed, took it, I spent a while walking around the heart of the town before going back to Eli's house. Seeing my father was always strange. I knew him better than anyone, and barely at all. He and I had found peace in our dim house after my mother left. Beyond the day of her leaving, I didn't remember much about what my mom was like, only a faint sensation of brightness glinting like a threat, like something too easily shattered. I used to wonder often if her grand escape plan had worked out for her, or if it was yet another scheme that fell apart faster than it had come together. She had always moved fast, like a tiny fish, flickering.

BETH

I was named after my mother, in a fashion—her, Elizabeth; me, Bethany. Her end is my beginning. Elizabeth means *consecrated to God*. Bethany means *house of affliction*. I have always preferred its second meaning: *house of figs*. When my mother was young, she did not live her life as if it was consecrated. She'd had ambitions, had gone to a good college, had met my father there. After my father led her to convert to the kind of Christianity that baffled her Catholic parents, he led her back here, where they'd had me. She called me Bethie, made me into a doll, her mini me, dressed us in the same long prairie frocks, all buttons and ruffles and minuscule flowers. Both our glare-blonde hair falling in thin strands down our backs.

She was a staunch Christian, and so was I, too. She told friends and neighbors that I was too smart for public school. But once, I pressed my father after a rare third beer at a Fourth of July barbecue until he revealed that my mother had longed to birth me a sibling; after four miscarriages, she had mostly stopped eating and washing her hair. They had talked about adopting a child from elsewhere, as so many white Christians did. I had a vague memory, as he mentioned it, of my mom, her voice bright as a soap bubble, asking me if I'd like to have a little sister from Africa.

He'd decided he didn't want the added responsibility. Still, he had been worried about her being alone in the house all day. If I stayed home from school, I could be her companion, and he figured if she ever did anything dangerous or unsettling, I would get help.

Hearing this, I gnawed corn off the cob and told him this would have been useful to know at the time. He sighed; he was always sighing. So, my mother taught me. She also made all of my meals from scratch, cut my hair, sewed many of my clothes. If she ever knew the true reason behind my staying with her, her understanding must have warped over time. When I disobeyed her, she would mutter with tight lips, "I had a future, you know, and I gave it all up for you." She hoped I would never find out what it felt like to pour my whole life into a child only for that child to disobey me.

Years later, when I had Preston, I heard echoes of her voice. It was easy, once he existed, to pretend to myself that my life without him would have been grander, how I might have made myself more significant with all that time. After Annabel, even more so. I remembered mere hobbies—my theater stint in high school, my middling ability to sew—with new suspicion that a childless version of me could have pursued a life of fame or usefulness. I knew how that kind of love could corrode a person, and I cared more about keeping them safe. So I stopped imagining alternate futures, any future.

Now, I find that the time I've spent away from the kids—along with my notable corporeal shift—has changed my thinking. Or maybe it's just the fact that they can't see me, can't need me, at least not in any way that I'm able to fulfill. I know this sounds heartless. Other mothers would surely claim themselves incapable of looking at their own children and feeling very little. Surely, given the chance to haunt their offspring after death, these mothers would cling to their little ones' shadows, clamor in their dreams. But none of those moms are me, and none of them know what it's like to be a ghost. I don't enjoy my children's lack of recognition. But it is also a relief. Love is a responsibility, and it's one we choose over and over again in life. In death, though, we get different choices.

At first, in Cassie's body, I reveled in being around them again— I urged Annabel onto my lap; I hugged Preston and scooped him up into the air. When I was alive, I was broader and stronger than Cassie; I was used to the motion of lifting a child. She could lift boxes of books, but those don't wiggle. There were other differences; her senses were slightly dissonant from what I remember; I think I experienced the whole world just a little sweeter than she does. Once, as I considered this, Eli looked at me, and I felt Cassie's rush of tenderness, and I thought, well, not the whole world.

CASSIE

On the anniversary of Beth's death, Eli went to work and I took the kids down into town, where we stopped by the playground at the elementary school. A cloudy haze hung over the fields. No one was there, and we felt so lucky, although it was a little eerie how abandoned the place was, swathed in fog. Then the bell rang and they all poured out like bright vomit, and the kids and I shuffled the few blocks toward the graveyard alongside the church, picking flowers from the side of the road on the way. I didn't know how to pay my respects. *Sorry you died; thanks for the husband.* I wondered if what they believed was true, if she was united with God in heaven, looking down. I wondered what she thought of me. A wave of strange feeling surged in me, a searching, desperate, panicked. The sight of Preston calmed me like medicine. I wanted to pull him into my lap, to stroke his sweat-damp hair. "Tuck in your shirt," I told him absently.

"Since when do you care?" he grumbled.

As I looked at the grave again, I had an inexplicable impulse to laugh; I pressed my mouth shut. What was wrong with me? I took a furtive photo of the grave and texted it to Nessa. *Literally dead,* she wrote back. As we stood to leave, a man jogged up to us in the parking lot. Preston and Annabel knew him—they greeted him and introduced me as their stepmother. The man introduced himself: Pastor Jack. He leaned back to take me in. Finally, he laid a hand on Preston's shoulder and said that the congregation missed his family, and that they were welcome back anytime.

On the walk home, I asked Preston, "Do you want to go back to church?"

He half shrugged. "Dad stopped going."

"You could go without him."

He looked older than he had all day when he said, "It wouldn't be the same."

The next morning, I shuffled downstairs, listless and overstimulated from staying up late, scrolling through all 246 of Beth's Facebook pictures, clicking onto the profiles of the people who'd commented on them. Annabel sat at the TV, too close, the light painting her features as she watched a show about two ten-year-old fashion tycoons.

"You shouldn't watch TV all day," I said.

She rolled her eyes, then smiled. "Want to play dress-up?"

"Sure."

I followed her upstairs and into a coat closet I'd barely paid attention to. In the corner was a small door leading to the attic. I stepped inside, the scent of asbestos choking the air. I had never been in here before. The room was stacked with boxes, and a rack of dresses hung in the corner, a vanity across from it. Annabel was already taking a heap of dresses from the rack, struggling under their weight. She spread them over the floor, petting them like cats.

I felt a frisson of panic—being here, surrounded by her things, felt invasive—but I was also curious. I wanted to feel one of Beth's dresses against my skin, the gaps and the tight spots revealing to me the differences between her body and my own.

The attic light flickered as Annabel lifted a sleek yellow halter dress off the top of the pile. "This one's my favorite. She used to wear it on date night with Dad."

"Yeah?" I asked. My voice cracked on the upswing. I could imagine the dress on my body—or on a body not quite mine, could feel the fabric slipping over softer curves, could see the way it would glow against warmer-toned skin. I blinked a few times. "She would put makeup on me while she was getting ready." Annabel hopped off the bed and opened a deep drawer on the side of the vanity. A trove of shimmery powders stared up at me, organized prismatically on a series of shelves.

"She liked this row," Annabel said, sweeping a hand over the light colors, the barely there glosses. "I like this one." She pulled the shelf out to reveal brighter colors. The last shelf of makeup held the dark colors, barely used.

"That's cool," I said.

"Dad built it."

I imagined Eli presenting Beth with his creation, bashful and excited. You asked for this, I reminded my burning chest.

At the dusty mirror, Annabel smeared cream blush over her eyelids, tongue stuck a little bit out. When the door creaked open and sneakers climbed the stairs, I raced through excuses (she wanted to! She begged!) but it was only Preston. He took in the dresses. "Those are Mom's."

"Nice job, Sherlock," Annabel said, as she rouged her cheeks with purple lip gloss.

"You look like an alien," he told her.

"I look glamorous," she corrected.

He sat down on the bed, shoving heaps of satin and linen away to make room.

"Are you upset?" I asked.

He looked down at the dirty floorboards. "Can I play?"

Eli would get home eventually. But with both of the kids doing it together, it would be easier to make the case that I was hardly involved. "Sure," I said. "Of course."

"Not fair," Annabel muttered. She watched the mirror, focused on mascara, which she was applying correctly, perplexingly. "Mom would never let him."

"Whatever. I have to do school anyway." He stood, smoothing the dress with care.

"No, it's fine," I said. "Come on. Let's play."

Preston was a different person in the dress: or maybe the same person, suddenly revealed. He chose white, a cotton A-line with a high neck and a gathered waist. Underneath it, he wore his boxers and an undershirt, but we tucked in the undershirt so it wouldn't show around the neck or armpits. The result was a little bulky, but fine. In white, his eyes were luminous blue, his pale hair soft as cornsilk. He stared at himself in the mirror. I pushed his bangs to the side, evoking a pixie cut, and he touched the flipping-out ends.

"This is boring," Annabel announced. She lifted her dress off, letting it fall on the floor, then shimmied back into her T-shirt and ran out, all unbelievably fast.

"Wash your face," I called downstairs, and I heard a door slam.

When I looked back at him, Preston had taken his sister's place at the mirror. He sat with his back ramrod straight, like a Victorian girl balancing books. His hands were laid flat against the nightstand as he looked at himself, then down, then back. He pressed his thumb into the spilled powder and turned it, watching the eyeshadow sparkle under the light.

"Do you want me to make you up?"

He closed his eyes and nodded.

BETH

I first talked to Eli on the last night of the school play. I was the Baker's Wife in *Into the Woods*. Every night, I'd stared out into the light-blurred audience, imagining that Zeke had come back to see my performance. Every night I'd emerged after the show, hair still stiff with spray, to find a room of strangers waiting to congratulate other people. The night after my last performance, I was stacking chairs in the cafetorium with the rest of the cast and crew. I was back in my normal clothes, my face still exaggerated with makeup, still wearing the basketball under my shirt as a joke. Eli was leaning against the vending machine. When I lifted a stack of four chairs and carried them past him, straining with effort, he spoke so quietly that I stopped. The basketball fell out of my shirt and bounced away. Behind me, someone laughed.

"What did you say?" My bangs were stuck in my eyelashes. He looked sorry he'd spoken.

"You were very good," he said. I noticed his voice first: a little raspy. Then his sad eyes.

"Thanks." I waited for him to leave, but he didn't. Everyone else was headed to the cast party, but I didn't want to go; there would be drinking and talk of sex, and they would see my every refusal as a challenge. I said, "You're a senior, too, right? Do you have college plans?" I tried. I still didn't know how to talk to kids my own age; I sounded like someone's aunt.

He said, "I think I'm staying here."

I brushed my bangs out of my face and watched his eyes track my movements. "You don't want to see the world?"

He laughed. "I don't know why everyone acts like this town is going to eat them. I actually think it's kind of shitty when people ditch it the second they turn eighteen."

I leaned back against the machine. "Me too."

A week later, Eli took me out on a date. I had never been on a date before, unless I counted the diner nights with Zeke, or the times we walked across the bridge to get ice cream from the shop that specialized in floral flavors, or the night we'd decided to get fancy, me wearing a lacy dress that belonged to my mom, him in a satin thrift-store button-down that might have been a woman's shirt. Those nights felt different, never awkward. With Eli, I didn't know what to wear and I couldn't rely on a lifelong store of inside jokes. "Your hair looks nice," I said bravely, upon entering the car.

"Thanks," he said, blowing a strand out of his face. "I'm growing it out."

Eli asked polite questions about my classes as he drove me to a Chili's in the adjoining town. "I like the nachos here," he said, and I filed that information away as we ate them in silence, me picking out the barest chips, leaving him the good ones. "So you were homeschooled," he finally said once we were down to the last chip. "What was that like?"

I wiped salt from my mouth. My lips burned from the jalapeños, and I hoped that made them redder. I wasn't allowed to wear makeup, but my dad didn't know how to notice concealer or clear mascara. Still, lipstick was too obvious. I wasn't allowed to go on a date, either, technically, but he'd been so glad I'd finally made another friend that he didn't ask questions. Really, that was what being homeschooled was like, but that sounded pathetic.

"I loved it," I said. "I could decide when school started and ended, as long as I got my work done. I could do all of my math lessons on Monday and then not do math for the rest of the week. When I was little, learning how to bake counted as a chemistry lesson as long as I could explain the principles behind what I was doing to my mom."

He nodded. He looked tired. I was annoyed that he'd brought me here, eaten all the good chips, and asked me about my life only to be bored by the answer. I knew I was boring. Public school had made that abundantly clear. I didn't know how to hang out with other kids. I didn't get their jokes. Everything I said seemed unintentionally funny or way too serious. Well, that was fine. I was a serious person. Bad things had happened to me. "She was a good teacher, my mom. Before she died."

That woke him up. "Shit, I'm sorry." He looked at me. "Is that why you came to West?"

I shook my head, embarrassed. "No, it happened years ago. By then I was old enough to teach myself, and my best friend, Zeke. Well, we learned together. But I made sure we did our tests and stuff."

"Is he in school now, too?"

"He moved away last year. To Philly."

Eli said, "My best friend moved, too, for college. New York. Her name was—is—Cassie. Everything feels so different without her. Emptier."

"It sucks, doesn't it?"

He laughed. I'd made him laugh. "It really sucks."

Zeke's absence had sucked a dimension out of my world, and Eli had an absence, too; our missing people soldered us together like new parts. I invited him to church the next week. Pastor Jack preached about the end-times—my favorite of his sermons. I liked imagining the drama of Christ's return. I thought it would feel nice to be revealed as one of the true believers in a world of mindless drones. Eli didn't say much about that sermon, but he came back the next week, when Pastor Jack talked about the power of forgiveness. I'd heard that one enough before, and I hadn't been wronged by anyone in a way that felt relevant. But after the sermon, Eli asked me to pray with him in his car. He cried, and for the first time since Zeke left, I felt like I had a purpose in someone else's life, and therefore in the world. After a good twenty minutes of rubbing his back while he wept, he said, "I don't think I've ever known a girl as kind as you."

By the end of my senior year, Eli and I were serious. We spent every day after school together, talking about our future. Eli was well ensconced in the church by then, and the elders told us it was better that we not waste time before getting married and starting our family. He had a job lined up already at the machine shop where a couple of his friends worked. My dad was already planning to build his cabin and let us have the house, and Eli said his salary would be enough for me to stay home, as long as we were careful. I liked the idea of staying in the house where I'd grown up, building a life that didn't involve that much change. Zeke's voice was indignant in my head. Heeding it, I still applied to colleges in secret, but only to the best ones. I didn't tour anywhere, or interview. Sometimes I still imagine the laughter in the admissions offices at all those Ivies.

Not long before our wedding, after a fumbling night of mutual curiosity and happy laughter, if not quite passion, I became pregnant. I still remember the feeling after seeing the positive test. It wasn't a disaster, I told myself; I would still fit in my dress, and God willing, no one else would know. I placated myself with these facts as if to guard against some oncoming panic, but as the moments passed, I remained numb. Not quite relieved or disappointed. Ready, I guess, to walk down the path that had unfolded in front of me so neatly.

CASSIE

Joan had arranged for a field trip at the machine shop, where Eli used to work. His former boss showed the kids the tumbler, the lathe, the drawers of screws and nails in smaller and smaller increments. The kids liked the shipping station, which housed rolls of bubble wrap wrapped around tubes as thick as their bodies. All over the floor, spirals of razor metal lay in tight, shiny locks. In the car, I caught Annabel tonguing the smooth edge of a coil she'd looped around her wrist like a bracelet, and I shrieked; I scared everyone. "Honey, no," Joan said with a saner amount of urgency, and held out her hand for Annabel to drop it into, saying, "But it's so pretty."

It was, I had to admit, all spiral and glint. But in the car home, my fingers still shook, and when I touched them to my pallid face, they were ice cold.

"You need a drink," Joan decided.

We sat on her back porch sipping lemonade I'd brought over, made with water and a neon-yellow powder I'd found in the back of a cabinet, and bourbon. Joan swirled her drink, not hiding her distaste.

The sky had become splendid, a rich layering of gold-pink ribbons. On the porch stairs, Annabel hunched over her iPad, playing a game. Preston and Felix stood in the backyard, practicing an intricate, ever-changing handshake. The other day, I'd watched them build a fort together in total silence, practically telepathic as they draped blankets over furniture, stacked books and toys to create infrastructure. I wondered what it was like to feel so close to someone that you stopped needing words.

"I love your name," I told Joan.

"Joan," she said doubtfully.

"Joan," I said, forceful. "Joan of Arc is my favorite hero."

"She's not a hero; she's a martyr."

"You can be both."

"Maybe *you* can," Joan said. "I want to make muffins before the berries go bad. Mind bringing this party inside?"

The kids scampered upstairs while I settled at the kitchen table and Joan assembled the ingredients. "I'll make the batter first, then chill it while I clean the berries," she said.

"Do you want help?"

"You can mix."

But I couldn't, it turned out—every time I touched the mixer, it turned off. "I'm sorry," I finally said, feeling helpless and stupid. "I don't know what's happening."

"Power must be going out," Joan said as she took over. It worked fine for her.

Mixer to the face; that's how I would kill Joan. Full speed, right in her mouth—I could see the blood, hear the horrible clacking of metal on teeth. I sat desolately as she blended the batter, exhausted by my horrible brain.

"I don't know if I'm interested in being a hero," Joan said as she scraped the batter down the sides of the bowl.

"I can't imagine not wanting to be a hero," I said, staring at the yellow light in the oven. When I blinked, I saw blue. "Or at least, like, good."

"I used to be more like that," she said.

"What happened?"

After a moment, more quietly, she said, "Beth."

I wondered if Joan meant Beth's existence or her death. I didn't want to pry. Carefully, I said, "You guys were close."

She pulled the beaters from the mixer and ran water over them. "We didn't know each other long. But I did—care, for her."

I joined her at the sink, feeling better now that the mixer was unplugged and dissembled. I started on the other dishes in the sink, wanting to be useful. "Do you and Eli ever talk about it?" I asked.

"Not these days."

The bowl I was drying was heavy enough to crack a skull, and I kept checking my hands to make sure that I hadn't already done it, that the water I felt wasn't blood.

Joan was picking stems off a gigantic Tupperware of mulberries the kids had collected from the big tree over her driveway. The berries were ripe on the brink of rotting, their smell pervasive. She poured them into a colander in the sink. The water ran through them, turning a dark purple-red. She shook the colander lightly, flecking my white shirt, and my brain went fuzzy—why is your shirt stained red, did you do something terrible, could you do the most terrible thing and forget?

I stepped out of the water's reach. "Kids," I called upstairs. "It's time to go."

Before we left, Preston and Felix clung to each other, begging for more time, even though they would always see each other tomorrow. Still, they tried to finagle evenings into sleepovers, sleepovers into the whole next day together. I couldn't remember what it was like to want someone around so much. Sharply, I said we were leaving, it was final, and all three of them tilted their heads, staring at me like broken clocks.

As we walked home, down the dark street, I apologized for snapping. "I'm having a hard day," I confessed.

"Why?" Preston asked. Annabel put on her headphones.

I imagined explaining what a spiral felt like to another person. I thought I might say, It's like all of my skin is wrapped around a thin layer of eggshell, and some days all it does is shatter, or, well, it's like wearing noise-canceling headphones and the only noise is myself telling me how terrible I am, or, like the sun gets sapped from the world, like everything around me is both blurry and starkly cold, like the opposite of the soft, sunlit feeling of love.

And other times, I got so desperately sick of myself and my over-eager romanticization of my experience of the world, sick of the part of myself that still hoped anyone might want to hear about the nightmares that danced wildly inside me. I wanted to yell at this poor, imaginary person who never deserved my honesty or my wrath: It's just fear, you fucking idiot, don't you know what fear feels like? Hasn't anyone else ever felt fear before, besides me?

That night, I swore I heard whispering in the walls. This had happened a few times in the past few weeks; one morning, I'd asked Preston if he and Annabel talked to each other when they couldn't sleep, but he didn't answer.

Sometimes, lately, when I walked by the TV, it turned on for no reason. Or the channels changed while I was watching—usually to cooking shows, sometimes old sitcoms. I figured the kids got a universal remote to mess with me. That was fine. I learned that biscuits require almost no kneading, that browning butter gives off a nutty smell.

Eli still had exactly one picture of Beth out, on the mantel. In it, she wore a floppy hat that covered one eye, the other brilliantly blue. Her hair was a filmic gold in the sun, her lips a dusty rose. Sometimes I imagined that one eye was watching me.

Often when I got spooked, I went outside and sat on the wraparound porch, surrounded by peeling paint and creaking boards. Outside, I could breathe better. Still, shadows lengthened long across the lawn. Each night, when the sun set behind the trees, there was a moment when every branch glistened, just before they sharpened into claws.

BETH

I didn't set out to homeschool my children. I wasn't sure that homeschooling had given me more than it had taken from me, and I wasn't the type of mom who was instantly obsessed with her newborn, who needed him near her at all times. Nursing was painful, and excruciatingly boring. But when Preston said his first word—bird, while pointing up—something unlocked in me. By the time he was speaking in sentences, he had become the sun in my days, his waking the reason for mine. Eli was lovingly perplexed, watching us babble together in a language half made up. Once, he said he was glad I had taken to "all of this," with a twitchy hand gesture.

Eli didn't know that Preston's presence in my life had thoroughly usurped his, that often, the only reason I wanted to look into Eli's face was to search it for the resemblance. They were alike, sometimes, but in Eli, the whining sounded petulant. The wonder so perfect in Preston's eyes seemed like a bad parody of innocence in my husband's gaze.

Eli had wanted a girl. "I'm used to girls," he'd told me. He had grown up with a mother and a sister. They still lived together two towns over, had come to visit a few times shortly after Preston's birth. Once, while Kim was holding Preston and Eli was checking on dinner, I took the rare opportunity to linger in the bathroom, marveling in the mirror over my changed face. When I opened the door, Eli, halfway up the stairs, looked at me, then at the closed bedroom door. "You left him with them," he said, his voice strange and strangled. He took the rest of the stairs two at a time, me bobbing helplessly like seaweed in his wake. He burst in. Kim was still holding him, and both women looked up. Nothing seemed wrong. Eli never explained what had terrified him so much. A few weeks later, I asked if they wanted to visit again, and he said they were probably busy. I hadn't seen them since, and I figured that was intentional.

When Annabel was a baby, I waited. I knew the boredom was part of the process, that eventually my heart would plummet into place and I would see her for the magical creature she was. But whenever she and Preston interacted, I was watching him learn her. When Annabel said her first word—car—I felt nothing new. Eli, perhaps sensing this, loved her extra. I hadn't known that he had held himself back from Preston all along, but now I could see it as clearly as words on paper. He brought her to the shop, where all the guys made hand puppets at her. On Saturdays, he strapped the car seat in his truck and took her grocery shopping. He wasn't a baker by nature, but he made a hummingbird cake for her second birthday. He held her over the bowl of batter as he stirred, watching her eyes trace the smooth circles of the spoon.

I decided Preston didn't need preschool. He learned constantly, breathing in the world and transmuting it into information. I told other people about it, amazed—the moment when he learned numbers, when he spelled his own name without me telling him how. I knew raving about one's child's specialness sounds like doting, and I was, but I was also basking. He was so special, so smart and so lovely and so much mine. I had spent my whole life feeling less than other people, and here, this small part of me was so clearly spectacular.

I promised Eli that I would send him to kindergarten, but then I couldn't bear to. Eli and I had mostly lost each other by then anyway, hiding our ambivalence for each other by turning our faces toward our respective children.

* * *

Four years ago, on a Sunday while I was home with Preston, who had a stomach flu, Rosemary Blake showed up at our church.

Rosemary and her husband, Dan, a dairy farmer who'd been hired in the adjoining town, were parents of four tall freckled boys, the youngest two years older than Preston. She was older than me— than all of us; the moms were all around the same age, in our early twenties. Until Rosemary's boys, Preston had been the oldest child in the group since I'd been the first one of us to get pregnant, at eighteen. I'd married Eli in time to avoid scandal, for the most part, though Beverly and her girls didn't talk to me for a while. Once they started having their own children, they came to me for advice I felt barely qualified to give.

I was relieved to be replaced in my role as oldest and therefore wisest. It had never suited me, and Rosemary took to it well. She was slight, quick moving; she talked with her hands, and her eyes flitted around the room like she saw bugs we didn't. Her features were soft, like she'd been coated in a thin film of dust. She often looked uncertain, and her voice was quiet, but her laugh was loud and braying, and she could be cutting when nobody expected it. Beverly had been the most popular mom in the congregation, with her careful blonde waves and her backyard pool. But after a few weeks of mean-girl bravado, trying to spread rumors that wouldn't take about Rosemary's origins and proclivities, Beverly gave in, scurrying around Rosemary like a clumsy mouse, and the rest followed her, like always.

Rosemary was always putting her hands on other women's shoulders and knees, laughingly, coaxingly. She never touched me in those early weeks, not once, but sometimes I caught her watching me like she wanted to drink me down. It fascinated and unsettled me. I was always choosing carefully where to sit when she was in the room; never next to her, but never far. I wasn't clumsy, but I broke things in her presence, stammered out even my simplest ideas: that

I might buy an ice cream maker to teach the kids; that we could take them to the nearby sculpture garden on a field trip. Stupid things. When I spoke, she would quiet the room, and I was never sure if she did it to bolster or to humiliate me.

One time during the Women's Bible Study, Beverly had been blathering about the pool feature she was putting in, remarking on how blessed she had been, that her husband's work was going so well. Rosemary turned to look at her—I remember the turn well; it was so slow and composed, like a stone coming to life. She'd said, "And next time you get sick or hurt; next time something happens to your child or that husband you love talking about—will you then consider yourself cursed? Or will God have simply turned away from you?"

Beverly stammered something about God's ways passing human understanding. Someone cleared her throat, and the study went on. Later, I asked Rosemary if she wanted to help me decorate for next Sunday's Easter potluck.

I liked baking more than I liked most things, and for church pot-lucks, I always brought the sugar cookies that I was famous for among the congregation, along with something a bit more ambitious and persnickety—cream puffs, florentines, linzer hearts with homemade jam. For that Sunday, I made petit fours iced in purple, pink, and green, each with their own tiny buttercream flower. The task was arduous. While making them, I snapped at Preston for being underfoot in the kitchen; with a simpler recipe, I'd have solicited his help, and as I drove to the church on Saturday night, I was annoyed at myself for the sweeter, more affectionate afternoon we could have had. Instead, when Eli got home from work, I'd over-heard Preston asking him, "Is Mama still mad at me?"

And now I was running late to meet Rosemary, the petit fours precariously balanced on the passenger seat—I would stash them in the church fridge overnight. Sometimes I tried to tell stories with my decorations, to invoke my own soul's questions into them; that year, I was preoccupied by the pain of crucifixion. I brought maroon hellebores, also known as the Lenten Rose, and bloodroot, which looked cheery, almost like small daisies, but produced a natural red dye. I also brought a roll of butcher paper and markers so the kids could make a banner during Sunday school.

A spring rain was falling heavily against the windshield, and I felt bad for having dragged Rosemary out in this weather. Once I arrived at the church, if she wasn't there, I would call her and tell her not to come. But when I pulled up, she was sitting in her car with the lights on, reading her Bible. When I knocked on her window, she started. A smile crossed her face like a wisp of smoke, there then gone.

I unlocked the side door to the church and turned on the kitchen lights, then after we shucked off our wet coats, the sanctuary's. I always liked the feeling of knowing where a place's light switches were. Rosemary followed me soundlessly. "What were you reading?" I asked.

She cleared her throat. "The Easter story," she said. "John's version. I like to prepare my heart before the day begins."

"Me too," I said, nodding at my bags of flowers. I ducked into the pantry to retrieve a few vases.

"So acts of service is your love language?"

"And quality time," I said. "What about yours?"

She was standing behind me in the pantry. "Physical touch," she said bluntly. I blushed. "And gifts," she added as I handed her a vase.

"Not many people have gifts."

"Not many people admit to it," she corrected. "Why don't you do the first one and I'll catch up."

"It's nothing special," I said, arranging a few stems of flowers in a vase. "I just make them look nice."

"I don't have an eye for that stuff." She copied what I'd done. "That's great," I said. She nodded, pursing her lips skeptically at her creation. She often seemed a bit dissatisfied—I'd noticed this at the ladies' Bible study, too—and I wanted to put a calming hand on her shoulder. As always, I refrained.

I can't remember much of what we talked about as the rain built into a proper thunderstorm, lightning blinking white outside the window. I remember wanting to impress her, to make her laugh. In remembering, I think I transpose the ease that we had later. On that first night, we must have been more awkward, me stammering and unsure of how to arrange my body. I do remember being grateful that I had something to do with my hands, and I remember my damp hair drying against my neck in the warm room.

The power went out. Rosemary gasped and I laughed. "Now it's a party," I said. She didn't respond.

"Are you okay?" I asked.

Her voice was small. "I don't like the dark."

"I can go to the basement, try to flip the circuit breaker."

"You don't need to do that."

"I'm already doing it," I called back from the basement doorway. "You don't have to worry."

I picked my way down the stairs by the light of my phone. A childish part of me would always be wary of a basement in the dark, but the nervousness in Rosemary's voice made me braver. When I was halfway across the floor, the lights came back on, accompanied by a sharp crack of thunder with a groaning finish. I heard a shriek upstairs and took the steps back up two at a time.

"I'm so sorry," Rosemary was saying, aghast. At first I wasn't sure what I was seeing—deep red blotches laid around her. Flowers, floating in pools of water and broken glass. She took in a shuddery breath. "Forgive me."

"There's nothing to forgive," I told her as I walked toward her,

glass crunching horribly under my sneakers, glad to have a reason
to wrap my arms around her shoulders.

Eli never asked me to have sex with him outright, but I could always
tell, his fingers trailing slow over my shoulders, his breaths blooming
into sighs; he would tell me I was beautiful while I was wrapped in
a towel, picking out a nightshirt, and I would know that he wanted
me to leave it off. I knew it was my duty as a wife to submit to him,
just as it was his duty to love me as Christ loved the Church; he was
honor-bound to sacrifice his life for me, should the need arise. In
comparison, the price I paid was almost nothing. Only the small
choices I made every day.

Eli went to church because he knew it was important to me. He
believed, but he didn't care much about the doctrine; what I inter-
nalized from my religion was hardly his fault. He knew that, and
I think he pitied me, knowing that I would bend myself to follow
rules he would never enforce. Still, without having to ask, he got
more than I wanted to give. I had been taught to bend my body to a
husband's will long before I met him.

CASSIE

JUNE

A heat wave undulated over the mid-Atlantic region, and the kids cycled in and out of various tantrums all day. At one point in the morning, Annabel had burst into a fit of laughter that wouldn't end. Eventually, tears streamed down her cheeks. She locked herself in the bathroom for an hour, giggling through the door, the pitch rising with her panic. After lunch—Annabel had emerged, still hiccupping softly—Preston and Felix had fought passionately, with biting and hair-pulling. They wouldn't tell us why, but when Joan threatened to just take Felix home, she screamed; a keen like a siren, loud enough that I was relieved there were no close neighbors. Only I saw Preston dig his jagged thumbnail into his wrist. At dinner—Joan cooked, I cleaned up—that tiny mark was still there, deep purple and indented.

After we'd all had the ice cream Eli brought home for dessert, we caved to the kids' begging and agreed to let Felix sleep over. Once they were in bed, Eli went to the cabinet over the stove and pulled out his bottle of Maker's. "I think we all deserve a drink," he said. Joan let her sunglasses clatter on the table and collected three snifters from the high cabinet over the sink. I was still thrown off when she knew where something was before I did.

The day—the past few days, really—had been so exhausting that my intrusive thoughts had mostly left me alone. I was trying not to celebrate or even acknowledge this, lest I summon them. I imagined them seeing my relief and shooting in through my ears, like the arrows of angry gods. Drinking would likely bring them back, not in the moment, but the next morning, but I didn't want to be a spoilsport. Besides, they'd return eventually, anyway.

"Porch?" I asked, and Eli brought the bottle, holding the door open for me and Joan. "My ladies," he said, and Joan frowned at him, as she often did. I'd wondered if she blamed Eli for Beth's death, or resented him for still being alive. Or maybe it was me she didn't like. But I didn't think that was quite it. Sometimes I caught her watching me with a curiosity that felt birdlike, empty of any human feeling.

Eli drank quickly and poured again. Joan savored hers, and I tried to take the tiniest possible sips—a private game. We troubleshot the day, debating whether we could have handled anything differently. Not really, we concluded; the various emotional turmoils underneath each child's misbehaviors were all natural, due to age or change or abiding grief. Still, our words felt like wallpaper over deep cracks; we were all tired.

Now, the night was cool and misty, the woods a haze of twisting shadows. Something rustled, but Joan and Eli didn't notice. I resettled in my chair. Crickets chirped under the porch, and the occasional bat swooped overhead. In the direction of Joan's property, an owl hooted.

"Felix loves that bird," she said. "She named him Oscar."

"Oscar the owl," I said.

Eli leaned against the rotting porch railing. "Careful," Joan said, and he came back to the table. "You guys ever look at your life and realize you have absolutely no clue how you got to where you are now?"

We all looked out into the woods. I wondered what nights like this had been like when Beth was alive. I imagined an easy intimacy to their banter, their love for the kids unstilted and natural. They probably made plans—field trips, summer weekends. Beth might have made cupcakes or a pie. Three parents drinking on a porch on a June evening—it was an idyllic picture; my presence was the only thing fucking it up.

"I should get to bed," I said. I gathered the blanket I'd wrapped around my shoulders and took my glass inside. The faucet turned on before I touched it, like it sometimes did. While I rinsed my glass, I listened for sound floating into the open window, wondering if they'd talk now that I was gone. But I didn't hear anything.

I peeked in on the kids—Annabel was asleep, her face belying none of the day's chaos. Felix and Preston had made a fort out of Preston's bed; Christmas lights glowed around its edges, and I pulled out the plug. In Eli's bed, I curled up with my phone, scrolling through news, book recommendations, opinions about TV shows I hadn't watched, until I fell asleep. I didn't know what time it was when Eli slipped in under the covers, his toes cold against my calves. I kept my face turned away. His breath smelled like whiskey and his fingers crawled around my ribs, pulling me back against him. Sweat gathered where our bodies touched. I waited for his breathing to steady before I eased out of his grip.

Later that night, I woke to a sound that I couldn't understand at first. Eli was quietly asleep beside me. I went to the stairs and looked out over the family room; Joan was asleep on the couch, buried tightly in a nest of blankets. The sound persisted. I walked down the hall—nothing in Preston's room. I pushed open the last door. The lights were out, the shape in the dark still. But in her dreams, Annabel was laughing.

The next morning, I woke up buzzing, fresh and new. The sky outside was clear, the kind of blue that made the leaves look dull. I eased out of bed so Eli wouldn't wake up. When I stepped down the stairs, I realized that no one was awake but me. This hadn't happened during daylight in weeks. It felt worth savoring. I could make a big, indulgent breakfast. I could drink a steaming coffee, black, while gazing out the window, listening to birdsong. I could read a book or lie in a pool of early sunlight, quiet and alone. Instead I laced my boots, tucking the hems of Eli's pajama pants into them, and traipsed out to the woods.

Mist hung suspended in the air, reached coolly into the cracks and crevices of tree bark, and of me. A dead squirrel lay along the footpath, its little hands curled under its chin, face closed in eerie peace. My chest splinted, tightened. I searched for the sense of well-being that had lured me out here from the house, but it had melted away.

By the time I got back to the house, it was a box full of noise. Preston chased Annabel up the stairs but tripped, and she taunted him, pulling the skin of her face down with her hands into a droopy sad clown mask, the reds of her eyes rimming the whites. He screeched, and Eli burst out of the bedroom, bellowing them into shamed submission. He saw me at the bottom of the stairs, calmly unzipping my boots, my hair wet with dew.

"Where were you?"

"Outside."

He sighed. "Can you handle breakfast?"

I nodded.

Later, when I went back outside, Preston and Felix were lying face down in the dirt. My world tilted sideways. I ran toward them, fell to the ground, turned Preston over with clammy hands.

"What?" he asked, annoyed. His cheek was stamped with grass, and a dandelion petal clung to his nose. Felix turned over, too.

"What are you doing lying out here like that?"

"Corpsing," Felix said.

Right. I was surprised the trend was still going. I hadn't walked down into town in months, I realized. "Who's recording?"

"We were practicing," Preston explained.

Back in the house, I ran cold water over my wrists, hoping to calm my jumpstarted nerves. My mind reliably replayed the moment when I didn't know yet that they were safe. When I worried that I could unpeel a flap of my brain, look up under it, and see a cleverly buried memory of a double murder. I had poisoned them, probably, or there were stab wounds through their stomachs, blood melting into earth. Their pain ran through me even now, even knowing that none of it happened. It didn't matter. The thoughts were there, as real as memory.

Preston was letting Thunderbolt the hamster play on the kitchen floor when Felix's snake slid out from underneath the oven and struck. Preston grabbed at the hamster's nub of a tail, screaming, but it was too late.

We held a funeral, minus the body. One particular section of lawn that lined the woods, sitting between two oak trees, had long served as a small pet graveyard. No proper headstones, just distinctive rocks pulled from one of the creeks, either the one across the street or the other one that I hadn't seen yet, which ran farther back in the woods. There was still so much of the kids' matter-of-fact world that I had never seen. "That's Charles Wallace, the parakeet," Annabel said, pointing to a smooth red rock. "Frodo ate him. That's Frodo, the cat, next to him. That gray one is Mabel, who escaped in the winter and froze to death. What animal was she, Preston?"

"Guinea pig," Preston said. Once they had listed all the graveyard's dwellers, Preston read Matthew 11:28–30. Felix recited a poem she'd made up on the spot, rhyming "protested" with "digested."

That night, I couldn't sleep. I still heard Preston's scream on repeat, my brain insisting on getting the intonation exactly right; there had been one scream in particular that went shrill and then shredded, hoarsening, that was stuck like a song in my head. As it went on, more tears came to my eyes, even though I was dehydrated, my skin hot and dry. The kids had been fine by the time they'd gone to bed, Preston reassured that he would see the hamster in heaven, Felix quietly pleased to have her snake back. But I was still stuck on the bad moment, unable to feel the relief of its end. And why did I need to replay Preston's screams? Did some part of me like the sound? I texted Nessa. *I don't think I can keep doing this*, I told her. *I feel like I stepped into someone else's life, like I don't fit in her clothes.*

No shit, Nessa said. She followed with, *Come home.*

I held the phone against my chest and tried to imagine going home. My roommates had filled my room; I saw the exchange on Facebook. The new me was an actress. She and my roommates sung show tunes at karaoke, toasted on rooftops, went shopping.

I asked Nessa, *am I an imposter wherever I go?*

I stared out the window awhile. I texted Nessa, *what if I'm ruining this family?* I thought if she told me that I wasn't wrong for having these worries, maybe the worries would evaporate. Maybe she would tell me that I was a good person, incapable of harming anyone, ever, and maybe I would believe it.

Nessa wrote back, *I thought being married meant you'd get laid more.*

BETH

I know it must have taken weeks, maybe months, but I remember my friendship with Rosemary as if it sprang into being fully formed. I was different around her. Usually, in every room, I felt cowed by my lack of life experience. I had never left the country, barely left the tristate area. I hadn't seen most movies, I didn't watch TV, and even the books I'd read were old, harkening back to different times. "You're like an artifact," a boy told me once in high school. "Is that an insult?" I'd asked. "I don't even know," he'd marveled.

But Rosemary was not unlike me. She hadn't gone to school either; she'd grown up on her parents' small dairy farm, which she and her husband had lived on until a few years ago. The way I knew baking and sewing, she knew animals. She rhapsodized about waking up to milk the cows and collect the chicken eggs. They had kept bees, too. Rosemary had loved them, reveling in the feeling of them floating around her in what she called her spacesuit. When her parents had passed away, one shortly after the other, she had gone out to tell the bees. She hadn't cried when they died, she told me, but she cried years later, when she had to sell the bees.

Beverly was much more fun to be around when I could laugh about her with someone later. When I told Rosemary about my first pregnancy, she was horrified to hear how mean the other women had been. "Good thing you don't need their friendship," she'd said haughtily, "now that you have me."

I let myself believe it. And I believed more than I had any right to. I had never had a girl best friend before. I kept every compliment she gave me, playing them over in my head as I fell asleep. I double, triple texted. I showed up at her door and let myself in. I hugged her hello and goodbye, holding her bones tight against mine, breathing in the smell of her hair, like cilantro and mist.

I'm sure there were warning signs. I didn't see them. In total, Rosemary lived in our town for six months. In early September, I saw her out to lunch at a pizza place with Beverly. Even now, shame crawls through me when I think about how I walked right up to them and sat at their table. Beverly left shortly after. "You're welcome," I said. She gave me a tight smile, her eyes a strange green, as uncertain as a bruise.

"I should get going," she said.

"I can come over. I don't have plans."

She tapped her fingers against the table, a nervous habit. I reached, unthinking, to cover them, like I had so many times with Zeke when we were children. She yanked her hand away and set about shredding a napkin into long strips.

"I'm sorry," I said. I wanted to explain, but I didn't know what to say. The air smelled like pepperoni. By the counter, two children fought over the gumball machine.

"Beverly said," she said in a high, strained voice, "that God laid it upon her heart to tell me that our closeness is inappropriate in the eyes of the Lord."

I laughed. She didn't. "She's jealous," I said.

She flinched. "That's an interesting choice of words."

I folded my arms and hunched over them.

"I hope I haven't communicated unclear intentions toward you," she said.

"No," I said. This was happening too fast for me to understand, and I wasn't even sure I was interpreting her words correctly. I had never met a lesbian, wasn't even sure I understood what one was. But what else could she mean?

"I'm not—" I said. I stopped. I thought of how blithely comfortable I was in her presence, how often I'd wanted to linger in her hugs. I'd smiled over my phone as we texted. I'd sung in the shower, thinking of her smile. Sexual desire had always felt to me like a flickering light, something to be approached sidelong, by gently touching the right places. The way I'd wanted Rosemary was different. It warmed my whole body, as undeniable as the sun.

"It's just as well," she said while I reassessed my whole life in front of her. "Dan found a better job. We're planning to move at the end of the month."

This brought me back to the present moment. I felt slapped, cracked open. "When were you going to tell me?"

Then she looked angry. "I didn't have to tell you at all." She wadded up her pile of napkins, shoved them in the trash, and left.

CASSIE

JULY

The toilet was clogged and I fixed it, feeling superhuman, but then the sink was clogged, the stopped-up water bile colored, like the whole house was one body, digesting our waste for us, and it had gotten sick, plus I found a nest of spiders I'd somehow missed in my cleaning binge under the full, bloated sink while looking for something to dissolve whatever probably crawled into our pipes and died. I found two different brands of drain cleaner and used the last of one, but it wasn't enough, and Preston informed me that you couldn't mix differing brands of drain cleaner, as they might spit hot water in your face, leaving you burned and scarred, might release a poisonous gas into your home, might even explode. I got the three of us ready to walk down into town. "Why can't you drive?" Preston whined.

The clouds hung low and dark in the sky, a little more ominous than the typical Jersey gray, lilac in spots and yellow in others, like a disease. Why can't they just be clouds, I scolded myself. At CVS, Preston got Oreos, fine, but Annabel wanted these horrific radioactive-looking chips that I knew would get noxious savory dust everywhere. I asked politely if she might want to consider any other snack. She said no. I begged. I promised her three snacks, as long as none of them were those chips. Preston wanted three snacks, too. While he dithered over options, Annabel wandered the store with her face buried in her tablet. I asked what she was watching, and she displayed the screen: a YouTube channel in which two six-year-old girls ran through a series of "kidnap" scenarios where their dad pretended to torture them while wearing low-rent Halloween masks. There was a lot of fake blood and fake vomit. The whole thing had the bright, weird quality of home-video porn, and I could feel myself not really feeling it, could objectively observe myself slotting it away for later, when I would take it out and force myself to watch it in horror over and over until it became part of me.

"Annabel. Where do you find this stuff?"

Disdainfully, she said, "It's one of the most popular channels on YouTube."

"I think you should put it away."

"No."

"Annabel, please. Just while we're in the store." Flashes from the video kept blinking in my head: the girls tied up, their father pretending to chop one's arm off with a plastic ax, the severed plastic limb spraying fake blood. Was I suitably horrified by this image? Or did I get some secret, sickened thrill? I thought the former, but I couldn't be sure; I had to be sure. I watched it again.

My brain stood, shaking its head sadly at me, drowning in the whirlpool. *You're checking*, it said, arms crossed. I was checking. I was. I couldn't stop.

"Annabel," I said, trying to restrain my voice. "Turn it off, now."

Preston strolled over from the next aisle. "What's going on?"

Annabel thrust the tablet in his face. "Cassie says I can't watch freaking YouTube? She just fucking flipped out on me."

"Language. Annabel," I said calmly. "I did not flip out. If I'd flipped out, Preston would have heard me. He was only one aisle over. Preston, did you hear me flip out?"

"I didn't hear anything," he said. "But you're being kinda weird now."

The girl with her arm chopped off again. The girl with her arm chopped off. I blinked.

"What is it?" Preston asked, reaching for the tablet.

I closed my eyes. "She can watch something else if she wants! I told her she could watch anything else, just not that."

"She did not tell me that."

"I meant to. I'm sorry if I didn't say it out loud."

She rolled her eyes. Preston watched the video now, the air humming with fake screams. At the end of the aisle, a man turned his cart in, then changed his mind and rolled on by. What would it feel like to chop through an arm? I shivered. I didn't want to know, and the shiver proved it. But I could have faked the shiver, just to pretend to myself that I didn't want to know. *You're checking,* my brain told my brain. *You know that makes it worse.* Preston laughed. I would not look at the video to see what he laughed at, even though I wanted to.

"We're leaving," I announced, and both of them stared at me.

When we got home, Eli had fixed the drain. It was late afternoon, no school had gotten done, and both kids were hyped up on sugar and destined to crash. I wanted to go to bed and start over. I wanted to evoke any expression on Eli's face except for this one: disappointed, exasperated. There was still a yellow ring around the sink. This, at least, I could fix. I grabbed a sponge from the kitchen and started to scrub.

"What?" I said to Eli's look.

"It's fine. It's—that was the dishwashing sponge."

"Well, not anymore," I retorted, and Eli laughed, but not with me, so I hurled the dishwashing sponge, now the bathroom sink sponge, one step closer to being the trash can sponge, right at his face. Yellow scum stuck in his eyebrow.

"Oh my God," I said as he grimaced. I started to cry, but then I heard a sound, I prayed it wasn't the sink, gaseous and restless, ready to explode. But it was Eli, laughing.

He was a good husband. I wanted to love him for this, to fall into him and forget everything. But the yellow scum was still stuck to his shining face, and looking at it was activating my gag reflex. This was the type of moment that inevitably happened with every person, the moment that made me wonder if, when it came to other people, there was a right decision for me. No part of me loved the sight of Eli's face right then. His whole body heaved with emotion, and there were sweat spots in his armpits, and his heavy breath smelled like vinegar and rot. I have always hated the way breath smells, all breath, teeth just brushed, mouth just washed, Listerine just swirled, gum just popped, wine just drank, cum just swallowed, Eli's breath, Lavender's breath, the children's breath, all of it, all of it.

Make an effort, I scolded myself. I swallowed and kissed Eli, hard. When I drew back, he was smiling. "You're lucky you're pretty," he said.

BETH

Two years later, Joan moved in next door. I brought her a plate of cookies on her first day, and I was relieved to find that she looked at me like she looked at everybody else, and she talked about her ex, Trent, with the fury of the truly brokenhearted.

Soon, Felix and Preston were best friends. Joan was always around, offering rides, offering vegetables from her abundant garden. She helped out with the kids. She observed them with me, laughing at their games, amazed with me at their growing. And Eli—I could roll my eyes at her when he was being absurd. With Joan there, I could take a moment away from the table when he irked me. I could take whole Saturday afternoons away, walking through the woods alone. She never minded watching the kids when Eli was gone, or when he was there. Early on, when I'd asked about Felix's name, Joan explained that it had been Felicia, that Felix had asked to change it when she'd learned the boy version. "I think it suits her," she said with a shrug. "Maybe she'll change it again when she's older; maybe she'll change other things."

Joan was nothing like Rosemary; there was none of that magnetism glowing under our words and movements. I often wondered if the current I'd felt with Rosemary could have existed without two conductors. She still followed me on social media, though she never engaged. A few shameful times I tried to goad her by posting Bible verses I knew she loved. Once, I posted a blurry picture of Joan, just to see if she'd notice. For all I know, she never saw it.

For a while, I'd been afraid of what making a new friend might awaken in me. My heart felt like a lurching toddler, impossible to hold in place. I posted in comment threads on queer websites only to delete seconds later. I blushed talking to the college-age barista with a pink triangle necklace; I was afraid to interact with any of the lesbians who lived in this town, afraid they would see my embarrassment, my eagerness. I watched them through my screen instead, combing through all the social media profiles of people I knew even barely, tangentially, who had come out. There was the field hockey player a year younger than me who had lent me a tampon once, who now lived across the river with her wife. The school librarian who was—as far as I knew—single, but posted a picture of herself with a group of laughing women at DC Pride. A bassist who used to play on the Worship Team, who had been friends for a while with my childhood best friend, Zeke, had transitioned and now lived in San Francisco. And of course there was Cassie Jackson, now McKean, like me.

CASSIE

AUGUST

For weeks now, I had been noticing my vision going funny, almost doubling; sometimes I had to shut one eye to make it down the stairs. A feeling came with the dizziness, like a new sense of orientation, an inexplicable familiarity. I looked at Preston's face and I saw it fatter, toothless. Annabel smaller, wrapping her arms around her chubbier legs. I looked out into the darkening yard, and the swing set waited a beat before blinking into focus. I felt my nipples sore against my cotton T-shirt, and I remembered distinctly the feeling of them leaking milk. I jumped back, dropping a glass in the sink. A crescent-shaped shard had broken out of it; it shone in the drain like a crooked moon. When I looked at the window again, my reflection gave me a cheery smile. But I wasn't smiling, was I? I touched my lips, my teeth. The features were the same, but I'd never seen this face in any mirror. As I tried to figure out what made this expression mine, it dropped from my face. I was staring at myself again.

I'm used to my brain feeling like a person separate from me, deviously grinning. This wasn't that. I didn't think this was that. How could I ever know anything for sure? I scraped a chair out from under the table and sat down. "Fine," I said out loud to the empty house. "Don't hold back."

A hesitation, and then memories poured through me like excited puppies, tripping over themselves, almost not making sense. Crying in this chair, and over that stove, and in the doorway. Eli coming up behind me and slipping his arms around my waist, but my hips are softer, and damp wisps of short hair cling to my neck. I can see my nose in a new way. My nails, manicured, cobalt blue. The ring on my finger holds an oval stone. I wear a gingham dress.

I thought I might throw up. The memories responded, lightening like diluting ink. "It's okay," I whimpered. "I can take it."

I knew then. I could feel her in my head, shaking hers knowingly. "Can you talk?" I asked. "It might be a little easier for me."

There was a long pause, then a voice issued from my own mouth, breathy and transparent. "It's—"

I screamed, then clamped my hands over my mouth. "Sorry," I whispered. There was no response. That was fair. I took in a long breath and said, "Okay. Try again."

"It's hard for me to talk."

"Right, I'm not crazy about this either, actually. But I need some answers." I said, "Okay. Let's start with how you're here. Do you know how you came to be here?"

A memory seared through me—me, eating the flower, only this time it was from the perspective of the flower. I felt my fingers around my petals, saw my own face get gigantic, felt crushed under my past self's teeth. In the real world, my knees buckled. I caught myself just in time to lower myself to a seat and grip the chair underneath me. "Jesus. Can you please warn me before you do that?"

I could feel her affirmation in my body, quick as an expression—like looking at someone's face, only without the looking and the face.

So you were in the flower? I switched to speaking in my head, since the sound of my own voice in the house was still giving me the creeps.

She sighed in light frustration. Although in those first few days, even when she expressed annoyance or sadness, or later true rage, I still felt the exuberant undercurrent of joy under everything she said and showed me. Something like a person whispering "finally!" over and over in the background of my brain. Even though the fact of her was existentially terrifying, I think it was made easier by her joy, as clear and earnest as an open door.

She asked if she could show me. *It's easier than trying to explain in words*, she creaked.

I'm gonna lie down first.

The tile was cool against the backs of my arms and my cheek. I didn't have anything to hold on to down here, just the earth, gravity pressing me closely to its surface, and even these things felt unsteady to me in that moment, like everything else did. But I didn't have time to change my mind. She was showing me the woods; all her days there, infinite in their sameness; she flowed into a tree and I squirmed at the feel of bark knitted with my skin. She dove into the earth, and I held my breath until I realized I didn't need to. All around me, the complicated root systems communicated to each other in shifts and sweet groans. Back in the kitchen, tears sprang to my eyes, and Beth flickered like a warmth in my hand before retreating to my head.

It feels nice to show someone, she told me, her voice soft and full of dirt.

I still had many more questions to ask, but my thoughts struggled to gather. She seemed to be doing something that I didn't really understand inside my head—like she was reaching into the top of my spine and smoothing something out. I felt calmer, then so tired.

When Eli and the kids got home, I was teased for falling asleep in the middle of the floor, but fortunately I had set enough of a precedent of being a fucking weirdo that nobody actually seemed concerned. I thought Beth was gone. Without her presence in my limbs, under my skin, I felt lighter, but more tired. I wasn't sure what to do with myself. Logic told me to self-soothe—either I had been briefly possessed or I'd had a mental break; either option suggested havoc on the nervous system. I took a bath. I couldn't relax. My thoughts zinged around my head. When I forced myself to breathe deeply, I thought I could still feel her. I was pretty sure. She was sleeping, or maybe meditating. So we didn't have to be in conversation all the time. This was a relief; it felt easier to live with. Looking back, I think it's funny how I was already trying to find ways to make it—to make us—work.

The next day, she was there again, tugging me awake, excited to bask in the sun that streamed in through the kitchen windows. She enjoyed washing dishes—unfathomable—and wanted to get them done before the kids were awake. I groused at her, but it was hard to stay mad; she was still elated to be in a body, and her ebullience lifted my mood. I resented this, too; it felt like wrestling a balloon. *You're too happy*, I groused.

Sorry, would you rather scroll through your whole morning like usual?

At least I was me.

You weren't, really. You were like a dopamine-seeking machine. All pleasure, no joy.

So how long exactly have you been stalking me from the inside?

Long enough to watch you click through every comment on my legacy Facebook page.

That night, I kept us awake late, scrolling and wandering the quiet house, but my body was tired. I started taking afternoon naps. Beth loved naps. Sometimes when I woke up, I felt so strongly rooted in her self-image that I had to stumble to the mirror and make sure I was still me. I was still me, wasn't I? Beth's expressions worked my features a little differently; her smile was softer, she was more likely to raise her eyebrows in a question than to furrow them in a scowl. Some mornings when I woke up, my face felt sore from working in new ways.

Now that I knew Beth, I could see her in the whole family. Annabel's short, double-jointed fingers. The curl in the fine wisps of
hair at the nape of Preston's neck when he sweated. And it wasn't
just genetics. I saw behaviors, too, picked up reverently or unthink-
ingly, like pretty stones. The way Joan tilted her head one way, then
the other, when she considered something. Eli's upside-down smile
when he thought he was being funny.

She helped me. She knew the kids and Eli so well, and she
could see more quickly when upset was brewing. With her encouragement, I stroked Preston's hair, gave Annabel impulsive hugs.
She was their mother. I didn't have to doubt her impulses the way
I doubted mine.

One night, she asked me whether Joan and Eli had fought recently. *They won't look at each other*, she said.

They're always like that.

She laughed. *No, they're not.*

Then, she didn't want to talk.

The next day, I found myself watching Joan more closely, and I noticed new things. The way her shoulders freckled in the sun. The
flecks of green in her eyes.

Did you have a crush on her? I finally asked.

She wrinkled her nose, making mine itch. *I found her interesting.*

It's okay if you did, I said gently. I realized that I hadn't told
her about my bisexuality, and I didn't know how to raise the subject
now. What if she felt weird about being in my body?

I already know. I see your dreams.

I blushed. Then, horror-struck, I asked, *Does that mean you see
all of my thoughts?*

Beth went very still. *I can*, she said quietly.

Does that mean you can also not? Like, can you ever opt out of certain ones? I didn't want to have to say which ones, but she probably already knew.

I don't think so, she said. *They're so sudden, a lot of the time.*

Tell me about it. I breathed a long breath in, trying to fill my lungs completely, then exhaled a gust of warm breath. *So how does it feel, being trapped inside the body of the worst person alive?*

I don't see it that way.

How can you not see it that way? Did your thoughts work like that when you were alive?

No, she said, and I heard a rush in my ears. This was proof: There were normal brains out there, and I didn't have one, and how was I supposed to know which kind of fucked up I was? Maybe it was OCD, but maybe it wasn't, maybe I was just evil and perverse, haunted in ways beyond the obvious.

But, Cassie, she said, so kindly that I knew she could hear me spiraling, *they're not your fault.*

"You can't know that," I whispered out loud.

I can—

Why don't you take a break, I said dully, in my head. *Save yourself the next few hours.*

She went, and I stayed in that room, barely moving while the sun moved to touch the trees, then sink among them, then below.

I had a lot of thoughts that I never told anyone. Not just the intrusive ones. The mean ones, the unfair ones. Beth saw them all. I didn't have a choice. She watched quietly as I sent Nessa snarky texts, and when I apologized for them hours later, Beth said nothing, just gathered her cool weight in my shoulders and sank them down, away from my ears. She heard me mutter "bitch" at the librarian who wouldn't let Preston take out more than twelve books, and she snickered so abruptly that I whirled around, thinking it was someone real.

She had a mischievous side. She liked to play little tricks on Eli. She would urge me to do things that she used to—walk my fingers over the back of his neck, push his hair back from his forehead. I didn't realize at first. One night, we were kissing sweetly when I was seized by the desire to puff out my cheeks and blow air into his mouth. When I did, he yanked away from me and went to the bathroom, muttering. In my head, I heard a giggle.

At my suspicion, she sighed with a sinking in my shoulders. *I never get to have fun anymore.*

For the first time, I felt invaded. I curled up under the comforter and turned toward the window. Outside, it was dark, and the wind flipped the leaves silver under the full moon. The floorboards creaked as Eli came back to bed; I was turned away from him and I could feel his wide back against mine. Beth's apology radiated through me, but I held still and focused on feeling nothing.

In the morning, Eli was gone, and I could hear the TV on downstairs. Beth had let me sleep, but now that I was awake, I could feel her waiting. *Can we talk about it later?* I asked, and she receded.

That night, I called her back. She responded right away, alert and on edge. I pictured her rattling around in my skull, just waiting for me to summon her. Did she get bored or lonely? But I didn't want to feel bad for her. I hadn't asked for this situation either.

I'm not so sure about this arrangement, I said slowly. I had avoided thinking the words—any words to do with her—all day, in case she was listening, so now my speech was unrehearsed.

What happens if I don't like it? I asked. *If I reject you?*

When she spoke, her voice was thick, and I realized that somehow, she'd been crying. *I don't know,* she said. *I've never done this before, either.*

I could kill myself, I said dryly, and she shuddered. *I wouldn't recommend death, so far.*

Right, I said. I didn't want to ask, but I wanted to know. *So, you don't have to tell me, but—*

I don't remember, she said.

Her presence felt charged inside me—wary, and ready to bolt. Then she asked, *What did Eli tell you?*

Only that you fell.

Fell, she mused. *Does that sound right to you?*

I'm not sure. She gathered herself. *Anyway, I think if you made yourself uninhabitable enough, I would—maybe not leave, but fade? I can feel that your attention makes me stronger. If you ignored me completely, eventually I wouldn't have the ability to . . .*

Move my body around without my knowing?

She paled. *Yes.* After a moment, she added, *Or talk to you.*

Would you ever be gone completely?

I don't know. I think, after enough time, yes. I would be a memory.

I considered this. So far, her presence was like a fun new game in my body, absorbing and occupying. It felt strange, but I had been curious about her for so long. I loved getting to see a version of her for myself. Still, part of me wanted to kick her out just to assert my dominance, my ownership over this body. But if she was gone, who would I be proving myself to? I was still interested in this new way of living in the world. And I liked her. I liked that she was so excited to be alive, in a manner of speaking. I felt lighter with her spirit lifting mine.

I could feel her realizing this as I did, and I didn't mind.

I warned her, *It's still my body, and my mind. I can change it later if I want to.*

She twirled in happy circles until I fell back, grinning dizzily, feeling fluttering through me. I thought I must seem ridiculous, lying there with happy laughter on my lips in the empty bed, alone but not really, not anymore.

CASSIE

SEPTEMBER

On Preston and Annabel's first day of school, Eli took the day off. We waited together at the end of the driveway for the bus. After it came, and the two of them climbed on, the brand-new backpacks bright and sturdy, and after we waved until the bus was out of view, Eli took me in his arms and danced me in a complicated pattern, then dipped me until my hair grazed the wet grass.

"Where did you learn to do that?"

"Around," he said.

For our wedding, Beth clarified. *We took lessons.*

"Why are you looking at me like that?" he asked.

I shook my head, trying not to laugh. Eli went on. "I thought we could go into town? Get coffee and take a walk by the river to celebrate your new freedom."

"We could go to Franklin's?" I asked. I still hadn't figured out how to feel about my newly empty days, and I wondered if Hank's offer of a bookstore job still stood.

"One-track mind, this girl," Eli said to no one.

At Franklin's, Hank stood at the register, stickering a stack of hardcovers. "Happy Tuesday," he said. "Just got a box of new releases."

"I won't know what any of them are," I warned.

He waved one at me—the cover a photorealistic close-up of a toothy mouth. "This one's supposed to be great."

Eli read the cover copy while I made my way toward the back. *What's your favorite book?* I asked Beth.

A lot of the modern stuff was too sinful, or sin adjacent. I loved classics, or just things that felt old. Jane Eyre, Rebecca. I Capture the Castle.

The kind of thing you should read wearing a long dress in a field of flowers, I said.

I do love long dresses.

I know. I've seen your closet.

"Boo," Eli said from behind me, and I whirled around. He leaned against a bookshelf, his hands in his pockets. Sometimes, for weeks, I forgot he was attractive, and then in the right light, I remembered. I kissed him briefly. He held on to me, prolonging the moment.

Have fun, Beth said. She vacated the forefront of my mind.

He said, "Are you ready? I thought we'd get lunch."

On the way out, Hank nodded at me. To Eli, he said, "Say hi to Joan."

We ate at a tapas place across the river. Eli ordered a beer. "We're celebrating," he said.

"Why not," I said, and ordered a glass of wine. The day was lovely, the leaves turning, the air crisp. I hadn't even thought of murder once that morning. Of course, as soon as I had that thought, I saw myself smashing my wineglass and jabbing a shard into Eli's throat. I breathed in slowly, and out.

"You're really cute," he said. "You know that?"

I forced a smile. I took another gulp of wine. "How did Beth die?" I asked.

Eli coughed hard and pounded his chest. He swallowed. "Sorry," he said. "I wasn't expecting that."

"Right. Sorry!" I said. "You don't have to—"

"It's okay." He cast a glance around the room and knitted his fingers together. "I told you. She fell."

"Okay, but like—and I'm sorry, you don't have to answer if you don't want to—fell how? In the house? Or . . ."

He cleared his throat. He looked down, fiddling with his napkin. He said, "In the woods. From a treehouse."

"What treehouse?" I had never seen a treehouse in the woods.

"We took it down, after. Me and Joan. Because obviously it was dangerous. The kids had made it, and she went up there one night. I don't know why."

"She went up there alone?"

He met my eyes. "Yes. As far as I know. Joan and I found her."

"Did she— Do you think it was on purpose?"

"I don't know. I don't think I'll ever know."

I searched my mind to see if Beth was around, but I couldn't feel her. I put my hand on Eli's. "I'm so sorry."

"Me too," he said. He held my hand for a moment, then said, "Your fingers are so cold."

"Cauliflower tacos!" the waiter announced. "And should I top off your wine?"

"Sure," I said mechanically. "We're celebrating."

Later, Beth came back, openly yawning and saying that day had been the best sleep she'd gotten in weeks. I thought I would ask her immediately, outright, if she had killed herself, but I couldn't. I forced myself not to think about it. Days passed. I was turned inward. Beth showed me the house the way she had known it, telling stories of her childhood playing in the attic, sleeping in the room that was now Preston's. *I thought it was haunted*, she told me, a smirk in her voice. *A premonition, maybe*, I suggested. I let her play piano through my fingers—confusing at first, but easy once I learned how to stop trying to understand it. She told me about her friend Zeke and showed me their favorite hiding places—a nook in the basement, a weeping pine at the edge of the woods, its low branches cloaking them from view. I sorted through the china cabinet that stood mostly forgotten in the dining room, and she told me the origin story of every knickknack—some of them pieces that had been in her family for decades, passed down. Alive, she'd been connected to a lineage in a way that I couldn't imagine.

Do you miss them? I asked.

Hmm, she said, concentrating. *I'm not sure.*

Before I could ask further questions, Eli snapped his fingers in front of me, his face concerned, and told me he'd called my name six times. "Where were you?" he asked, and I could not answer.

Eli had to work and Joan wasn't answering her phone, so I brought Preston and Felix to Annabel's talent show, where I met Preston's history teacher in the audience. She spoke to me earnestly while Preston pretended to melt out of his seat, oozing bonelessly to the floor.

"And you homeschooled them?" she asked. I nodded. It felt strange to explain Beth while she was listening. Anyway, Mrs. Tibbits was talking to her, too, even if she didn't know it.

"Well, you've done a wonderful job," she said. "Preston is so smart, curious, and kind." Beth preened. "Thank you," I said.

After the talent show was over, the parents walked in no particular order up and down the hallways, visiting various classrooms. Squeals of recognition bounced through the hallways. Being back in this school reminded me that once, I'd had friends besides Eli; not close ones, but locker buddies, other girls who sat with me as we read through lunch. I thought maybe I'd recognized a couple of them there that night, but I couldn't be sure. Every teacher always seemed deeply involved in a heartfelt conversation with another parent, so I hung around the doorways, peering at children's drawings and poems.

I couldn't remember if my dad had ever gone to these nights, or if he and my mom had gone together, when she was still around. Her leaving had solidified my childhood into two parts; I rarely thought about the first. But I was a child in this town. My fingerprints had once been all over these doorknobs. I had been a girl here, and in this moment, I didn't like that I had so thoroughly disconnected myself.

Other parents hugged, laughed. And I understood that Eli had chosen to disconnect himself while still living here. I wondered why that was.

Probably because of me. Beth's voice floated through my thoughts.

Why?

She shrugged, and I tamped down the lifting in my shoulders, not wanting anyone to see me acting out a conversation with no one. I moved to the dark window. Lately, I liked looking at my reflection while I talked to her; I thought I could almost see her expressions moving across my face.

I've never really known how to connect to other people, she said.

What about Zeke?

That's different. I made him need me.

I stepped outside. The school was one story, a long building set next to a playground, a football field, and a baseball diamond, all backed by a long woodsy hill that rose starkly enough to act as backdrop, as if this school, the field, and the town across the street were all part of a play. Now, in the play, the sky was cobalt and deepening. Kids tumbled on the field. Annabel was surrounded by a group of girls in dresses; in the parking lot, Preston and Felix talked over each other while a boy their age in glasses and costume pearls listened intently. Beth sighed. Walking through the halls, she had been intently curious, almost wary. Now, outside, she relaxed. *That was sweet.*

You sound surprised, I said.

Growing up, I heard a lot about how schools were like prisons for kids, stifling their creativity, teaching them horrible lies about evolution. I know, she said, before I could interject. *Anyway, even once I knew better, I always pictured something very bleak.*

Preston and Felix bounded over to me. The other boy watched them, then stuck his hands in his pockets and went back into the school.

"Making friends?" I asked.

"Theo's already our friend," Felix said.

"Our best friend," Preston added.

"Besides each other," Felix reminded him, and he nodded.

"That's nice," I said. "What's he like?"

"He's depressed," Preston said.

"Like us," they both added in unison. They fist-bumped, then tilted their heads to touch. I pictured myself smashing their heads together harder until their skulls splintered.

"Who isn't?" I said.

Later, Beth was pacing in my head.

What's wrong? I asked.

He's been through a hard time. He's not depressed.

I tried very hard not to think any words.

And you're not exactly helping, she told me.

Plenty of people with depression live long and fulfilling lives.

And plenty don't, she snapped.

I tucked myself into my phone.

* * *

Later, she asked, *How do you manage, with yours?*

OCD isn't the same as depression, I warned her.

Still.

I sighed. *I have good days and bad days. Sometimes good years and bad years. Some things almost always help. Exercise, cutting out caffeine. Exposure therapy.*

You drink more coffee than anyone I've ever met.

I'm sorry, I didn't realize I was talking to the only person alive with no vices.

We were both silent as the silliness of this statement settled. *Sorry,* I said.

You don't have to quit coffee. But I do think you should go back to therapy.

Look at you, telling me what to do.

I'm serious.

I knew she was right. For a long time now, I had been pretending that this life was different from my old one, that I didn't need the same things, or that they wouldn't work. But it was all my life, and I was me no matter where I went.

Except I go with you now, Beth pointed out.

I tried not to think the words "for now," but I still worried that she could hear them.

BETH

Since I died, I've been questioning my faith. I was raised to believe that God cares deeply about me, personally, about my life and trajectory. But I don't know that I feel that anymore. Not going to Heaven negates a lot of what I was taught.

If you take from God the moral imperative, the goodness. If you don't even feel sure about the creation narrative, then what do you have, really? Just an omniscient being, watching. Waiting, I guess, but for what? And why? Does God feel urgency? Is he hoping for some grand culmination of the human species? Or is he dispassionately perusing us, like a person flipping through the channels?

When I was alive, faith was my animating force. My days turned around it. I lived in prayer. Every time I witnessed beauty, cosmic or granular, a mountain or a kind act among strangers, I converted it into ardor and funneled it toward God. Even the things I loved about myself were his. Only my faults were mine.

Like many faithful children, I couldn't wait to die. I daydreamed often of the afterlife, thumbing the thin pages of Revelation, my hands shaking with desire. I longed to see what world he had created for me. I knew it would be more beautiful and perfect than this one. As a small child, I imagined rooms full of candy, a reunion with my dead pet bunny. As I got older and more existential, I hoped Heaven was a world without grief or fear, a world where I would feel close to him, the being who loved me most. Once I became a mother, Heaven was the ability to still time, to lie forever with the small bundle of Preston napping on my chest, without stiffness or fatigue. But still, no matter how much I loved my life on Earth, I held a quiet, separate anticipation for the moment when I would cross over into the better world.

And I had been so patient. I had sacrificed. My life was small because I told myself, over and over, that faith should be enough. It should sate my thirst for every other thing. I didn't let myself want outside of what I'd already been given. I tried not to. Sometimes I woke with the desire to claw out of my life, to leave the house and never come back. I did nothing. Then I died, and I woke up still here. In this world, in these woods, behind this house, and I still couldn't leave.

I've never met another ghost. I wonder if this world brims with them, all lonely, passing each other by without knowing. Or if other people do go somewhere when they die, but I didn't. These questions didn't bother me as much when I lived in the woods. Now, surrounded by other humans, I feel disturbed by questions of belonging.

I try to be grateful. Not to God, but to something. It makes my days better, now that I can't bury myself in faith.

But you miss God? Cassie prods.

I don't know why you care, I say. I'm embarrassed to discuss it with her. She's never believed. She must think I'm an idiot.

I want to defend myself. I feel like a stupid girl who lost her favorite doll, the adults around her trying to console her, but half-heartedly, because they can't feel her pain.

I refuse to tell myself that God was a childish thing. But I feel more grown-up, now that I don't believe. I hate thinking about it. I can't think about much else.

I remember teaching the kids about God. I did lean on him, sometimes, for easy explanations. In the same way that I used him to explain things to myself.

I think the world is more beautiful now that I know there's nowhere else to go, after. I want to try harder to see it, to hold it, to save it.

Cassie says, *I've never believed in a being that unconditionally loves me.*

That makes me sad for you.

But you don't believe in it anymore.

No, I say. I breathe through the brief guilty cringe of denying him. *But I think I'd still rather remember the feeling than never have known it.*

Suit yourself, she says.

CASSIE

One night, we were talking about God, and then we were talking about the idea of being wholly known. I tried to explain why the thought of being seen completely made me squeamish. *My last girlfriend kind of fucked me up*, I admitted. *Or, I fucked her up and now I'm too afraid of it happening again.*

Beth nodded. *What was she like?*

I've never been closer to anyone, I said. Why not be honest, I figured. Who was she going to tell? I said, *Being with a woman is more intimate than being with a man. You're closer. You can be kinder to each other, and also meaner. You can have a whole fight just with facial expressions. You can make love with words. You say embarrassing shit like* make love *and you don't feel corny because what you're doing, even by being together, is brave and powerful. You're not subservient. You're making it all up together.*

That sounds overwhelming, she said.

It is! I laughed. I felt almost giddy. Talking frankly about Lavender felt like curling back up inside my old self, but more comfortably, now that so much had changed. *One time, early on, I asked Lav if it was normal for both of us to cry every time we hung out together, and she just told me, "Welcome to your first lesbian relationship."*

Beth was quiet for a moment, and I wondered if I'd said too much. Finally she asked, *Did you prefer that?*

Obviously not, I said, gesturing toward her house.

Sorry. I just wondered.

It's fine.

But later, she was back again, like her questions were a toothache she couldn't stop prodding. *Was it the intimacy? Was it too much? I don't know. Probably there's something wrong with me,* I sniped. *Oh.*

Later that night, she suggested mildly, *Maybe it was just her, specifically. Maybe with a different woman—* She stopped. *Well, I wasn't with a different woman. I was with her. Oh,* she said again. I could feel more questions. *There's not enough time in life to try every person and make an objective decision,* I said defensively. *You of all people must know that.*

And then she was crying, and I felt bad, and I wondered.

Beth, I said carefully, a few days later. *Were you queer?*

Then she was the one who was annoyed. *I guess I'll never know, will I?*

What were you like as a kid? Beth asked. *Before your mom left?*

I was fussy, I said, already regretting the word choice—it made me sound like a colicky Victorian. *Easily scared,* I added. I remembered that clearly—how shadows on the wall would seem wrong, keeping me awake out of fear that when I flicked my eyes away, they moved. *At one point, out of desperation,* I told her, *my parents told me that the shadow on my bedroom wall was an angel watching over me.*

Did that help?

I laughed. *It made me afraid of angels.*

She nudged gently. *What about the good parts?*

I'm not trying to be self-pitying, but I don't remember much.

I remembered some moments, out of context, haloed in sun. *Playing at the wing dam by the river. I had a best friend, Eleanor— she moved away before my mom left. She was the kind of really beau-*

tiful that made random strangers give us things. She still is. I found her online, but we never reconnected.

What did you do together?

I don't remember. I have images—climbing a tree, being on a trampoline. I don't even know if I was with her. We weren't friends for that long, I clarified. *I just remember we had a best friends necklace that gave me a rash.*

What about your mom?

I sighed. *Nothing. It's like there's a wall there. Why, do you remember your whole childhood?*

Lots of it, she said apologetically.

Like what?

So much with Zeke. We also climbed trees. Once, he put up a tent in his backyard and insisted on sleeping in it all summer. I would hang out in there with him. It smelled disgusting, like mold and preteen boy. Every time I left it, I would take in a deep clear breath and feel like a whole new person.

But you kept going back.

She nodded. *I remember a lot about growing up in this house. Learning how to bake. My mom teaching me to fold clothes the right way. My dad was always on a ladder, fixing something. He loved this house. Let's see, I remember church. I was always sleeping in and missing breakfast beforehand, and I would be so hungry by the time we took Communion. When I was a teenager, I started sitting in the back with the other kids my age, and we would write notes to each other in our study Bibles. That was how Zeke and I really became friends. He was so funny.*

It sounds like a good childhood, I said.

I think it was. She sat up straighter, and my spine uncurled. *Can I try something?*

I barely nodded before she was darting like a minnow through my thoughts; I could only feel it in the flashes of light where the sun caught her scales. She went deep for a while—I couldn't sense her at all. Something floated to the surface.

I knew I was small, because everything looked big. I was in Franklin's Books, holding my mother's large, cool hand. Her palm was faintly greasy with the Kiehl's lotion she used to wear. "Here, I put on too much," she would say, swiping my hands with hers, leaving the extra. She used to do that, I marveled. She wore a long green skirt. "I'm going to look around here for a while," she told me, gesturing at the New Fiction section. After I grew out of children's books, I had grown up reading the books that lined our walls. I hadn't considered the fact that they had been hers, that they had been anyone's. My grown-up self wanted to stay with her, but in the memory, I was already running to the back of the store, picking out an Edith Nesbit book, sitting on the floor, and opening it against my knees.

A while later, my mom came back.

"Can I get this?" I asked.

"But you're already halfway through," she said, laughing. "How about you pick out another one, too, just to be safe."

Stop, I said to Beth. *Stop.* I was crying. And I was humiliated that Beth had seen my young self, so innocently in love with my mother, so wholly unaware that she would leave me, that in some quiet corner in her heart, she probably already had.

Oh God, I'm sorry, Beth said. *I tried to choose a nice one.*

It was—nice. It was just a lot.

I won't do it again.

But I held my mother's face in my mind like a rare jewel. I said, *We can go slow.*

CASSIE

OCTOBER

If you can drive, I can drive, I said.

That's a theory. I'm not letting you drive my kids over the bridge based on a theory. She sighed. *But we could practice.*

Obviously, I couldn't leave the kids alone after school, and I didn't want Joan or Eli to know—I didn't want one of them taking it upon themselves to play instructor. Especially because I quickly learned that Beth teaching me to drive would look, to the outside observer, like me arguing passionately with myself. So we practiced at night. I would sneak out of bed while Eli slept, take the car, and Beth would use my body to drive us over to the church parking lot, where she receded and became only a voice again. It was strange, letting her fill my body and move for me. Sometimes while she drove, I would force a small movement, a finger tap or a wink, just to remind myself that I could overpower her. She was annoyed by this—she said it was distracting—which was a relief to me. It told me that she wasn't letting me do it. After a few days, she let me out on the mostly abandoned country roads.

You're drifting, she reminded me tensely.

Then take over.

You have to learn this for yourself. What if I fall asleep? What if one day I'm not here anymore?

I pulled over. *You think there's any danger of that?*

I don't think anything. I just take it all day by day.

So you don't have any plans?

Plans for what?

I don't know, I said, pulling back out on the road.

She hesitated. *I guess I'd like to try to find out why I'm still here.*

I've been thinking about that, I said. *You know, since you can see my memories, maybe I could see the memory of when you died.*

No thanks.

Okay, it was just an idea.

I was thinking more along the lines of psychics, maybe find a witch. Find a way to travel. I know it sounds stupid.

That's not stupid, I tell her. *It's awesome. A ghost tour of the world? I would do that.*

Really? She pinked, a flush on my cheeks, and I remembered that my opinion was important to her, not because she liked me, but because she couldn't do anything I wouldn't do.

Sure, I said lightly, backing off. *Someday, if you want.*

She could sense my cooling. She said, *I would have to do a lot of research first.*

Through the windshield, the sky was clear and dark, the twisting road flanked by woods on one side and a cornfield on the other, the stalks that eerie pale color of crops under the moon. I thought about how I, too, didn't know how to explain the person I'd become.

New Orleans is supposedly super haunted, I offered. *I've always wanted to go.*

Maybe one day.

I guess you want to stay until the kids go to college.

I could feel her surprise, a light breeze in my mouth. *I don't . . .* She trailed off.

You would leave them?

I already have, she reminded me. *And I don't really understand how time works anymore.* She shook herself, and I tried not to be annoyed at the jolt. *You don't want to stay with Eli?* she asked. I felt myself recoiling from the question. I laughed. *What, so I can't go on vacation?*

Alone, without your husband? People would think it was strange.

What would you think?

She smiled wryly, and I tongued the crack in the corner of my lip. *I'm on the ultimate vacation,* she said.

I found a fun one, she told me a few days later.

What?

But the memory was already there, surfacing. I was a little older than I'd been in the other memory, maybe ten. I wore a red sundress over yellow leggings, and I was crouched in the shade of a tall oak, on the roof of a low shed in the cemetery. I'd climbed up via a stack of trash cans leaning against its side.

"Can I come up?" someone called below me.

"Sure."

The boy was faster than I was—I'd stumbled and skinned my elbow on the first trash can; I kept blotting out the blood on the hem of my dress. He was climbing, and then he was standing over me. "What's your name?"

"Cassiopeia."

"I'm Eli," he said. Present-me wanted to stare at him, to know every detail, but ten-year-old me barely looked. "What are you doing?" he asked.

"Watching people go by. Sometimes I drop these." I revealed a handful of acorns. "Not on them, but just so they look around. They don't look up, though."

He settled in with me. "Do you go to West Elementary?"

"No, I live in town."

"We'll go to the same high school, then."

"Maybe. If I still live here."

"Are you moving?"

"I might go live with my mom one day. Or maybe I'll explore the world. Antarctica, or outer space. I bet by the time we're older, they'll have cities on other planets."

"Space freaks me out."

"They could put you to sleep for the journey, so you won't be scared."

He considered this. "I like it here. Can I have an acorn?"

"You can have them all," I said. "I'll see you around." This was a phrase I'd picked up recently. I liked the way it felt coming out, swingy and carefree. I transferred them to his warm hand and shimmied down the tree. I heard an acorn land behind me, but I didn't look up.

Later, after we read Annabel a bedtime story, I asked Eli, "Do you remember when we first met?"

"Sure," he said.

"When was it?"

"We were kids," he said. "On the roof."

The next night, Eli was gone again and I couldn't sleep. *Beth*, I thought quietly, but she didn't seem to stir. I ran my hands over my thighs and my belly. I hadn't masturbated since I became aware of Beth's presence. I'd had sex with Eli, sure, but that felt less private, less personal. Usually—after her brief bout of messing with him had ended—she didn't interfere, so I assumed she had recused herself and would do the same here. Still, I couldn't figure out how to start. What if she stepped into my consciousness unaware and got embarrassed or disgusted?

What? she said now, her voice drowsy.

Oh, I said, flustered, *you know what, I actually forgot what I was going to say.*

She became alert, some of her attention spilling into my awareness: I scanned the room like it was hiding something.

You're lying, she said.

You're right. I just changed my mind.

You're embarrassed, she noted coolly. *Your cheeks are flushed.*

I sighed. *Fine. I was going to ask you if it was alright with you if I masturbated. Okay?*

You wanted permission? she said, amused. *Have I been stopping you?*

Well, yeah, actually. It feels—rude.

She laughed. *Really? Oh, you poor thing.*

Weren't you like, super religious?

I was an adult human being, she said. *And Eli was away, often.*

Great, okay. Glad to know that. I was glad. I worried a lot that being in my body forced Beth to live in the world in a way that she wouldn't have chosen to, alive—especially since she had been so devout. I worried that even my sex life with Eli was an affront to her.

She laughed.

I didn't say anything, I said.

Your thoughts are extremely loud, she said.

Do you have anything to contribute?

You may have slept with more people than me, but I was unsatisfied in my marriage for years. I tried everything, honey. Things you haven't even dreamed about.

You're really in a sharing mood tonight. I considered this information. I had never suspected that I might be less sexually open than a Christian housewife.

You're very guarded in bed, she explained. *You'll do whatever he wants, but only because he wants it. It's like you're performing for him.*

I didn't realize you were watching so closely.

She shrugged. *I find you interesting.*

Oh.

I can stop watching, if you prefer.

There were moments, with Beth, when I found myself ashamed of my carelessness with my own body, as if I was taking up an unfair amount of space in it. What did she do when I banished her, anyway? I knew my assumptions were too tangible, but I imagined her sitting by herself in an empty room, bored, waiting for me to allow her back.

You don't have to stop, I said.

She half smiled. *Then I won't.*

Do you want to watch now? I asked. I think I was joking, or I thought I was.

Do you want me to?

I couldn't figure out her tone. *This is getting weird*, I said. *Right?*

She laughed again, with less mirth. *It got weird a long time ago.*

I don't even really know what you look like, outside of old pictures. I can feel your expressions, but I don't know them on your face.

This startled her. *Does that matter?*

I thought about it. *Yeah, I think. We're getting—closer. It's strange that I don't know what your smile is like, or your eyes.*

Most pictures feature both smiles and eyes.

But I don't know—I don't know. How you look when you're surprised, or let down. You get all of my feelings in this raw, unfiltered way. But I don't even know if you can raise one eyebrow.

I can't. Couldn't, she corrected herself.

But you can see why I want to know those things, right?

I think so. She breathed in, long and slow. *Give me a second.*

After a moment, she told me to close my eyes. When I did, I saw Beth, standing in front of a mirror—my bedroom mirror. The drawers to the side were disheveled, a pants leg hanging out of one, the other half open. Beth wore a gray T-shirt and jeans, the cut a little outdated. She stood in front of the mirror, watching herself closely.

Is this a memory?

Yeah, she sighed. As her past self turned and frowned at her butt, Beth said, *Idiot.*

Me or her?

Her, Beth said. *You know when you see a picture of yourself as a teenager, or a child, and you remember hating how you looked back then? But looking back, you see how beautiful you were.*

You were beautiful, I said.

I know.

Mirror Beth sighed and pulled off her shirt. Her bra was white, an underwire with lace cups, her breasts perfect. I stayed very still and tried not to think as she stepped closer to the mirror and adjusted the straps. She squeezed her arms together to enhance her cleavage and stared at herself in the mirror. I couldn't tell if she was proud or dissatisfied. I could hear my Beth giggle as I tried not to blush.

I blinked, and she was standing in front of the same mirror, naked. She had a C-section scar, and her shoulders were sunburnt, and I wanted to touch her. Then she stood in the same mirror, younger, wearing a wedding dress. She was grinning, her face so full of joy it made me want to cry.

Stop, I said.

I want you to see me.

Why?

Because you're the only one who can.

The next morning, at breakfast, Annabel cleaned a spill with too much soap, so the floor was still slick moments later when I stood to bring our plates back to the sink. I slipped. Before I realized I was falling, my arm shot out and grabbed the table for balance. My other hand caught the plate before it could shatter. "Nice," Preston said, bored, and I looked at the plate for a long moment before resuming the task.

Later, I confronted her. *You took over.*

You could say thank you, she said mildly. *You might have gotten hurt.*

Can you do that whenever you want to? I asked.

I haven't tried. (*Out of respect*, she didn't need to say.)

Try now.

Why?

I need to know, I said, my voice shrill even in my thoughts. I felt a cool, unfamiliar desire flow down my arm. It wanted to pick up the mug on the table. I resisted it. It came again, but weaker. *I can't do it*, she said.

Try harder.

The desire came back, more like the first time, but it flickered out quickly.

And you're not just pretending? I urged. *You really can't?*

No. She sounded annoyed.

I'm sorry, I said later.

It's fine.

I just get freaked out at the idea of someone else being able to control me, I explained.

Trust me, I know the feeling.

That isn't really fair, I said. *It is my body.*

I know.

I like having you here, I said, trying to help. She laughed.

I do, I insisted.

I just don't know what I'm doing here, she said. *I don't know why I—stay.*

It might be in your memories. You could let me see more.

No, she said flatly.

Why not? You see mine.

I want to keep some things for myself.
I laughed out loud. *Are you joking? You get everything for yourself. You get my habits, and my thoughts, and my body—*
And all of that is yours, too. I have nothing of my own anymore.
Yeah, well, neither do I.

Later, Eli was still gone and I couldn't sleep again. This time, I didn't say anything to her; I just let my fingers explore my skin, light and almost unintentional. I couldn't tell if she was watching. I remembered the sight of her in the mirror—her breasts on the brink of spilling over her bra, her soft belly, her muscled thighs. Her sloped shoulders, the dimple under her chin. My hands felt liquid over my own skin. Then, I felt a movement that wasn't mine, a shift in my hips, then a twitch in my thumb. My hand changed direction, just slightly.

Is this okay? she asked.
Yes.

Possessed by her, my fingertips were new; the fingers I knew—the hangnail I'd bitten off earlier, the scab on the knuckle I'd been picking at for days—imbued with an unfamiliar, alien softness. I could feel her breath deepening in my chest. Later, when I pushed my damp hair back from my forehead, I swore for a second that it felt different. Silkier, softer than mine.

I feel kind of guilty, I said as the dawn grayed the sky and the grass underneath it.

Why? she said. She sounded awake, like she'd been ready for my questions.

I can't tell Eli.
That's correct.

So what's the plan here? I cheat on him with you, we keep it a secret?

Oh, you want to keep doing this? I figured it was more of an experiment, she said airily.

I remembered our orgasm and felt her shiver happily in my skin. *Nice try,* I said.

I don't mind lying to Eli, she said. *I think he deserves it.*

I know you two weren't happy in the end, I said. *But he's been nice to me.*

Sure, she said. *When he's around.*

You want him around more? I asked.

Nope. But don't you wonder? she asked. *What he's doing all the time?*

On Halloween, after a short bout of trick-or-treating the next town over, after bobbing for apples in the sink, Preston's hair plastered translucently to his skin, after watching *Hocus Pocus,* Annabel's sweaty hand worming into mine during the graveyard chase, after the adults had wine and the kids had cookies iced in spiderwebs and peeled grape eyeballs, the kids poured all their candy on the kitchen counter to trade for their favorites. Joan and Eli went to the living room to start a fire.

"Can we play Truth or Dare?" Preston asked. "My school friends are always talking about it."

"We don't really have enough people," I said. But Preston and Felix were already off their chairs and in the family room, chanting "truth or dare" at Eli and Joan until they agreed. I hovered in the doorway as everyone settled. I hated Truth or Dare.

"I'll start," Felix said. "Preston, truth or dare."

"Truth."

"No, pick dare."

"Fine. Dare."

Felix looked around. "I dare you to eat all of your candy right now."

"Absolutely not," Eli said.

"It's more for embarrassing things," I explained. "Like, I dare you to stand up and do a dance."

"I don't want to do something embarrassing," Preston said.

"You can dare me," I said to Felix. "Just as an example."

Felix tapped her fingers against her chin, looking eerily adult. "Preston, help me think."

He scooted closer. "We could make her do a dance."

"No, she just said that. We could make her and your dad kiss," Felix said.

Eli and I looked merrily at each other.

"Gross," Annabel said.

"And boring," Preston added. "They've kissed before."

"What about Mom?" Felix said. Her eyes rested on me. "And Preston's dad."

Joan started to laugh. "I don't think this is how the game works."

"You could kiss on the cheek," Annabel said.

"That doesn't count," Felix said.

"Okay, time for bed," Joan said. "Come on, kiddos."

"No, not yet," Preston whined.

"If you come upstairs now, I'll read you a scary story," Joan said.

"A Goosebumps one?" Felix cried.

"Okay, but only if you hurry," Joan singsonged.

Felix grabbed her mom's hand, Preston grabbed Felix's, and Annabel scampered after. I sipped my wine and stared into the fire. Halloween-themed pop punk droned in the background. Eli cleared his throat a few times. "Wonder why they suggested that," he finally said.

"Don't worry, I'm not jealous."

He adjusted to face me more directly, but he was backlit and I could barely see his eyes. "You're not?"

How much of Eli could I lose before I felt something, I wondered. And I thought of Beth, and how much I was keeping from him now. In my head, she didn't say anything. I told Eli, "You can do it if you want to."

"Really?" He didn't sound excited. Men rarely did when you set them free. But I liked to remind people that I held them loosely. Less pressure on me, then, to hold them well.

"Sure," I said. "Why not?"

Eli swirled his wine in its glass as the fire popped. "Well, I wouldn't want you kissing—"

"Joan?" I interjected.

He laughed. "Right."

Guilt spread like a rash under my skin. "I think you should do it," I said. "I really wouldn't mind."

"Right," he said, his voice humming with displeasure. He tossed the rest of his wine into the sink and went to stand by the window.

Moments later, when Joan came downstairs, he said her name like a command. I didn't think she would like his tone. I was surprised by her expression when she turned to face him. Unguarded, like I'd never seen her. He walked over to her, slid his hand around the back of her neck, and pressed his lips against hers.

She sank into him, and his hand moved behind her back, his fingers spread against her narrow shoulder blades. The movements were fluid, too easy. Her eyes were closed, then they blinked open to meet my gaze. Beth exited my consciousness like a light turning off. I hadn't realized she was watching.

Joan backed away to the front door, fumbled behind her for the knob. Like I was a predator, and she knew she couldn't turn her back. I wanted to say I was sorry, but my throat was full of ache, and I didn't trust myself to speak. There were so many ways to hurt someone. I didn't think I'd ever learn how to guard myself against them all.

After Joan closed the door behind her, I went to the kitchen. Eli followed me. "Are you going to say anything?"

"I have nothing to say."

"Well, maybe I do." He was agitated, fidgeting. "I haven't been honest with you."

I faced him, waiting. He pressed his palms against his cheeks and pulled his hands down, like he was trying to drag his features off his face. I realized numbly, almost in slow motion, that this conversation would change everything. The way I thought about him, maybe the way I thought about the world. He said, "I'm in love with Joan."

I laughed. "After one kiss?"

He looked down, and I knew that it hadn't been one kiss. Beth was back, sitting grimly in the corner of my mind. I sat down, too. The room felt too still.

"I think I need to be alone," I said to Eli, my voice uncertain.

Coatless, he stepped out the front door, closing it gently behind him.

It's often said that anxious people are good in a crisis, eerily calm, since they already expect things to go wrong. But what about anxious people who are so stupidly myopic that they can only see one possible villain? I could have killed my most naïve, sweet self. Poor, stupid, self-absorbed me. I had flung myself into someone else's world, convinced that I was the danger, forgetting to look for it anywhere else. And what else didn't I know? Secrets flourished here, even living in my own body.

Whoa, Beth said, putting her hands up against the force of my thoughts.

You have to show me what happened, I said.

I'm not ready. Since when is this your decision?

I don't care.

I don't like this, Beth said.

If you can stick yourself in my brain whenever you want, I get the same privilege.

She was angry and sad, maybe scared, too. Maybe she'd trusted me to let her have what little space she was capable of occupying. But she didn't understand. I needed to know what she knew. It was a precaution, I told myself; I needed answers to keep myself safe. But more than that: I felt ruined, and I wanted to ruin someone else. I don't know how much of that she knew. I didn't care. Still, she let me in.

BETH

First, the invasion, then the clarity. Letting Cassie root through my memories is like reading my own diary alongside another person, only much worse. I'm reliving the moment, and I know she's watching me.

The night I died, the kids had spent the day building a tree fort behind Joan's house, then begged for a sleepover. Once they were in bed, I was sitting at Joan's kitchen table, waiting for her to get bored of me. Instead, she asked if I wanted to go back out to the fort. She brought a bottle of whiskey. I was always surprised when Joan decided to drink—she usually didn't, but when she did, it was with merciless determination.

We ended up lying on the treehouse floor—really, it was only a floor; eight wide planks nailed to parallel branches, with a rope ladder hanging down the trunk—twelve feet up, yards of tree branches between us and the night sky. We weren't looking at each other. I was losing the thread of her rambling; she was talking about how she didn't know what she'd do when Felix grew up. "She's bound to abandon me," Joan said, a dreary slouch in her voice.

"Will you stay here? If she leaves," I asked.

"Where else would I go?"

"You could go anywhere," I said, almost reverently. "You don't have roots. You can do anything you want."

"I'd like to believe that I've become a valued part of the community here," she said.

"Oh—you have. I just admire how many places you've lived in—what, four? Five years?"

She shrugged.

"You know the farthest away I've ever been from Elwood is Washington, D.C.? On a field trip, when I was twelve. I've never been to California, to the South, anywhere. And places like Paris or Africa might as well be made up. I know so little about anything outside of this house, this town. How am I supposed to teach them?"

"You teach them about outer space, don't you?" Joan asked dryly.

"I'm afraid that I've lived my whole life only being able to see out of a tiny window." It was only partly the whiskey talking.

"You worry too much."

"Do you ever wish you could go back to the beginning of your life and make entirely different choices? Or that you could watch two different lives unfold in front of you, so you could see what you were choosing?"

Joan grunted noncommittally.

I went on. "Every choice I've ever made felt right in the moment. I liked Eli, so I dated him. I came to love him, so I married him. I got pregnant, so I had Preston. Then again, Annabel. The church told me to homeschool, so I did. I wasn't qualified; I was hardly educated. When I finally went to school that one year, I realized that I wasn't a good student, and it was way too late for me to become one. It was too late to apply to college. And then I met Eli. And he never wanted to leave. It was like after Cassie leaving, his mom and Kim moving, like he felt like he had to stay, to hold on to the one thing that wouldn't change. That used to be so comforting."

"When did it stop being comforting?" Joan asked.

"When I realized I was trapped."

She didn't say anything.

"Preston was getting old enough that we could do trips if we wanted to, so we went for some weekends down the shore, a museum day in Philly. Eli hated it; he was so tense. I'd ask, could you imagine waking up near the ocean? And he would say, What's wrong with waking up in Elwood?"

Joan was nodding along. If I'd stopped there, she might have believed that was the whole story of my unhappy marriage. Just two people who wanted different things from life. A familiar, boring story. I had spent my whole life being boring. I took a big swig. My mouth burned as I said, "I fell in love with someone else."

Joan listened calmly as I tried to tell the story. I didn't tell it well. I had no practice. When I finished, she nodded many times, her motions jittery and lit up. She said, "So you're going to leave him."

"No," I said.

"Why not?"

I'd been hoping to intrigue her, maybe for sympathy. But Joan seemed offended in some way I couldn't discern or understand. She said, "What you're doing isn't fair to him."

"I have a good life. I love my children. I love Eli."

"No, you don't," she said. "Nothing you've told me tonight sounds like love."

"Fine," I said. "He gives me a life that feels safe. I'm grateful. Maybe that's all I deserve." I was finally saying out loud the thoughts I'd let circle in my head for years. "Maybe being with him forever is a kind of penance."

"Wow."

"What?"

"All that talk of wanting a bigger life, going out into the world. I guess it's just talk. You say you're trapped, but you've trapped yourself and decided he's your captor. And you don't even have the guts to tell him." She was more passionate than I'd ever seen her.

"Why do you care so much?"

She wore an unhappy smile. "Your husband is a good man. He deserves better than you."

"Whose side are you on?"

"His."

I laughed awkwardly. "Maybe you should be with him, then."

Her face. Her mouth a round, wet O. I think I really shocked her for a second. That made me feel good; it was never easy to unseat Joan. Then I realized that without meaning to, I'd seen right through her.

She turned serious. "If you don't tell him, I will."

That pissed me off. I shoved her against the tree trunk, feeling childish. And maybe more; maybe I wanted to provoke a reaction. She pushed back, hard. I veered to the side. Below the plank I lay on, I heard a clean, loud snap.

When I landed on the ground, I was still there, I was alive with pain, the rock under my head, my neck too warm and oily wet. I could hear Joan's voice like background noise, crying, "Oh my God, I'm sorry, oh my God."

I wished she would stop. I was feeling every nerve in my body. Until, with a horrible suddenness, I wasn't.

BETH

Now, I can still feel my death reverberating through me. Cassie
has retreated. She's numbing out on her phone, giving me space. She
feels bad. Well, she should. I didn't want to relive those moments.
She shouldn't have forced me to show her.

I can't distract myself from a bad feeling the way I used to in life.
I can't clean the house or bake something complicated enough to require my precise attention. I don't want to convince Cassie's body to
do anything, either; it would require too much interacting with her.

Instead, I scan her body, too deep in her subconscious for her
to really feel. I know that when I leave her thoughts, she thinks I'm
sequestering myself in some quiet room in her brain. More often,
I'm swimming in her body, exploring. I do this sometimes while she
sleeps, too. I coax tense muscles to relax. Once, I spent the whole
night healing a pimple, draining moisture in infinitesimal increments. In the morning, she grinned at the mirror, marveling at the
place where it'd been. I didn't tell her it was me. I loved her delight
so much; I didn't need her gratitude.

Now, I search for pain—the kind so low level that she wouldn't
notice. I find a small bruise on her thigh, a thumbprint-size cluster
of damaged blood vessels, and I set about knitting them back together. It's calming work, meditative. The body already knows what
to do; I am just helping it along. I can't see her skin from the outside, but I imagine the purple changing to green and faint yellow
as I work. Hours later, I am done, and I feel better. Working to take
away her pain has come with the strange side effect of forgiving her.

I used to rely on God so much; I realize it now. When I walked alone at night, when lightning cracked the sky. God was my protector, my confidante. When I had a frustrating day. When Annabel gnawed the edge of the table like a dog and screamed when I scooped her up away from it. *What is God teaching me through this?* I used to ask myself, with diligence, and the asking forced me to find an answer.

When I think of God now, and what he used to mean to me, sometimes I feel like I'm circling around something I can't quite touch. I look at my life, and I try to remember what it was like, that centrifugal force that kept me steady. As soon as it left me, I struggled to remember it. People talk about childbirth like that, as if the hormone flood is magical, and it is; at least, I think I remember it being so. But I also have a hard time holding on to sense memory—even in life, I struggled with this. I assume everyone does. I have to put it into language in order to keep it, and even then, it's like holding on to a shadow of the thing itself.

I miss my God shadow. And I'm angry at it, still, for seeming so real, and for making me a different person than I would have been without it.

I think that I have lost my faith, but now I see how beautiful the world is, how improbable. How we exist not because we were lovingly created, but due to a series of compassionate accidents. We are a wonder, and I don't think that makes us less. And I love that when I look at the world through a lens absent a creator, I get to see that we are the creators. That we can heal each other.

Cassie stirs. She says, *But we create terrible things.*

Sometimes, I say.

CASSIE

NOVEMBER

The next morning, Eli came back. He wouldn't look at my face as he spoke, and his words came out dry and monotone, as if he had removed all feeling from them before speaking. He and Joan had fallen in love while he was still married to Beth. She had died in an accident, he maintained, in the woods. Joan was the only witness. He did wonder if she'd killed herself and Joan had decided to protect him from that truth. He had made his peace with not knowing.

In the version of the story that the police knew, Eli was there, too. He saw her die. He confirmed it was an accident. They were cleared. But they couldn't be together, not after having been the only two witnesses to Beth's death. They needed time, or some kind of buffer. And besides, things were strange between them. Joan was distant and closed off. Eli tried to comfort her, but she couldn't bear his kindness. She still helped with the children, but she kept herself separate. And he had wondered if he would ever be able to be with her without Beth's memory standing between them. Maybe they both needed to move on and build new lives, he thought. Or maybe they just needed time. Then I had showed up.

I would have to leave this house. I didn't know where I could go. I wondered if I could convince him to let me stay in the attic, like a deranged nanny. Had I not proven my usefulness over the past year? And Joan and I got along. I shook my head at myself. Warmth prickled over my neck as I thought about how often I had assumed this new life was permanent. But the only permanent part of human life was the chasm of meaninglessness we were all trying to climb out of. We built ladders out of jobs and relationships, family and friends and passions, all hoping that enough narrative would lead to meaning, and enough meaning would hoist us out above the abyss. But the second we started to climb, we made ourselves vulnerable. The lightest wrong breath could ruin us.

I was thinking about this when Joan walked across our lawn, her hair copper in the sun, bright as fire. She saw me and slowed, then regained speed.

"Why are you here?" I asked.

She just looked at me. Her face was impassive, though I thought I could detect pity there. Maybe I was projecting.

"Did you think I was stupid?"

Joan licked her dry lips. A petty part of me wondered how Eli found her attractive—I could see what made her attractive to me; her boyish bone structure and taciturn, wry way of speaking. But if Beth and I were like apples and oranges, Joan was a socket wrench. I didn't understand. I was scrutinizing her face, trying to find a wisp of softness, when she said, "I didn't think of you much."

The next day, Beth and I cleaned the house with bright, fast motions, though I had barely slept and couldn't stop yawning. Felix came over in the morning, and I kept sneaking glances as she and Preston played. They must have known all along. Kids so often knew the things adults hid from each other.

That night, one of Preston's new school friends was hosting a sleepover, and Felix and Annabel trundled along. Once the house was empty, Eli, Joan, and I avoided each other until we gathered helplessly in the kitchen. "We should sit down and talk all of this over," Eli suggested.

"Let's go out," I said. They looked at me oddly. "Come on," I said. "You guys deceived me for months. You owe me many drinks."

This logic was difficult to argue with.

Once we were at the bar where Eli had, a century ago, puked in my bag, I could feel how the balance between us had shifted. Eli and Joan sat close together. He went up to get drinks and forgot to bring mine back. I wanted to remind them that Eli and I were still legally married, that paperwork meant something to someone, but I also wondered if it did. I got drunk. They were right there with me—we got another round of bourbons, then we were doing shots. Beth was a silent bystander at first, snarking at everything they said, but she delicately eased out of my mind at some point. We were all pretending to have a great time. Maybe they actually were. They kept collapsing together like fallen toys. I made a joke about how I should just leave them to their lives, and they looked at each other.

"Should I do that?" I asked, feeling a few drinks behind. "Should I just go?"

"I'm going to get some air," Joan said. She slid out of the booth.

I turned to him. "So let me just get the timeline right. You fell in love with me and left Joan to rot, letting her provide free childcare while you did whatever you wanted? Just like you did with Beth before her?"

"No," he said. "I still loved Joan all along." He didn't even look sorry.

"You could have told me," I said.

He laughed. "Really?" he asked.

"I'm good at weird shit. I could have helped. We could have been friends," I said.

"I didn't want to be friends."

"So you figured it'd be better to spend a solid year fucking with my head?"

"That wasn't my intention. I didn't plan any of this."

But I didn't believe him. He had hoped or known all along that it would work out like this—that I would spin in distracted circles of self-loathing, distrusting myself until I ran smack into the stone wall of his love for Joan. He knew it would take me a while to do this, and that this would buy them time. He knew me. He always had. He twisted his ring on his finger, and I wondered why he was still wearing it. I slipped mine off under the table and dropped it in my purse. I asked, "Did you ever love Beth?"

Eli leaned back. "I know I've been shitty, okay? I know that. To you, to Joan. To Beth, even, in other ways. But yes, I did once love the mother of my children."

"I don't believe you," I said. "You know Joan pushed her, don't you?"

"Stop." He looked around furtively, then he leaned in close to me. His eyes were kind, pitying. "I love her," he said. "It doesn't matter what she did."

I went to the bathroom. After I peed, I braced myself against the sink and stared at myself in the mirror. I hadn't seen my drunken face in a while—I always thought that girl was pretty, her hair falling in wavy, sweaty strands around her face, her eyes like black holes. I reapplied my lipstick and smiled. The smile didn't feel like mine. Joan stumbled in. "I'm sorry," she said.

"It's okay. I was just leaving—"

"But you don't understand," Joan said, her voice firm. "This whole year has been like some game to you. You're here for your own reasons, and I don't understand what they are, but they're not good enough for me."

"This is a really shitty apology," I told her. I was so tired. I was about to leave when I stopped. "It must have been hard for you, when he kept choosing Beth."

"Excuse me?"

"Especially when she didn't even want him anymore. Man, that must have sucked! And then after you got rid of her, and you felt so guilty and alone, you had to watch him choose someone else again."

She laughed. "You have no idea what you're talking about."

Then Beth rose up like a wave inside me, knocking me to the ocean floor of myself. I could still see it happening, like I was watching a movie—how she stepped forward and slapped Joan across the face, hard. She fell back against the counter, banging her elbow on the faucet.

I was me again by the time Joan pulled away. She was holding her cheek. Her tooth had gashed her bottom lip, and it shone with a spot of blood. I drew back, horrified.

Sorry, Beth said, but she sounded proud. I gagged over the trash can. I had slapped Joan. I had made her bleed. No, I told myself, Beth had slapped Joan. I would never hurt another person. I didn't want to hurt anyone, not like this. Joan licked her lip and spat in the sink.

Look, she's fine. I'm sorry, Beth said, meaning it this time.

"Get out," I said out loud. I didn't care if Joan heard, or what she thought of me. "You're supposed to be dead."

Cassie—

"Leave me alone!" I yelled. "Get the fuck out of my head."

Joan shook her head at me in the mirror. "You need help," she muttered. She left.

In the Lyft, Eli and Joan studiously avoided the subject of Joan's face. They talked about how they would best tell the kids. They wanted me to be there, so I could pretend to sanction everything that had happened. I pressed my temple against the cool window and watched the gray town move past me.

Cass . . .

A tentative voice scratched open in the back of my brain. *No thanks*, I said. *I think you and I are done.*

She tried to respond, but I blocked her out. I kept remembering the moment she took over at the bar, and bile hit the back of my throat. I couldn't risk that again. More accurately: I couldn't think too hard about what she felt like, all the time, helplessly under my body's control. I couldn't keep doing that to her. It was for her own good.

When we got home, I went up to the bedroom while Eli heated up leftover pasta and poured Joan a glass of water. I sat on the bed for a moment, looking out the window to see the woods. I didn't have to go back to New York. I could go anywhere. I had some money—I'd barely paid for anything in Eli's house. I could take a train somewhere, even fly. I could be anonymous. I didn't know what tethered someone to a community; I had tried. I had thought for a while that Preston might need me, but he had Felix, his dad, Joan. He had enough.

I crept to the top of the stairs and peered out over the family room. Joan and Eli were spooning on the too-small couch. As I watched them talk quietly to each other, I felt a sticky, longing curiosity that I wished I could dig out of myself and fling far away. I didn't want to care about them. I wanted my hatred for them to feel clean and simple. Not only for Beth, but for myself. This house, this life, was supposed to be mine. Or, sadder and more embarrassing: I once thought it was, and I was wrong the whole time.

The next morning, the house was a mess I refused to clean. The children orbited around me, got food, took out toys, left them strewn, turned on the TV, left it on. I sat at the table nursing a cup of coffee, then another. I wanted none of this to have happened. I sent the kids to Joan's—they weren't my responsibility anymore. I scrolled until my phone was drained of battery, and I let it die.

I opened my laptop and turned to my old emails with Lavender. After skimming a few, I plugged in my phone and clicked through all the pictures of me and her—there we were, laughing on the subway, in Riverside Park, a flower tucked behind her ear. We were candlelit at a dinner party, drunk and beaming on someone's rooftop. My arms were a belt around her waist and she was doubled over. It was a simpler life, I reminded myself. I hadn't taken too much from her or showed her anything so true it made me sick. I hadn't forced her to look at memories that hurt; I hadn't made her relive her worst traumas so I could understand them. I had made myself into a series of gifts for her. She never saw the hours of toil it took to turn my personality into something consumable. Look, honey, I had always wanted to say. This still life, if you look closer, you'll see the rot in the apples, the cracks in the porcelain bowl. Sweetheart, I never told her, the orange lamplight warming the scene is a fire. Stay in this room long enough, and you'll find there are no survivors.

Eventually, jumpy and light with hunger, I went to my room and started packing. Had I ever really planned to stay? To live my entire life here, with these people? To be Eli's wife until we were old, mother Preston and Annabel into high school, college, beyond? I was meant to be an old lady living in an improbable rent-controlled apartment in the city, covered in tattoos, still dyeing my hair black late into my seventies. I would totter around the city in spike heels, going home to an apartment choking with cats, spending evenings on my fire escape in a red silk robe, breathing smoke into the smog-blurred sky. I had never been a family woman. Desperation and decent sex had led me astray for a while, and this would be a good story: the year I was married. Maybe there would be another marriage, or more, but none would stick. I knew who I was.

I wandered through the house, picking up errant books and notebooks, the few tchotchkes I'd placed on shelves and in corners. I had tried to make the house feel like mine. I could feel something straining in my chest, trying to get out. I thought of the woods, that flower, all the dumb ideas I'd had.

Eventually, I had everything gathered up except for my side of the closet. This poor little section of hangers and drawers I'd tried to fit my whole self into. I wrapped my arms around my dresses, squeezed them in a giant bear hug, lifted them off the rack, and that was it. There was nothing left of me.

The woods were dark, but they were always dark. The setting sun cast a slant of deep gold across the grass, etching them in light. Eli wasn't home yet. Here I sat, in a pool of honeyed light, drinking blush wine with the glass rim afire. My life was more beautiful than it had ever been. The knowledge beat in me, like moth wings against closed palms: I was going to destroy it.

As always, the woods welcomed me. I tried to stop thinking, letting only my subconscious guide me. I felt led down a series of paths, turns I wouldn't have expected. There was Beth's tree. I touched its trunk and felt nothing. I wanted to curl up in its roots and slumber for centuries. I sat on the cold ground. Maybe I would stay here forever. I could dig a hole in the ground and fall asleep, and simply stop thinking about everything that had ever happened to me, and about everything I had done. Around me, the sky deepened and grayed, and snow began to fall. My fingers went numb and color leached out of the tips. My nails were a faint lilac under the chipped polish. I couldn't summon the desire to go back to that house, or to go anywhere else. The snow dimmed, or everything around it did. Dusk slipped into my vision like a tune that had been playing faintly all along.

I heard something strange, like an animal. I stood and listened. Far behind the tree trunk, somebody was crying, calling out. I followed the sound. I was farther away from the house than I'd ever been; I couldn't see any human light or structure. Snow fell more thickly around me. I had started to follow the sound hoping I could help, but as I walked, I realized that I also needed help; I was thoroughly lost. Unease leached the strength from my arms and legs. My numb fingers shook, and I tried to keep the rise of fear tamped down, even as I felt myself gasping with panic. The sound kept on, and I kept moving toward it, picking around wet rocks. I tripped over a splintered tree, pulled myself up, and continued onward.

I saw the lump of a body in the snow. I stared at it, unable to resolve its presence with my understanding. It stirred and said my name.

Eli had been caught, his ankle stuck in an animal trap.

"But what are you doing here?" I asked. His body was all curled around his ankle, trying to protect it. A thick chain slithered through the leaves from its loop around the tree trunk to the jaws around his ankle. He groaned. "I came to find you."

I said, "Where's your phone?"

"I forgot it. Do you have yours?"

"No. Fuck. Okay. Fuck. This can't be happening."

But it was. His face was red, shining with tears or sweat. The trap looked evil, its jaws like a caricature, rusty and stained. I had no idea what to do. I wormed my fingers into the prongs of the trap and tried to pry it loose, but it dug into the flesh, and there was no way to pull it away without tearing Eli's heel open. He kept his jaw clenched, his hands gripping each other white. A vein throbbed terribly in his forehead. The pain of watching him suffer was excruciating. I thought this was the most I'd ever loved him.

"I'll stop touching it."

"Yeah," he eked out. "Good idea."

It wasn't, though, because there was no other way to get him free.

I sat with him in the dirt. The woods were dark, the leaves damp under our thighs. Around us, crickets scraped, and the occasional bullfrog bellowed. I pictured him on the bank of his creek, singing to the wilderness around. I said, "I can hear the creek." As if to agree with me, the frog crooned again.

Eli grunted. Even now, the rust could be poisoning his blood, the trap's bite could be already fatal. I wondered if Eli was thinking all of this, too, but I didn't want to scare him by asking. I only knew because of all the Civil War study. Without thinking, I said, "Beth would know what to do."

Beth, I called in my head. I listened, but all I could hear was the sound of Eli's jacket as he twisted against the ground. "Shush," I told him.

Eli glanced toward me, perhaps confused, though his expression was too warped by pain to tell. "Maybe. She's the one who put this thing here. There was a bear sighting across the river, and she got all freaked out."

"Oh."

"Wish she'd marked it better," he said. He winced, the trap biting in.

"We can't stay here," I said.

His voice was blurred. His eyes closed as he said, "Let's figure it out in the morning."

But I knew about rusty traps. I knew he might have already lost his foot, and I knew that if I did nothing, he would likely be dead by morning. I couldn't tell him this. I could only stroke his face as his eyelids fluttered.

Once he was asleep, I stood quietly, worried about waking him, but he didn't stir. I set off in the direction of the creek. But the sound was confusing; it seemed to bounce off the trees. I walked by the maple with the twisted branch that touched the ground. I thought I heard another frog. I thought I heard rustling nearby, so I walked faster, almost tripping on an exposed root. I stared up through the bare branches, hoping I could figure out where I was going based on the stars, but they were blocked out by the clouds, and anyway, I didn't know how to navigate based on stars. Some time later, I passed it again. A while after that, I almost tripped over Eli. He was still asleep, and still breathing.

I sat again and waited a while, watching the blood congeal around the trap's teeth. Maybe somehow the wound wasn't deep. It occurred to me that if I was actually a violent psychopath, maybe I would revel in the sight of all this blood. But in real life, it didn't hold the sick thrill that it did in my head. It was too tactile, somehow fake, and I didn't like what its loss did to Eli's face. This whole situation continued to feel more absurd than dramatic. I kept waiting for an obvious answer to emerge.

"Eli," I said. His eyelashes stirred, but he didn't say anything.

I stroked hair away from his clammy forehead. If Eli died tonight, out here in the cold, losing more blood every moment, nobody would ever have to know that I had left him here. These woods had swallowed one death's secret; it could stomach another.

Around us, the trees smelled like cardamom and must. The snow was melting fast, in patches. The dust that coated my shoes was orange, and it clotted in my throat. I thought of the flower in my body, of its petals folding and unfolding. I thought of its roots winding around my bones. I was so sick of being afraid.

A new image came into my head. The boy was blonde, blue-eyed, with a birthmark on the side of his nose. It was Preston; I knew him immediately, even though I'd never seen Preston as a toddler. Not quite a toddler yet, I guessed, because in the image that rose up, like a video playing in my head, he was holding fiercely to the edge of the coffee table in the family room. No one else was in the room except me, and he didn't seem to see me. He pulled himself up and took one step, and then another, alone and so determined.

More images came. I saw Preston holding Annabel—tomato red, with a thrush of black hair—for the first time, saw the mix of trepidation and familiarity in his eyes as he looked up, and I heard his young voice say, incredulous, "*My* sister? All mine?"

I saw Annabel asleep, twisted in her blanket. I saw Preston collecting rocks in the creek, his little-boy shorts sagging, he had put so many in his pockets. I saw Annabel eat a piece of candy for the first time, her eyes boggled with joy. I saw Eli, younger, though not as young as when I first knew him, swinging Annabel around the room. I saw him trudge up to put the kids to bed, and come back down, and approach me, a soft, sweet tiredness in his eyes. He murmured and I murmured back, with a different voice.

You're back, I said.

I'm sorry. Her voice was faint with disuse, and I felt a pang for having caused it.

I missed you, I said.

She shrugged this off and looked through my eyes. She had never done this with such focus before, and it was an uncanny feeling—I could see everything she saw, but the movements of my eyes weren't mine. She avoided looking at Eli's flesh. Instead, her gaze traced the contours of the trap. Finally, she said, *The trap was my dad's.*

You know how it works?

You're not going to like it.

Try me.

You can disengage the springs by pressing down. Hard.

I thought of forcing the trap's teeth deeper into Eli's skin, his already-broken bones. I recoiled, a hard shiver wracking me. Bile rose in my throat, and a panicked buzz in my ears. My brain asked: Did you arrange this? Isn't this the kind of pain you secretly long to cause?

Can you do it? I asked. A horrible thing to ask, but Beth didn't respond. My hands shook, my thoughts fragile and too fast. I remembered Arthur in his office, his body draped over his chair. I remembered backing out of the room. *I don't think I can do this.*

It doesn't matter what you think.

I moved his leg as gently as I could, and he did not stir. I whispered his name, tapped his shoulder. I checked for a heartbeat and it was there, but faint. The blood around the trap was drying thickly, but some still flowed from the part where the trap's tooth bit deepest. For a moment I sat, holding his limp hand.

I could still go for help. When I came back, whatever might have happened during the time I was gone would not be my fault. I was alone, and whatever I chose would be mine to live with. To remember, to doubt. To make part of the story I told myself about who I was.

I knelt down hard on the trap. I heard the crunch of bone and gagged. The trap pressed back up against my knees, and I yanked it off of Eli's foot, its teeth scraping blood down the ruined canvas of his shoes.

It was then, finally, that I had to crawl a few feet away to throw up in a great heave. I spat hard, afraid to wipe my mouth and make this process any more unsanitary than it already was. I wiped the blood on my hands off in the snow. Eli was awake, it seemed, muttering nonsense, his eyes rolled into the back of his head.

"We're going to take you to the hospital," I said. He gritted his jaw and let it slacken. His eyelids fluttered closed again. I kicked away the trap, glossy with blood. I packed clean snow against the wound, then took off my shirt and tied it tight around his ankle, holding the snow in place. Eli's heart still beat, but sluggishly. As I stepped back, his outline looked dead against the ground. I gasped back a sob, then crouched and hoisted him up onto my back. His clothes were rough and damp against my bare skin. I could feel melting snow or blood dripping down my calf, drops running into my boot. I wanted to angle him so the wound was above his heart, his body slung across my shoulders, but I couldn't carry him like that. I started walking.

I knew you could do it, Beth said. Her pride felt as warm and soft as a hand holding mine.

"Yeah, well, he's lucky you're trapped in my head."

She stopped. Like always, her stopping mid-thought felt like a disappearance, like she couldn't just stop talking; she had to block herself out of my mind. After a moment, she blinked back in— warmer, a little flustered. *I don't think I'm trapped*, she said. *I think, given the choice to go back to my old life or this, I would choose this.*

We crunched through dead leaves. Now in the graying dawn, I recognized our path. We reached the creek; I walked downstream until I saw the fort like a flag amid the trees. I turned and walked toward Joan's.

The sun inched closer, closer, and then there was a boundary, and then we had crossed it. Into the backyard, sun hanging mundanely, clouds nothing special at all. As soon as we were clear of the woods, I let out a mangled yell and stumbled to the ground, Eli's body over mine. A light went on, then another, then the door opened and Joan ran toward us, almost tripping in her haste.

NOW

Eli is unconscious, still. Joan leans like a shadow over him on the lawn. She has called an ambulance, and now she strokes his face, her hands shaking, her voice frantic as she murmurs his name. The kids sit in a tight knot around him; Annabel has pulled his head into her lap.

I don't know what happens next. Eli might still lose his foot. He might get tetanus or an infection. I fought so hard to drag him here, and it might not have been enough. I might still have failed this family. And even if I didn't, I stand apart from them as they bend over his inert body, and I know that none of them are mine anymore.

That's okay, Beth whispers, her voice soft and alive, a snail curled in the shell of my ear. *We have each other now.*

I remember what my head felt like without her in it. Too sharp, and so lonely.

Down the road, I hear sirens coming closer, their shrill whine cutting through the mist of the morning. Wet grass streaks our ankles as we turn away from the others.

No one watches us as we leave. We walk casually past the swing set, into the house to grab our bags, then out past clusters of chirping birds on the front porch, welcoming morning. The lightening sky gapes over us, Beth's-eye blue and piled with pink clouds. Dreamlike, we walk toward Eli's car. We deserve the car, we think, after everything. We climb in. The seat is cool, the windshield glimmering with dew. We breathe in, feeling the cold air shock and settle in our lungs as we rub our hands together to keep warm, as we reach out and turn the key.

ACKNOWLEDGMENTS

Sarah Bowlin: This is the best iteration of our working relationship so far. Thank you for loving this book, and for teaching me so much about writing and editing over the past decade. I truly can't begin to express how grateful I am to you on this page alone, so here's to many more opportunities to thank you in the future. Thanks also to everyone at Aevitas, especially Maria Cardona Serra, Erin Files, and Mags Chmielarczyk.

Thank you, Olivia Taylor Smith, who *got* the book so immediately and thoroughly, and who has honed it so lovingly into its ideal form. Thank you, Brittany Adames, for all of your excellent work. Thanks to the rest of the team at Simon & Schuster: Martha Langford, Danielle Prielipp, Amanda Mulholland, Olivia Perrault, Lauren Gomez, Morgan Hart, Crystal Watanabe, Andrea Monagle, Dominick Montalto, Carly Loman, Meryll Preposi, Alicia Brancato, Samantha Cohen, Mikaela Bielawski, Jackie Seow, Emma Shaw, Tom Spain, Raymond Chokov, Nicole Moran, Michael Nardullo, Mabel Marte Taveras, Lyndsay Brueggemann, Winona Lukito, Sean Manning, Irene Kheradi, and Tim O'Connell. Thanks also to Sylvie Rosokoff for the loveliest park walk and the best author photo. Thank you, Emily Mahon, for the gorgeous cover.

Thank you to Josh, Mom, Dad, and Cindy for the endless support. Thank you also to Alex and to all of my brilliant cousins for showing me so many different ways to work in and alongside artmaking. Special thanks to Mom for your nursing expertise and your willingness to answer many questions about wounds. And extra special thanks to Josh for knowing all of the settings.

Thank you, Dr. Alex Camargo, without whom the writing of this novel would not have been possible.

Thank you, Ethan Labourdette, for reading the most unformed first draft and gently telling me not to show it to anyone else. And for reading so many later drafts. I'm sorry I didn't write you into the book—or did I?

Thank you to Cory Leadbeater and Amy Feltman for your wisdom and encouragement on so many Wednesday nights, and for the very best group chat. Thanks also to Sam Graham-Felsen.

Thank you to Peter Kispert, for reading such an early draft and treating it like a book. Thank you, Kelli Trapnell, for always getting the weirdest parts.

Thank you to Sanaë Lemoine—a most-trusted reader for over a decade now—Forsyth Harmon, and Kirsten Saracini for the insightful reads, and the long talks, and the ice cream. Special thanks to Kirsten for introducing me to the cinematic masterpiece that is *Moonstruck*. That has nothing to do with this book except that it did change my life. Thank you to Lynn Steger Strong for the early read (you were right about the blood) and for so much more. Thank you to Jenni Milton, Carrie Esposito, Cait Emma Smith, and Brittany Newell for the wise notes. Special thanks to Christine Vines for reading at a crucial moment and for understanding everything, always.

Thank you to Megan Cranford for all the voice memos and so much more. Thank you Michael Shirey and Angela Elia for the workdays. Thank you Jared Cranford, Cam Gowdicott, Ryan Kerr, and Larissa Rhodes, for listening to my fake podcast. Thank you also to Logan Gowdicott, Jackie Labourdette, Andre Leverett, Shiomara Gonzalez, Josue Ledesma, Audrey Yeoman, and Amanda "Mousecakes" Mouzakes for attending readings, for having such great fashion sense, and for all the late-night talks about art over the years. Thank you, Courtney Preiss, for the encouragement and for reintroducing me to Asbury Park.

Thank you so much to the friends who constantly inspire me and who have listened to me go on about this (and other) book(s) for years, especially Avi Silber, Dan Birnbaum, Emilie Palmer, and Lee Gomila.

Thank you to my teachers, especially Mom, Melanie Kaminski, Bay Pedersen, Dr. Cotton, Tom Piazza, Mark Yakich, Chris Schaberg, Janelle Schwartz, John Biguenet, Boyd Blundell, Laura Hope, John Wray, Stacey D'Erasmo, and Deborah Eisenberg. All of you showed me new ways to understand reading and writing, and I think often of your wisdom. Thank you to the late Doc. P. for introducing me to the horror section. Thank you to Tony Tulathimutte and the CRIT community.

Thank you to Hannah Tinti, Maribeth Batcha, Patrick Ryan, and the rest of the One Story universe, for building and caring for my favorite corner of the literary world. Thank you, Adina Talve-Goodman—who is loved and missed by so many—for all the pie.

Thank you to the publishing mentors and colleagues who have generously shared their know-how with me: Elizabeth Harding, Katherine Fausset, Libby Burton, Caroline Zancan, Jon Cox, Barbara Jones, Kenn Russell, Rachel Mannheimer, Jana-Maria Hartmann, Danny Yanez, and Alanna Feldman. Thank you to Madeline Jones, Ruby Rose Lee, Ryan Smernoff, Eleanor Embry, and Olivia Croom for every gchat message. Thank you, Fiora Elbers-Tibbitts, for all the book talks. Special thanks to Margo Shickmanter and Caitlin Landuyt for reading with such care. Thanks also to Literary Thicction for the word-count challenges.

Thank you to the Posner family for all the loving support over the years.

Thank you to Amos Posner for finishing this book on the way to your bachelor party, and for marrying me after. Thank you for listening to all of my thoughts, and for building a life with me.

To my readers, thank you for existing. I often have a terrifyingly overactive imagination, but imagining you was my favorite part of writing this book. I hope you love Elwood, and I hope every one of you has an excellent dessert in your near future.

Lastly, Exposure and Response Prevention Therapy (ERP) is considered by many to be the gold standard treatment for OCD. From a personal standpoint, this treatment changed my life and I am grateful for it every day. If you would like to research treatment for OCD, some resources include the International OCD Foundation, BeyondOCD.org, and NOCD.

Kerry Cullen's fiction has been published in the *Indiana Review*, *Joyland*, *One Teen Story*, and more. She earned her BA at Loyola University New Orleans and her MFA at Columbia University. She is a freelance editor and lives in New York.